BOOK 1

THE RELUCTANT ASSASSIN

BOOK 1

THE RELUCTANT ASSASSIN

# EOIN COLFER

HYPERION
NEW YORK

Copyright © 2013 by Eoin Colfer

Printed in the United States of America

First Hyperion paperback edition, 2014

1 3 5 7 9 10 8 6 4 2

V475-2873-0-14015

ISBN 978-1-4231-6495-1

Library of Congress Control Number for the hardcover edition: 2012048160

Visit www.un-requiredreading.com

*To Finn, Seán, Grace, Jeremy, and Joe*

BOOK 1

# W.A.R.P.

## THE RELUCTANT ASSASSIN

# 1 » THE KILLING CHAMBER

THERE WERE TWO SMUDGES IN THE SHADOWS between the grandfather clock and the velvet drapes. One high and one low. Two pale thumbprints in a black night made darker still by blackout sheets behind the thick curtains and burlap tacked across the skylights.

The lower smudge was the face of a boy, soot-blackened and slightly shivering inside the basement chamber. This was young Riley, brought this very night on his first killing as a test.

The upper smudge was the face of a man known to his employers as Albert Garrick, though the public had once known him by a different name. His stage name had been the Great Lombardi, and many years ago he had been the most celebrated illusionist in the West End, until during one performance he actually sawed his beautiful assistant in half. Garrick discovered on that night that he relished taking a life almost as much as he enjoyed the delighted applause from the stalls, and so the magician made a new career of assassination.

Garrick fixed his flat murderer's eyes on Riley and gripped his shoulder, long bony fingers pressing through the fabric of the boy's coat, pinching the nerves. He didn't say a word but nodded once, a gesture heavy with reminder and implication.

*Think back*, said the inclined chin, *to your lesson of this afternoon. Move silently as the Whitechapel fog and slide the blade in until your fingers sink into the wound.*

Garrick had instructed Riley to haul a dog carcass from the Strand to their Holborn rooms and then practice his knife work on the suspended remains so he would be accustomed to the resistance of bone.

*Novices have the mistaken impression that a sharp blade will slip in like a hot poker through wax, but it ain't so. Sometimes even a master like myself can come up against bone and muscle, so be ready to lever down and force up. Remember that, boy. Lever down and force up. Use the bone itself as your fulcrum.*

Garrick performed the move now with his long stiletto blade, tilting his wide, blackened forehead at Riley to make certain the boy took heed.

Riley nodded, then took the knife, palming the blade across to the other hand as he had been taught.

Garrick nudged Riley from the shadows toward the large four-poster bed, on which lay the nearly departed.

*Nearly departed.* This was one of Garrick's witticisms.

Riley knew that he was being tested. This was a real killing, a fat purse paid in advance. Either he snuffed out his first candle or Albert Garrick would leave an extra corpse in this terrible, gloomy chamber and swipe himself a new apprentice from the gutters of London. It would pain him to do it, but Garrick would not see any other option. Riley must learn to do more than fry sausages and polish boots.

Riley swept his feet forward, one at a time, tracing a wide circle with his toes as he had been taught, searching for debris. It slowed his progress, but one crackle of discarded paper could be enough to awaken his intended victim. Riley saw in front of him the blade in his own hand, and he could hardly believe that he was here, about to commit the act that would damn him to hell.

*When you have felt the power, you can take your place as my junior in the family business,* Garrick would often say. *P'raps we should have cards of business made up, eh, boy? Garrick and Son. Assassins for hire. We may be low, but we're not cheap.*

Then Garrick would laugh, and it was a dark, faraway noise that caused Riley's nerves to throb and his stomach to heave.

Riley moved forward another pace; he could see no way out of it. The room seemed to close in around him.

*I must kill this man or be killed myself.* Riley's head started to pound till his hand shook and the blade almost slipped from his fingers.

Garrick was instantly at his side like a ghost, touching

Riley's elbow with one crooked icicle of a finger.

"'From dust thou art . . .'" He whispered so softly that the words might have been formed from the gusts of a draft.

"'And unto dust thou shalt return,'" mouthed Riley, completing the biblical quote. Garrick's favorite.

*My own last rites*, he'd told Riley one winter's night as they looked out on Leicester Square from their booth in an Italian restaurant. The magician had polished off his second jug of bitter red wine and his gentleman's accent had started to slide off his words like fish from a wet slab.

*Every man Jack of us crawled forth from the filth and dust, and unto that stuff we shall return, mark you. I just send 'em back quicker. A few heartbeats early so that we may enjoy life's comforts. That is the way of our situation and if you have no steel in you for it, Riley, then . . .*

Garrick never completed his threat, but it was clear that the time had come for Riley to earn his place at the table.

Riley felt the crack between each board through the thin soles of his shoes, which had been painstakingly shaved down on the lathe in Garrick's workshop. He could now see the mark in the bed. An old man with a thatch of gray hair jutting out from under a puffy quilt.

*I can't see his face.* He was grateful for that much.

Riley approached the bed, feeling Garrick behind him, knowing his time was running out.

*Unto dust. Dispatched to dust.*

Riley saw the old man's hand resting on the pillow, the index finger a mere nub due to some old injury, and he knew that he could not do it. He was no murderer.

Riley cast his eyes about while keeping his head still. He had been taught to use his surroundings in times of emergency, but his mentor was behind him, observing Riley's every move with his eerie, non-blinking intensity. There would be no help from the old man in the bed. What could a gray-hair possibly do against Garrick? What could anyone do?

Four times Riley had run away, and four times Garrick had found him.

Death is the only way out for me, Riley had thought. Mine or Garrick's.

But Garrick could not be killed, for he was death.

*Unto dust.*

Riley felt suddenly faint and thought he would sink to the cold floor. Perhaps that would be for the best? Lie senseless and let Garrick do his bloody work; but then the old man would die too, and that knowledge would weigh on Riley's soul in the afterlife.

I will fight, decided the boy. He had little hope of survival, but he had to do something.

Plan after plan flitted through his fevered brain, each one more hopeless than the last. All the time, he moved onward, feeling the frost of Garrick on his neck like a bad omen. The man on the four-poster grew clearer. He could see an ear now, with holes a row of rings must have once pierced.

*A foreigner perhaps? A sailor?*

He saw a ruddy jaw with tallowy runs of flesh tucked underneath and a lanyard that ran to a strange pendant lying on the quilt.

*Look for every detail* was one of Garrick's lessons. *Drink it all in with yer eyes, and maybe it will save yer life.*

*No chance of saving my life, not tonight.*

Riley took another sweeping step and felt his forward foot grow curiously warm. He glanced down and to his surprise and confusion saw that the toe of his shoe glowed green. In fact, a cocoon of light had blossomed around the frame of the sleeping man, its heart an emerald blaze emanating from the strange pendant.

Garrick's words gusted past his ear. "Hell's bells. Trickery! Dirk him now, boy."

Riley could not move, petrified as he was by the spectral light.

Garrick pushed him farther into the strange warm glow, which immediately changed hue, becoming a scarlet hemisphere. An unnatural keening erupted from somewhere in the bed, piercing and horrible, rattling Riley's brain in the gourd of his skull.

The old man in the bed was instantly awake, popping up like a windup Jack from his box.

"Stupid sensor malfunction," he muttered, his accent Scottish, his eyes rheumy and blinking. "I have a pain in my . . ."

The man noticed Riley and the blade emerging from his fist like an icicle. He allowed his hand to trail slowly down toward the glowing teardrop pendant resting on his scrawny chest, then tapped the center twice, silencing the dreadful wail. The pendant's heart displayed a glowing series of numbers now, seemingly written in phosphorus. Flickering backward from twenty.

"Now there, lad," said the old man. "Hold on to those horses. We can talk about this. I have funds."

Riley was transfixed by the pendant. It was magical certainly, but, more than that, it was familiar somehow.

Garrick interrupted Riley's thoughts with a sharp prod in the ribs.

"No more delay," he said briskly. "Make your bones, boy. Unto dust."

Riley could not. He would not become like Garrick and damn himself to an eternity in the pit.

"I-I . . ." he stuttered, wishing his mind would supply the words to extricate both himself and this strange old man from these dire straits. The man raised his palms to show they were empty, as though fair play was on offer in this dark room.

"I'm not armed," he said. "All I have is unlimited currency. I can run you up whatever you need. Easiest thing in the world to print a few thousand pounds. But, if you harm me, men will come to make sure you didn't take my secrets—men with weapons like you have never seen."

The old man spoke no more, as there was a knife suddenly embedded in his chest. Riley saw his own hand on the hilt and for a sickening moment thought that his muscles had betrayed his heart and done the deed; but then he felt the tingle of Garrick's cold fingers releasing his forearm, and he knew that his hand had been forced.

"There it is," said Garrick as the warm blood coated Riley's sleeve. "Hold on tight, and you will feel the life leave him."

"It wasn't me that did it," Riley said to the man, the words trickling from his lips. "It was never me."

The old man sat stiff as a board, the pendant's cord fraying against the dagger's blade.

"I do not believe this," he grunted. "All the people on my tail, and you two clowns get me."

Garrick's words crawled into Riley's ears like slugs. "This is not credited to your account, boy. Mine was the hand that found the gap between this pigeon's ribs, but there are circumstances here, I'll give you that. So, I may allow you another chance."

"I do not believe this," said the old man once more; then his pendant beeped and he was gone. Literally gone. Fizzling into a cloud of orange sparks that were sucked into the pendant's heart.

"Magic," breathed Garrick, his tone approaching reverence. "Magic is real."

The assassin stepped sharply back, protecting himself from whatever the consequences of the vaporization might be; but Riley did not have the presence of mind to follow. Still holding the dagger, all he could do was watch as the cloud spread along his arm, dematerializing him quicker than a beggar could spit.

"I am going," he said, and it was true, though he could not know where.

He saw his torso turn transparent, and his organs were

visible for a moment, packed in tight behind translucent ribs; then all the workings were gone too, replaced by sparks.

The gas that Riley had become was sucked into the pendant's heart. He felt himself go in a vortex that reminded him of being tumbled by a wave on Brighton beach and of a boy watching him from the shore.

*Ginger. I remember you.*

Then Riley was reduced to a single glowing dot of purest energy. The dot winked once at Garrick, then disappeared. The old man and the boy, both gone.

Garrick reached for the pendant, which had fallen to the sheets, thinking, I have seen this device before, or one like it. Many years ago . . . But his fingers touched only a smear of soot left behind where the strange talisman had been.

"All my life," he said. "All my life . . ."

He mouthed the rest but did not say it aloud, as he was alone in this room of wonders.

*All my life I have searched for real magic. And now I know it does exist.*

Garrick was a man of turbulent emotions that he usually kept tucked inside his heart; but now warm tears of happiness trickled down his face, spilling onto his lapels.

*Not simply conjuring. Real magic.*

The assassin sank to the ground, his long spindly legs folding so that his knees were level with his ears. Blood soaked through the seat of his expensive breeches, but he cared not one jot, for nothing would ever be the same again. His only fear was that the magic had gone from this place forever. To have been so close and to have missed out by a whisker would indeed be devastation.

*I will wait here, Riley,* he thought. *The Chinese believe that magic often resides in a place, so waiting is my only card to play. And, when the men come with their fabulous weapons, I will avenge you. Then I will take the magic and bend it to my will, and there will be none who can stop me.*

# 2 » GYM GIRL

CHEVRON SAVANO HAD NEVER PARTICULARLY cared for the parable of the Prodigal Son. In fact it could be said that she hated that particular story and had to grit her teeth whenever some lecturing type brought it up.

*There is great rejoicing in heaven when a prodigal son returns to the fold.*

Really? Was that so? And what about the son, or daughter, who has stayed in the fold and worked through holidays and weekends to keep the fold safe from organized crime and corruption? What about the daughter who has sacrificed just about everything to make sure that *the fold* didn't come under threat?

What about *that* daughter? Well, apparently that daughter got shipped off to London to babysit an overseas witness-protection safe house, which seemed to be pretty much a career-killing assignment, as far as she could tell.

Special Agent Lawrence Witmeyer, her FBI boss in the L.A. office, had assured her that she was not being unofficially punished for her recent, very public embarrassment of the Bureau.

"This is an important assignment, Chevie. Vital, in fact. WARP has a thirty-year history in the Bureau."

"What does WARP even stand for?" Savano had asked.

Witmeyer checked the e-mail on his screen. "Er . . . WARP: Witness Anonymous Relocation Program."

"That sounds like they threw in *Anonymous* to fit the name WARP. Otherwise they'd have WRP, and what kind of acronym would that be?"

"I guess they wanted to make it sound cool. You know these name guys."

Chevie fumed. It was obvious that the Bureau was tucking her out of the way in London where the press might not find her.

"I did my job, you know? I saved lives."

"I know you did," said Witmeyer, softening for a moment. "Chevron, you have a choice here. The rest of the group accepted the decommissioning package. You're sixteen years old; you can do whatever you want."

"Except be a Fed."

"You were never a real agent, Chevie. You were an official source of intelligence. That's a very different thing."

"But it said *Agent* on my badge. My handler called me Agent Savano."

Witmeyer smiled at Chevie as though she were five years old. "We thought you kids would like a badge. You know, to make you feel important. But it takes more than a badge, Chevie."

"I was on the fast track to becoming a real agent. I was told that all I had to do was complete my assignment and a place at Quantico would be mine."

"You were *told*," said Witmeyer. "But there was nothing in writing. Take the deal, Miss Savano. It's a good one. And maybe, if you keep your head down, we can talk about Quantico in a few years."

Chevie was not interested in the deal but, if she wanted to be a real Special Agent, England was her only option.

"So I report to the London office?"

Witmeyer looked shiftier than usual. "Nope. You report directly to WARP. The London office works mostly on hate crimes, that kind of thing. What you'll be doing is not connected to their day-to-day operations. They won't even know you're in the country unless you call in." Witmeyer looked around excitedly, as though about to deliver *amazing* news. "In effect, you'll have nothing to do but study distance-learning modules for your high school diploma."

Chevie sighed. "So it's back to school for the little kid."

"I hate to tell you this, Chevie, but you *are* a kid," said Witmeyer, glancing over Chevie's shoulder, anxious to shut this meeting down and join the other agents *clack-clack*ing their weapons in the bustling office space beyond. "I'm giving you double years for your pension, Chevie. That's the best I can do. You can take the pension offer or not. Either way, if you want any chance of staying on at the Bureau, you're going to London."

So Chevie had been in England for nine months, babysitting a metal capsule that looked an awful lot like an Apollo landing module that had been stuffed into the basement of a four-story Georgian house on Bedford Square in Bloomsbury.

"What do we actually do here?" she had asked her boss on the first morning. His name, believe it or not, was Agent Orange, which she thought must be some kind of alias, and he was gray from head to toe, from his floppy coif to his sunglasses and his skinny suit, right down to his custom-made tasseled loafers.

"We attend the pod," said the fifty-year-old agent, his Scottish accent making the word *attend* about three seconds longer than it needed to be.

"What are we, podites?" said Chevie, still jet-lagged and feeling a little belligerent.

Orange took the question seriously. "In a way. Yes, Agent Savano. That pod downstairs is your church."

He led Chevie through the lobby area, which was decked out like a three-star English hotel, complete with andirons and a ship in a bottle, down into a basement with a reinforced steel door. Once they got past that door, things got real FBI real quick. Chevie spotted over a dozen cameras in the concrete walls; there were motion-sensor bugs all over the corridor; and every type of information cable known to man was threaded through a gray conduit.

"Nice conduit," said Chevie drily. "Goes with your . . . everything."

Orange coughed. "Agent Witmeyer did mention that I am your superior?"

"Negative on that," lied Chevie. "He said we were partners."

"I doubt that very much," said Orange. "In fact, I am only referring to you as *Agent* as a courtesy. From what I hear, you're being stashed in London after the ill-conceived *high school initiative* went south."

They passed a holding cell and a well-stocked infirmary; then the corridor widened into a circular chamber, which housed a ten-foot-tall pyramid-shaped metal pod covered with refrigeration tubes and complicated groups of blinking lights.

"This is WARP central," said Orange, patting the casing fondly.

"It looks like a sci-fi Christmas tree," said Chevie, doing her best not to be impressed.

Orange checked a number of readouts; it really seemed like he knew what he was doing.

"I was expecting this attitude," he said, without facing Chevie. "I read your file. Most informative. Graduated top of your special group. Record test scores in spite of your age. Problem with authority figures, *blah blah blah*, so movie stereotype." Orange turned finally to Chevie. "We both know why you're here, Agent Savano. Your group was an embarrassment to the Bureau and a potential legal minefield because of your age. You messed up for the cameras in Los Angeles, so they sent you overseas on a quiet posting; but, in spite of what you may think, what we do here is important, Agent. There shall be no cutting of slack because of your youth."

Chevie glared. "Don't worry, Agent. I don't expect slack, and I don't cut any."

Orange thrust a hand inside the pod, checking the temperature. "I'm glad to hear it. It is more than likely that your unslackened talents will never be called upon. On most days a man probably won't come out of the WARP pod, so you don't have to do anything except study for your diploma. But on the off chance that this very special man does emerge from that hatch when I am out, you need to keep him alive. Just keep him alive and call me. That's it."

"Is the man in there now?"

"No, Agent. The pod is empty at the moment, and has been for thirty years."

"So it's a magic pod?"

Orange smiled in a way that told Chevie that he knew quite a lot that she didn't. "Not magic, exactly. Magical, maybe."

"Yep, that makes a lot of sense."

"That's all the sense you're going to get out of me today, Agent Savano. Maybe when you've proven yourself as a serious podite, I'll share some details. Until then you live on-site, you never stray more than a mile from the house, and I watch the pod while you sleep."

"Where do I sleep?"

"The flat upstairs. You'll love it."

"Where do *you* sleep? In bonnie Scotland?"

Orange smiled again. "The top floor. I get the penthouse. One perk of being the boss."

He handed Chevie a smartphone. "All the numbers are preprogrammed. And there are apps for the alarm and surveillance. You see this alarm-button icon? Don't press that if you don't want all hell breaking loose. Got it?"

Chevie took the phone. "I got it, Agent."

"Good." Orange turned back to the pod, his fingers tripping across multiple old-fashioned plastic keyboards bolted to its surface. "If you do well here, keep your head down for a couple of years, then let's see if we can't sneak you back into the U.S. without the press noticing. By that time you will be almost old enough to apply for Quantico."

Chevie scowled at Orange's gray back. In two years she would be ancient. Almost nineteen.

"Wow, that would be great. Two years of babysitting. I am so glad I did all those firearms courses."

Orange left the pod chamber without looking back. "Keep trying, Agent," he called over his shoulder. "Someday you will say something that is actually funny."

I hate that guy already, thought Chevie Savano.

Now, several months later, Chevie had lost touch with most of her friends in California while she waited for some mystery guy to pop out of a space pod in the basement. She hadn't fired her weapon once, even on a firing range, which made her extremely nervous; and she realized that she was not only talking to herself on a regular basis but answering herself too.

"You need to stop that," she said to herself. "People will think you're crazy."

Really? What people? It wasn't as if she had talked to anybody other than Orange for over six weeks. She had even celebrated her seventeenth birthday on her own with a chocolate brownie and a single pathetic candle.

The house on Bedford Square had become like her second home, or maybe her prison. She knew every inch of the building better than she knew her own cottage on the Malibu bluffs, where she could legally live alone when she turned eighteen in less than a year.

There was one room in the Bedford Square house that she did love, and this was the studio. At some point in the house's history a dancer had converted a large part of the second floor into a dance studio, complete with a mirror wall and barre. Not that Chevie Savano was a dancer, but she was a gym girl; and it had only taken three weeks of nagging to get Orange to sign off on a few thousand pounds for weights and machines.

On this evening, which was to prove eventful but had started out pretty same-old same-old, Chevie had spent her last stress-free moments for quite some time looking at herself in the mirror and thinking, *Girl, where is your life going?*

It was hardly a mystery.

*You know where your life is going. Do your time watching the pod, and hopefully the powers that be back in the U.S. will forget all about Los Angeles and give you a shot at becoming a real agent. You still have friends in Quantico.*

Usually federal agents had to be twenty-three years of age minimum before they could wear the shield, but Chevie had been part of a trial program to combat the increasing problem of terrorist infiltration of high schools. A handpicked group of state wards had spent a semester in Quantico, and then had been placed undercover in various schools attended by suspected sympathizers, in a strictly observational capacity. No infiltration, no confrontation. Chevie had spent six months in L.A. keeping tabs on an Iranian family who the Feds believed were trying to start a cell in California. The assignment had ended with a public disaster outside a Los Angeles theater where Chevie had used her training to disarm a drunken teen who'd been threatening the Iranians. Unfortunately, the teen had been wounded in the process, and the entire fiasco was captured on a cell phone camera. The hothouse program was hurriedly shut down, and Chevie was whisked off to London for babysitting duty so a senate committee would not catch on to the fact that the agent involved in the Hollywood Center Affair was a minor.

Chevie did thirty minutes of cardio, thirty minutes of core, then shadowboxed in the mirror until her Lycra leggings and vest were dark with sweat. She was in good enough shape to whip the top ten percent of law-enforcement officers anywhere in the world. And she could shoot an apple off a tree at a hundred paces.

*Do I look seventeen?*

As far as Chevie could see, she looked pretty much the same as she had at sixteen. At five feet six she was a little short for an FBI agent, but she was lithe and fast, with a delicate oval face and the glossy black hair typical of Native Americans.

I am going to get through this assignment, she thought. They don't get rid of Chevron Savano so easily. There are worse things than boredom.

Which was the last routine thought she was to have for a while.

Riley could not for the life of him have described his predicament. Had there been a Bible handy, he could not have testified on it as to whether he was alive or dead. His thoughts were a jumble of fear and confusion, and he found that the tough, stoical core of his spirit, which had kept him going through the terrifying years with Garrick, was totally absent.

His senses were spun together like the muddy streams flowing into the Thames, and he felt an urge to vomit that was somehow in his mind and not his gut.

Is this the pit? he wondered. Has the devil claimed me?

He ordered his hand to wave, but nothing happened; or perhaps it did and he could not see it.

It seemed somehow that there was a light up ahead, glowing like a streetlamp. Though Riley could neither see the light nor calculate in which direction "up ahead" lay, he somehow knew these things to be true.

I am about to arrive, he realized.

Chevie stood in front of the mirror and watched her image split in two. For the briefest moment she thought that she had finally gone stir-crazy; then she realized that the mirror had cracked from roof to ceiling.

*That's bad luck for someone, probably me.*

Then more cracks appeared, jagged black lightning rents that divided the room into sections.

*Could it be an earthquake? Do they have those in London?*

The mirror cracked once, twice, a thousand times with a sound like automatic weapon fire. The cracks raced past the edges of the mirrors, streaking across the walls. Chevie finally moved when the lacquered floorboards beneath her sneakers began to splinter and fall in torn chunks through to the hallway below.

"What the hell . . . ?" she cried, picking a safe path to the door.

Overhead the lights flickered, then exploded, showering Chevie with glass and sparks. Through the window she could see streetlamps exploding all along Bayley Street and around the square itself. Beyond the square the blackout rippled down toward Covent Garden and Soho as though some giant night creature was swallowing chunks of light.

*What is happening to the power? Orange will know.*

But Orange was out. She was the on-duty agent.

A bulletproof front-facing window cracked, allowing noise in from the outside world. Metal shrieked as cars collided on Tottenham Court Road, and the cry of panicked people rose into the dark London clouds, which had lost their streetlight underglow.

*Whatever is happening, it started here,* Chevie realized.

She ran to the wall safe, punched in the code number, and pulled out her Glock 22 in the shoulder holster she wore with an extra strap to pull it tight to her left side for a smooth cross draw. She expertly donned the holster and drew her weapon.

Chevie held the gun straight-armed in a two-handed grip, staring fixedly through the green tritium contrast points of her night sight, hoping that nothing would pop up and force her to shoot.

*I don't even know what the guy looks like who might come out of the pod. If I shoot the witness, they will never let me back into California.*

Chevie ran down the upper landing, sticking close to the wall. Around her, bricks grated and plaster fell in chunks.

That chunk looks like Texas, thought Chevie, because you can't control what the mind throws up.

Emergency lighting blisters flickered on, bathing the interior in industrial yellow light.

Good, thought Chevie. I can see whatever happens, which will hopefully be nothing.

Something else occurred to her.

*Agent Orange. He's probably going to blame me for this.*

Chevie rattled her gun and told herself to focus, pulling a tight turn into the stairwell. She made her way carefully down the two flights of stairs. The basement steps before her were relatively intact, but the door had buckled and the central panel seemed to have melted.

What could melt a steel door? wondered Special Agent Savano, and this unspoken question was answered when a bolt of lightning sizzled through the glowing edges of the melt hole and took a good-sized lump out of the wall.

*Lightning. Okay.*

Chevie realized that she had squatted on her hunkers with her weapon aimed at the door.

*That's right, Agent. You can shoot the lightning.*

She gave it a few minutes, until it seemed as though the indoor lightning bolts were over and done with, then hurried down the remaining narrow steps.

There was nothing left of the basement door but its frame; the melted edges had already solidified.

In a move that would have made Cord Vallicose, her Quantico instructor, proud, Chevie dived through the frame, rolled, and came up with her gun pointed down the corridor. She would later realize that the sharp edges of the door had scraped her all down one side, but at that moment she didn't even feel the scratches.

There was no obvious threat beyond the ruined door, just dust and devastation. The WARP pod itself had broken free of its brackets and was pointing nose-first down the basement corridor. It looked for all the world like a small spacecraft had crashed into the house.

*Which would make about as much sense as what is actually happening: a big machine is sucking the juice out of central London.*

Chevie swore to herself that when Orange arrived, she was going to hold him at gunpoint until he told her exactly what this 1970s-style pod had to do with witness protection.

The pod usually reminded Chevie of a science museum

exhibit, with its retro design and faded metallic finish, but now the machine seemed alive and totally functional, whatever its function might be. The thick power cables at its base hummed and crackled like electric eels, and a dozen light clusters flashed complicated patterns in total unison.

*This must be the day the important man comes out of the pod, which is impossible.*

"You there, in the . . . er . . . pod," she called, feeling more than a little silly. "Come out with your hands up."

No one emerged from the metal pyramid, but a hatch vented gas, then dropped with a loud clang to the floor. Ghostly sheets of steam floated from the interior.

Well, that's new, thought Chevie, checking with her thumb that the safety on her gun was off.

Inside the pod, orange light flickered, casting weird, shifting shadows on the wall.

There's something alive in there, Chevie realized.

Riley felt every molecule in his body coalesce, compacting until his senses returned.

I am alive, he rejoiced, until the bitter cold settled upon him, and his teeth chattered violently.

His hand still gripped the murder weapon, which was even now lodged in the chest of the murdered old geezer.

I cannot let go, he realized. My fingers are locked.

Riley tried to take stock of his surroundings, as Garrick had taught him.

He was contained in a metal tank with numerous fairy lights a-flashing on the cold walls.

*I have brought this magical gent back to his people with a blade in his body and my hand on the blade. They will see me swing for this.*

*Escape,* his instincts told him. *Escape before you are in the dock for murder or, worse, Garrick finds a way to find you.*

But the cold held him like a boulder strapped to his back; and Riley knew that, like thousands of street urchins every winter, soon he would sleep and then he would die.

Chevie rose on her haunches, then moved stealthily toward the hatch, keeping her gaze pointed through the gun sights.

"Come out with your hands up," she ordered once more, but again nothing emerged from the pod.

It may have taken three seconds to reach the hatch, but to Chevie it felt like an age. Everything slowed down as adrenaline coursed through her system, stimulating her heart rate, dilating her blood vessels and air passages. She saw sparks tumbling slowly from the conduits and steam clouds seemed to stand still in the air.

*Keep your focus, Special Agent,* she told herself. *There is someone in that pod.*

She could hear scrabblings inside.

*Is it a dog? An animal?*

*How do I warn an animal?*

Suddenly time sped up again, and Chevie found herself in front of the hatch. Cold radiated through the opening and orange sparks moved unnaturally toward one another, coalescing into something solid.

*Am I aiming my gun at a ghost?*

But there was something else inside, huddled shivering in the cramped interior.

"Don't move!" shouted Chevie, using her most serious FBI voice. "Freeze, or I will shoot."

A weak voice came from somewhere inside the orange cloud. "I *am* freezing, miss. My word on it."

Before Chevie could wonder why the strange accent had her brain singing "Consider Yourself," the cloud dissipated, revealing the figure of a boy huddled over an old man.

The boy was alive but the man was not, probably because of the knife jutting from his chest. Being dead was not the only thing wrong with this guy: the blood congealing on his torso was yellow, and one of his arms seemed to be that of a gorilla.

*Don't think about it now. Do the job.*

"Okay, kid. Move away from the dead . . . thing."

The boy blinked, searching for the source of the orders. "I never done it, miss. We need to leave this place. He'll be coming for me."

Chevie made a split-second decision, reaching into the pod and yanking the kid out by his collar.

Chevie held him on the floor with the palm of her free hand.

"Who's coming, kid? Who's coming for you?"

The boy's eyes were wide. "He's coming. Garrick. The magician. Death itself."

Great, thought Chevie. First a monkey guy, and now Death itself, who is also a magician.

Chevie felt another presence in the room and looked up to see Agent Orange in all his gray glory moving down the corridor toward the pod.

"That's a good way to get yourself shot, Orange. What are you doing here anyway? I never pressed the panic button."

Orange pulled off his silver sunglasses and surveyed the devastation. "Well, Agent Savano, when half of London blacked out, I guessed the WARP pod might have been activated." Orange hesitated six feet from the hatch. "Did you look inside, Chevie?"

"Yes. I looked. Am I gonna die from radiation poisoning now?"

"No, of course not. Is there . . . a man in there? Is my father in there?"

*Orange's father? This posting cannot get any weirder.*

Chevie returned her gaze to the restrained boy. "There were two people inside. This boy and a man. I really hope the man is not your father."

*But the way this day has been going, I just bet that monkey guy is Orange's dad.*

Chevie realized that she had never really trusted Agent Orange, but at this moment she actually felt sorry for him.

# 3 » MACHO-NERDS

LBERT GARRICK SAT SLOUCHED ON THE COLD basement floor, eyes tightly closed, preserving the ghost image of the orange sparks.

*Magic is real.*

It was a revolutionary thought in this industrial age of logic and reason. It was difficult to maintain belief in what he'd just seen once the evidence had disappeared. It would be much simpler to dismiss the entire event as delusion, but he would not.

I am being tested, he realized. My night of opportunity has arrived, and I must find within myself the mettle to seize my chance.

Garrick's faith had always been in bone, blood, and

butchery—in things he could wrap his fingers around and throttle, substantial things. There was nothing ethereal about them, but this was something different, something extraordinary. *Magic.*

Garrick had been fascinated by magic for as long as he could remember. As a boy he had accompanied his father to the Adelphi Theatre in London and watched from his perch in the wings as his old da swept the stage and kowtowed to the talent. Even then, this deference had angered the young Albert Garrick. Who were these people to treat his father with such disdain? Hacks, most of them—hacks, hags, and hams.

Among the ranks of the players there was a hierarchy. The singers were top dogs, then the comics, followed by the chorus pretties, and finally the conjurers and animal acts. Albert watched, fascinated, as the petty dramas played out every night backstage. Divas threw tantrums over dressing-room allocation or the size of opening-night bouquets. The young Garrick saw cheeks slapped, doors slammed, and vases hurled.

One particularly vain tenor, an Italian named Gallo, decided that the magic turn was not affording him due respect, and so he decided to ridicule the man at his birthday celebration in the Coal Hole public house on the Strand. Garrick witnessed the encounter from a stool beside the fireplace, and it made such an impression on the lad that he could recall the incident even now, almost forty years later.

The magician, the Great Lombardi, was built like a jockey, small and wiry, with a head that was too big for his body. He wore a pencil mustache that made him seem a touch austere, and a slick helmet of pomaded hair added to this impression. Lombardi was also Italian, but from the southern region of Puglia, which Gallo, a Roman, considered a land of peasants— an opinion he shared often and loudly. And, as Gallo was the star turn, it was understood that Lombardi would stomach the constant jibes. But Gallo should have known that Italian men are proud, and swallowed insults sit like bile in their stomachs.

On that particular evening, having treated the assembly to a raucous rendition of the "Drinking Song" from *La Traviata*, Gallo sauntered across the lounge to the magician and draped his meaty arm across the little man's shoulders.

"Tell us, Lombardi, is it true that the poor of Puglia fight with the pigs for root vegetables?"

The crowd laughed and clinked glasses, encouraging Gallo to further mischief.

"No answer? Well then, Signor Lombardi, tell us how the women of the south borrow their husbands' straight razors before Sunday ceremonies."

This was too much: the taciturn illusionist quickly drew a long dagger from his sleeve and seemingly stabbed Gallo upward under the chin, but no blood issued forth, just a stream of scarlet handkerchiefs. Gallo squeaked like a frightened child and collapsed to his knees.

"On the subject of razors," said Lombardi, pocketing his trick blade, "it seems as though Signor Gallo has cut himself shaving. He will survive . . . this time."

The joke was most definitely on the tenor, who, humili-ated beyond bearing, took the morning ferry from Newhaven to France, reneging on his contract and ensuring that he would never work a music hall in Great Britain again.

It was a beautiful revenge, tied together with the bow of wordplay, and the young Garrick, perched by the fire, vowed to himself, *Someday I, too, will have the power to command such respect.*

It took six months of fetching and carrying, but eventually Albert Garrick persuaded the Great Lombardi to take him on as an apprentice. It was his door to a new world.

Garrick thought of his vow now, sitting in the killing chamber of the foreboding house on Bedford Square.

*Someday I, too, will have the power.*

And that day had finally come.

Garrick dipped his fingertips in the small pool of black blood on the bedsheets, then watched the thick liquid run down his long pale fingers. The patterns reminded him of war paint worn by the savages in Buffalo Bill's Wild West Extravaganza, which he had taken Riley to see.

Someone will come to clean this mess, he thought, and daubed his cheeks with stripes of a dead man's blood.

*They will come, and I will take their magic and their power.*

BEDFORD SQUARE, BLOOMSBURY, LONDON, NOW

Special Agent Chevie Savano was feeling pretty under-informed. The first thing she did when she got the strange boy under lock and key in a holding cell was to storm into the pod room and prepare to have it out with Agent Orange. Her indignation seeped out of her when she saw her partner kneeling at the hatch, staring morosely at the body inside.

"It's . . . my father," he said, without looking up. "He must have been dead or dying going into the wormhole. The rapid energy loss might explain the multiple mutations."

Chevie had never expected to hear the words *wormhole* and *mutations* spoken outside of the movies.

"You need to tell me everything, Agent Orange."

Orange nodded, or maybe just allowed his head to droop. "I know, of course. But first we have to call in a cleanup team. I don't know what my father left behind. Get me the London office and tell them to send a full hazmat team. It's probably unnecessary, but I have to go back and check."

"Go back where? What is that pod? Some kind of transporter? If we had that technology, surely the public would have found out."

Orange's laugh was hollow. "There are a thousand Web sites dedicated to suppressed technology; two have even posted blueprints of the pod. People believe what they see in the Apple Store, not what some nutjob conspiracy theorist tells them."

"So it is a transporter?"

Orange was finding these questions a strain. "After a fashion. I'm upgrading your clearance. Open my folder on the network. The password is HGWELLS. One word, all caps. Those files will tell you all you need to know."

Chevie was halfway upstairs to her computer when she remembered why the password seemed familiar.

H. G. Wells. *The Time Machine.*

A time machine? she thought. That's insane.

But then, no more insane than a monkey arm and yellow blood.

Chevie called in the hazmat team request to the London office and was given the runaround for nearly fifteen minutes, until she invoked Agent Orange's name; after that she was put straight through to the hazardous materials section and was assured that a team would be on-site in less than an hour. No sooner had she put the phone down than a brigade of London's finest firefighters burst through what was left of the front door, determined to hack their way through the building with large axes. They were politely but firmly turned away by a dozen black-clad Fed musclemen who had set up a perimeter around the house on Bedford Square before the hazmat team arrived.

Once Chevie was sure that the perimeter was secure, she told the chief muscleman's mirrored sunglasses that she was taking ten minutes in the operations center.

*Just enough time for me to find out what the blazes is going on here.*

Chevie was surprised to find that she was handling the evening's events pretty well. She had always been cool under pressure, but this was different. Something sci-fi was going on here. It seemed that the world as she knew it was not the world as it was.

*Hold it together,* she told herself. *And read the file.*

Orange's folder had been sitting on the local network's

shared folders list since she'd arrived in Bedford Square, but she had never been able to access it until now. Chevie felt a little nervous even floating the cursor across the icon.

*What am I going to find out? If there is time travel, then why not aliens? Why not vampires? I really don't want to turn into one of those movie FBI gals who hunt freaks of nature. Those gals always end up with a limp.*

Chevie opened the folder and was dismayed to find over two hundred files lined up alphabetically inside. Chevie changed the view so that the files were listed in order of date and picked one with the title "Project Orange Overview." She began to read, forcing herself to go slowly and absorb every word. After twenty minutes of absolute concentration, she leaned back in her office chair and covered her mouth with one hand in case a hysterical giggle leaked out.

You have got to be kidding me, she thought, then removed her hand and shouted toward the door, "You have got to be kidding me!"

Orange was downstairs in the small medical room. He had wrestled his dead father from the pod's interior and laid him out on a steel gurney, covering all but his head with a white sheet. When Chevie entered the room, he was gently sponging the old man's forehead.

"Why do you think that kid killed your father?"

"I don't know. The Timekey video doesn't show much. One second the boy is not there, and the next he is. More than likely he's a thief."

"A thief from the past. What are we going to do with him?"

Orange wrung the sponge till his knuckles were white. "Again, I don't know. No one has ever brought back a local before. We could shoot him—I have a gun."

"Shoot him, good one. Are you okay, Orange? Maybe I should take over as agent in charge?"

Orange smiled wryly, and Chevie thought, not for the first time, that her partner had a wide variety of smiles, none of them very happy.

"No need for that, Agent, I am perfectly fine."

"But that's your father."

"In name only. I haven't seen this man for a long time. The Bureau is my family."

"Wow. I think that's the saddest thing I've ever heard."

Another smile, this one rueful. "I think you may be right."

"Do I still have to call you Agent Orange?"

"No. Professor Smart will be fine. Or just Felix."

"Professor Felix Smart. Son of missing Scottish quantum physicist Charles Smart. You have the same nose."

"But not the same blood, thank goodness. Yellow blood sets off the scanner at airports."

Chevie ignored the feeble attempt at humor. "So what happened to Professor Smart Senior? I didn't get that far in the files."

Felix Smart gazed at his father's face as he spoke. "He discovered that Einstein's quantum theory was essentially correct and that he could stabilize a traversable wormhole through space-time using exotic matter with negative energy density."

"I knew someone would get around to that eventually," said Chevie with a straight face, then wished that she could activate the WARP pod so that she could go back five seconds and not crack a funny when her partner's father was lying dead and mutated on the table. "Can we talk about this outside?"

"Of course." Felix Smart led her into the corridor, talking as he walked. "The university in Edinburgh funded my father for a few years, then he moved to a larger facility in London in conjunction with Harvard Research. By this time I was already with the FBI in Washington. Once it became clear to me that Father was getting somewhere, I persuaded my section chief to take a look. You wouldn't know it to listen to my accent, but I lived in Washington with my mother after my parents divorced. The Bureau consultants loved the concept and threw money at Father, and I was appointed as project liaison. We saw real results, really quickly. We sent through cameras first, and animals. Then death-row prisoners."

Chevie was not shocked. She knew that it had been common practice for government departments to offer testing deals to condemned prisoners in the last millennium. The government had tested everything from rubber bullets to telepathy pills on convicts.

"The tests were pretty successful. There was a small number of aberrations, usually on the return trip, but less than one percent, so acceptable in a scientific sense. Then some bright spark had the idea that we could stash valuable witnesses in the past."

Chevie raised a finger. "Just say that last part again. I want to nail it down in the real world."

"Even John Gotti couldn't have put a hit on someone in the nineteenth century, right? We sent the witnesses back into the past with a handler and then we would bring them home to testify."

"So, the FBI does witness protection in the past?"

"Yes. Would you like me to say it one more time?"

"No. I got it."

"Of course it's incredibly expensive, and the power needed for a single jaunt is enough to light a small country, so witnesses were always huge security risks and involved in trials that were tied up for a few years. In the ten years that WARP actually functioned, we only sent four witnesses back to various periods. Certain high-ranking intelligence officers felt the government was being short-changed, and so it was strongly suggested by a Colonel Clayton Box, a very enthusiastic special-forces type, that the tech be used for black ops."

"Wet work? Assassinations?"

"Exactly. Imagine if we could go back and take out terrorists while they were still in high school. My father did not like that idea and, no matter how much I tried to reassure him, he grew more and more paranoid. He saw conspiracies everywhere and was convinced that his research was being stolen, so one morning he simply disappeared into the past, taking all programmed Timekeys and the access codes with him. Father could come back if he wanted to, but we couldn't go after him. Not without the precise algorithms and codes that my father kept in his brain. He invented the language that the pods speak, so without him WARP was finished. My father was the key, and even after all this time we haven't been able to hack his machines. We lost Terrence Carter, the key witness in a huge corruption case. And his bodyguard was stranded with him. Not to mention the fact that there are millions of dollars' worth of WARP pods lying around wormhole hotspots like so much scrap. The irony was that Colonel Box and his entire team were on a mission when Father escaped into the past. Box and his men never made it home, so the threat to WARP was effectively neutralized."

Chevie took a long moment to absorb this deluge of information, then asked a sensitive question. "So the yellow blood and the simian arm were two of your aberrations?"

Felix Smart answered calmly, as though having a dead father with ape parts were an everyday occurrence. "The odds against two aberrations were steep. Wormhole mutations happened a few times with some of the prisoners. Father's theory was that the time tunnels had memory, and sometimes the quantum foam got muddled. Molecules were mixed up. Our test subjects made it through without any significant mutations over ninety-nine percent of the time. But we saw extra limbs, extrasensory perception, a dinosaur head once."

Chevie found it a struggle to keep a straight face. "A dinosaur head?"

"I know—insane, isn't it? Velociraptor, I think. We never found out for sure."

"The dinosaur died?"

Felix Smart frowned. "Technically the velociraptor committed suicide. There was enough of the scientist still inside there to realize what had happened, so he grabbed a gun and shot himself in the head. Terrible mess."

Chevie felt a sensation something like jet lag settling around her mind.

It's mild shock, she realized. My brain doesn't believe a word it's hearing. Still, might as well play along; it will all be over soon.

"So, what's next, Orange . . . Professor?"

Before he could answer, Felix's phone buzzed with a message. He drew a flat silver communicator from his pocket and read the screen. "Hazmat is here. So, next we clone my father's Timekey to go back to wherever he was hiding, and maybe find some notes and clean up whatever mess he left behind. We don't want some local finding one of my daddy's designs and building super-lasers a century ahead of schedule. You stay here and review the video evidence on the original Timekey's video log."

Chevie watched her partner/boss as he strode toward the stairway, back in action mode less than an hour after stumbling on the body of his estranged father.

Cold, she thought.


Riley lay on a low bunk in the holding cell. He held his hands before his face and clenched them into fists to stop them trembling.

*I am in another world* was his first thought. His second was Garrick. *He'll be coming for me, you can bet your last shilling on that.*

Riley tried to think about something else.

He'd never had a friend, as far as he could remember, and he was used to bolstering his own spirits. But sometimes, in his dreams, he saw the tall boy with red hair and a wide smile, and he had developed a habit of talking to that boy in his head as a way of calming himself.

*I'm alive, ain't I, Ginger? And maybe this prison is far enough away. Far enough to flummox Garrick himself.*

But Riley didn't believe that, no matter how many times he repeated it.

Riley tried to stop thinking about Garrick, but it was hard to cheer yourself up when Garrick's mug was the main image in your brain.

*So think of something else, then.*

What about the yellow blood busting from that old geezer's ticker? And didn't he have monkey parts? And what about that shameless lass in the black undergarments? This was indeed a confusing new world, and a strange-looking prison cell.

*But every cell has a door and every door has a lock.*

Garrick's words.

Undeniably those words had a wisdom to them. Riley forced himself to stand and walk the half dozen paces to the door. If this was indeed a prison, then it could be escaped from, just as Edmond Dantès had escaped from the dreaded Château d'If in one of Riley's favorite novels, *The Count of Monte Cristo.*

In recent years, books had become Riley's passion and had helped him through the long, lonely hours in the Holborn theater that he and Garrick used as their digs. It was Garrick's custom to disappear for days on end, and on his return he expected a clean house and a hot dinner. And while the assassin sat in the kitchen, blowing on his beef stew, his knees knocking on the underside of the table, he would twirl a spoon regally, which was Riley's signal to begin the evening's entertainment. Riley would then regale his master with an approximate summary of whichever novel he had been tasked with reading.

*Lively now, son,* Garrick often called. *Make me believe that I'm in between the pages my own self.*

And Riley would think, *I am not your son,* and, *I wish I was in between these pages.*

When Garrick had initiated this storytelling practice, Riley had hated it and grew to resent the books themselves; but *The Adventures of Sherlock Holmes* changed all of that. The book was simply too fascinating to be despised. Riley could no more hate Arthur Conan Doyle than he could hate the parents he could not remember, though Garrick reminded him often that they had left him hanging in a flour bag on the railings of Bethnal Green workhouse, where the magician had found him and rescued him from slum cannibals.

*I could certainly do with some advice from Mr. Holmes at this present moment,* thought Riley, rapping on the door with a knuckle. *A genius detective is exactly what the doctor ordered—that or a housebreaker.*

The cell door itself was standard prison issue, heavy steel

with a window of sufficient dimensions for a medium-sized dog to squeeze through were it not glazed.

*Or an escapologist.*

Riley knew he could wriggle through that gap if there was a way to get the glass out.

*Garrick has forced me through tighter holes.*

But the glass extended into the door itself on all sides and was well milled, with no warps or bubbles.

These people know their glass, Riley had to admit. The lock, then?

The lock was of a design that baffled Riley. There was no space for even the narrowest pick to penetrate. Riley tested the keyhole with his fingertip and felt a nail crack for his trouble. The door had no visible hinges, and there wasn't enough room for so much as a draft to squeeze through underneath.

*This would be a challenge, even for Albert Garrick.*

Then again, Garrick would be coming in, not going out. And getting in was always easier, especially if you could knock off the person with the key and take it from them.

Riley shivered. He swore that he could sense Garrick drawing closer, and his approach seemed to chill the air.

The door clacked and swung slowly inward, and Riley held his breath, so convinced was he that Garrick had come to tuck him in for a Highgate nap. But it was not the magician; instead the half-clothed lass who had locked him in stood framed in the doorway.

"Step back from the door, kid," said the girl. "Lie on the bed with your hands behind your head."

Her tone was amiable enough, but there was a large pistol in her delicate fingers, and in Riley's opinion, this particular pistol seemed capable of shooting the bullet and perhaps digging the grave as well. This was not a pistol one argued with, so Riley did as he was told and looked sharp about it.

The girl seemed satisfied and stepped inside the room, leaving a tantalizing wedge of freedom on display behind her. Riley briefly considered bolting for the outside world, but then light glinted on the gun's barrel, and the boy decided he could wait for the next opportunity.

"Miss," said Riley. "Have I come to rest in a traveling Wild West Show? You appear to be a savage Injun."

Chevie glared down at the boy along the sights of her weapon. "We don't use the term *savage Injun* anymore. Some people take issue with being described as savages. Go figure."

"I saw Buffalo Bill's Extravaganza a while back. You have the look of an Apache."

Chevie half smiled. "Shawnee, if you have a burning need to know. Now, enough small talk. There's a bar behind your head; grab it with your right hand."

Riley did as he was told, and having an inkling of what was coming, spread his grip to widen the span of his wrist, but to no avail.

"Sure, kid. Oldest trick in the book. What? You think I graduated from Idiot College last semester?"

"Why do you refer to me as 'kid'? We are of the same age or thereabouts."

Chevie leaned across Riley and snapped a metal cuff over his wrist.

"Yeah? Well, I'm seventeen, actually. And you don't look a day over twelve." She ratcheted the cuff tight, hooking the other end on the bed railing.

"I am four and ten," retorted Riley. "And due a stretch any day. This time next year I'll be towering over you, miss."

"I am thrilled to hear that, kid. Until that great day dawns, you've got one hand for eating and scratching your behind, though I recommend you eat first."

Now that the boy was secured, Chevie wedged the door open with a chair so she could keep an eye on the pod room, just in case something else decided to come through.

Riley jerked his chain a few times to test its strength and Chevie grinned.

"Everybody does that, but let me tell you, those cuffs have a tensile strength of over three hundred and fifty pounds, so you are wasting your time." Chevie shook her head. "There's a lot of *time* wasting going on around here today; you have no idea."

Riley suddenly felt like crying, and almost as suddenly felt ashamed of himself. Crying would not get him away from Garrick; backbone was the order of the day.

"Miss, you need to let me loose before he gets here."

Chevie pulled up a steel chair, spun it on one leg, and sat, leaning her elbows on the back.

"Oh, yeah. *He.* Death, right? He is Death, and Death is coming. The bogeyman."

"No, no bogeyman. Garrick is flesh right enough. He done for old yellow-blood, and he'll be doing for us soon if we don't get a little wind under our sails and leave this place, wherever it is."

Chevie almost pitied this filthy urchin until she remembered the first time she'd laid eyes on him. "Tell you what, kid. Why don't we forget this *Death* character for a minute and focus on why you killed the old man?"

Riley shook his head. "Not me, miss. I never did. It was Garrick."

Chevie was pretty good at reading people, and this kid's face was wide, with heavy brows, a pointed chin, and a mop of hair that could be any color underneath the dirt. His eyes were a startling blue, at least the left one was; the right eye seemed to be mostly enlarged pupil. In short, an innocent kid's face, not a murderer's face. Unless he was a psychopath.

"Oh, yes. Garrick. Mr. Death. Or perhaps Mr. Nobody."

"You're mocking me, miss. You think I'm a liar."

Chevie scowled. "Stop with the *miss* stuff, kid. You're making me feel like a grandmother. Call me Agent Savano. Don't go thinking we're friends, now; I'm just being civil, and I don't want to judge you until all the facts are in. And, to answer your geographical query, we are in London, England."

The boy was obviously disturbed by this news. "London, you say? Is it true? But then he is already here. There is no time, Agent Sa-van-o. We must get away from here. Can you summon the orange magic?"

Orange magic. Agent Orange, thought Chevie, hearing the penny drop at last. Now I get it.

"Listen, kid. If this Garrick person does exist, and he is stuck on the other end of the *orange magic*, there is no way in heaven he's going to show up here. Understand?"

The boy's odd eyes grew no less wide or wild. "No way in heaven, but perhaps a way in hell."

Chevie snorted. "You Victorians are pretty melodramatic, aren't you? What's your name, kid? I can't go on calling you *kid* all day."

"I am called Riley," said the boy.

"Something Riley? Or Riley Something?"

Riley shrugged. "I don't know this, Agent Savano. Garrick never knew either. One name was all that was needed. The note left with me simply read, 'This is Riley, a waif in need. Look after him.' I was on the point of being boiled up by cannibals when he found me. Killed the bunch of them, he did, made the last one chew on a hunk of his own leg as a lesson."

"I am totally not liking this Death, magician, one-name-calling, alleged time-traveler killer."

Riley sighed. This lady was not giving Garrick his due, but how could she? Garrick was a unique creature, and his wrath could not be appreciated without being seen or experienced. Riley would have to grind a plan from his own brain, and perhaps distract his captor for a moment to buy time to think. Riley raised himself a little and nodded at a tattoo on Agent Savano's bicep.

"What is this arrowhead marking, Agent? Are you a sailor?"

Chevie tapped the blue mark. "This is the chevron, and I was named for it; but that's a story for another day, when I visit you in prison, maybe."

The lady had not fallen for his ruse.

"I am innocent, miss . . . Agent. You must let me go."

Chevie stood up, twirling the chair under her palm. "I'll have to get back to you on that, once I review the video. I'll bring you some McDonald's in an hour. Until then, don't go anywhere, time traveler."

Riley watched the door close, thinking, Time traveler?

And, What is a video?

And, Why would she bring me Scotsmen? What help would that be?

The hazmat team was unlike any hazardous materials team that Chevie had ever seen. There was no sign of the white virus overalls, or wi-vi suits as the Feds had nicknamed them; instead the four agents were dressed in what looked like synthetic rubber, and they seemed pretty ripped for a science squad.

Chevie jogged along the basement corridor to Agent Smart, who was strapping a crossbow across his chest.

"What are these guys? Chemistry ninjas? And why are you bringing that bow?"

"So many questions, Agent Savano."

"Yeah, well I've been a little out of the loop around here. Nobody mentioned time-traveling witness protection even once before today. Now everyone's jumping into the past except me."

"You don't have hazardous materials training, Chevie. This squad does, plus they have serious combat skills, too. As for our outfits and equipment, our clothes are hemp-based and will biodegrade in the open air, and the weapons are high-end design but not too sci-fi for the locals, should we meet any. We go back, clean up, and beam home. And if something does get left behind in the field, then there's no domino effect."

"With respect to the . . . er . . . domino effect, why don't you go back a little early and rescue your father? Now that you have his Timekey and know exactly where he was."

Agent Smart shook his head. "You didn't read the entire file, did you, Chevie? Wormholes are a constant length to the nanosecond. Think of them like straws; you move the front and the back moves too. So, if an hour has passed here, then an hour has passed there. This particular wormhole measures just under a hundred and twenty years, so that's how far we're going back."

"How long will you be gone?"

"Not long. Ten minutes, tops. Any more than that and we're dead, and you're to shut this thing down, dismantle the pod, and go home to California."

"Way to think positive, Agent. What are we going to tell the fire brigade this time?"

Smart pulled a full face mask over his head. "Not a problem. I've powered up the dampers; no blackouts this trip."

Chevie surveyed the time squad, clad head to toe in padded black body armor, bristling with blades and bows.

"You guys look futuristic, even with the old hardware.

What happens if you get caught before the hemp melts? The boy, Riley, swears there's some kind of magical killer back there."

Smart's voice was muffled by the filter over his mouth. "Ah, yes. The bogeyman. It's classic transference, Savano. Blame Mr. Nobody. Even if there is some Fagin person back there, I think my boys can handle him."

Chevie thought so too. These guys looked like they could take down a small country.

"What if there's an earthquake, and your boys are stuck in the rubble?"

"Well, that's what the red button is for, though these suits have been in storage for fifteen years, so I hope the mercury switches still work."

This statement brought the gravity of the situation home.

"Self-destruct?" said Chevie. "You *are* kidding me? This isn't an episode of *The Twilight Zone*."

Agent Smart's shoulders jerked as he chuckled. "Yes, it is, Chevie. That's exactly what it is."

Chevie did not chuckle; she had a sense of humor, but self-destruct jokes were not to her taste.

"So I gotta just twiddle my thumbs here while you macho-nerds are off straightening time dominoes?"

Smart froze. "Macho-nerds? Straightening time dominoes? Do you know something, Agent Savano? I think you have grasped the essence of what's going on here, and I never really thought you would. Some people's biggest muscle is in their trigger finger, but you have held it together admirably during this stressful time, and without shooting a single person."

Chevie stared. Was Smart taking the time to make fun of her? Or was he simply a robot?

"Are you sure you should be heading up this operation? Maybe I should relieve you?"

Suddenly the four ninja-nerds pulled their sidearms from holsters on the coat hanger.

"Don't say the R word, Chevie," advised Felix. "This mission is pretty important. Nobody wants to end up not existing because my father polluted the timeline."

Chevie backed down not one inch. "Yeah, well, you tell your boys that when they get back, I'll see them in the gym, two at a time."

The hazmat team lowered their guns, gazing at Chevie, heads cocked in surprise, like lions challenged by a little mouse.

"They don't say much, your lab buddies."

Smart opened a series of laptops on a metal table; thick cables flopped onto the floor from the rear of the computer bank and wound their way across to the WARP pod. He quickly tapped in long code sequences.

"That's why I like them, Agent. They just do their jobs, no small talk."

The laptops were old and chunky, with raised letters on the keyboards that glowed green and were not in the usual QWERTY order. Chevie tapped one casing, to check whether it was actually wooden.

Smart slapped her hand away. "Don't poke the equipment, Agent," he admonished. "This stuff is ancient alternative tech. We don't even have the parts to repair this anymore."

"Shoot, I got some wood in my room."

Smart ignored her comment and continued his systems check. As he typed, the pod shook itself awake, vibrating and venting steam like a very old fridge. The banks of square lights flickered in complicated patterns, and the fat power lines buzzed with barely contained megawatts of electricity. In spots, the rubber melted, exposing fizzing wires.

The entire setup reminded Chevie of sci-fi reruns she'd seen on cable.

*This is how people thought the future would look on last-century TV. Cheap and flashy.*

Laser beams shot out from several nodes on the pod, connecting to form a lattice around the ship.

Lasers? thought Chevie. It's a time machine, all right. I feel like I'm going back to the seventies.

It took several minutes for the WARP pod to warm up. It shrugged, coughed, and hummed into life, six electric motors clattering into action at its base. Chevie was quite glad that she was not among the group waiting to step into its belly to be dematerialized. Eventually the pod hovered maybe half an inch above its trailer and the various lights flashed in perfect harmony, except for the ones that popped and crackled.

"Okay," shouted Smart above the electrical din. "We have ninety-seven percent stability. That's good enough."

Ninety-seven percent? thought Chevie. I bet those hazmat guys didn't see the monkey arm, or they'd insist on waiting for a hundred percent.

The black-clad hazmat team climbed through the hatch

into the vehicle and sat on a low bench that ran around the wall. They were a cramped bunch in there and suddenly looked a little less tough, in spite of their scary suits and weapons. Chevie was reminded of her little foster brother and the night he and his buddies had camped out in the backyard, all tough as nails until something brushed against the tent at 2 a.m.

Smart gave Chevie the Timekey he was holding. "I've cloned keys for me and the team, but this is still the prime key with all the access codes. In fact, the entire history of the project is on this key. Don't lose it."

Chevie hung the key around her neck. "I'll keep it under my pillow beside my photo of you."

Smart lowered his mask, and Chevie saw that for the first time in nine months, he was genuinely smiling. "I'm going to miss you when this is all over, Savano. None of these guys ever gives me lip. Having said that, if you foul this up, I will have you stationed in the Murmansk office."

"We don't have a Murmansk office."

"Oh, we've got one . . . but it's really deep under the ice."

"I get the message. Don't worry, Felix. The boy is secure, and I won't let anyone else touch this Timekey."

Smart fixed his mask. "Good. Then in ten minutes, you get to go home early with a commendation and a clean record. But if any strangers come through that pod, remember your training: always go for the chest shot."

"I remember," said Chevie. "Chest shot. The biggest target."

They shook hands, something that Chevie did not particularly want to do, not because of any germ phobia, but because in the boredom of the last nine months she had developed a fondness for action movies—and as any film buff knows, when two cops develop a grudging respect for each other, then the supporting cop is about to die.

And if anyone's a supporting player around here, she thought, it's me.

Smart ducked into the pod, squeezing onto the bench beside his teammates.

He counted down from five with his fingers, then the entire team reached into the middle and overlapped hands. As they all touched, Smart tapped the pendant around his neck, the pod bloomed with orange light, and there was a loud whoosh, which immediately collapsed in on itself, creating a vacuum that Chevie could feel even from her position behind the computers.

The noise rose to hurricane level, and Smart's crew jittered as their molecules were torn apart. They turned orange, then split into orange bubbles, which spiraled into a mini-cyclone that spun faster and faster in the center of the pod. Chevie swore she could see body parts reflected in the bubbles.

*Reflected from where? Sub-atomia?*

The wormhole opened like a drain of light, a little smaller than Chevie had expected, if she was honest, yet it was big enough to slurp down the atoms of the hazmat team and their leader. The bubbles spiraled down, forcing themselves into the pulsating white circle at the pod's base. It shone like a silver dollar, then spun as though someone had flipped it, each revolution sending a blinding beam across the basement.

Chevie closed her eyes. When she opened them again, the wormhole had closed, leaving behind a wisp of smoke in the shape of a rough question mark.

*You and me both*, Chevie thought, stepping forward warily around the bank of computers to peer into the pod's belly. It was cold in there, and blobs of orange gel shivered on the steel walls.

*I hope those blobs weren't important body parts.*

Smart and his team were gone.

I didn't believe Orange's story until this moment, Chevie realized. Not for a second. I am not sure if I believe it now.

But there was no denying that her partner had disappeared, whether into a wormhole as planned, or boiled to jelly by old-school laser beams.

*I can worry about all of this when I am home in Malibu. Until then: act like a professional.*

Chevie decided to use the ten minutes to check through the video on Smart Sr.'s Timekey. See if there was anything more she could add to her report. And, you never know, there was always the ghost of a chance that Riley was telling the truth. But even if he was, there was no way the bogeyman he was so afraid of could make it to the future.

Chevie suddenly saw a flash of Riley's face: blue eyes wide, soot-blackened brow.

*No way in heaven, but perhaps a way in hell.*

She shivered. Maybe that boy wasn't telling the truth, but he sure believed he was.

# 4 » ALT-TECH

ALBERT GARRICK HUMMED A NURSERY RHYME he'd learned on the knee of an Irish woman who had nannied for half of the Old Nichol back in the dark times. If there was one truth that Garrick held like iron in his core, it was that he would never return to the Old Nichol, not even to dodge the noose.

"I would swing before I'd go back to that cesspit," he vowed quietly through clenched teeth, as he did most nights.

And in this case the term *cesspit* was not simply a storyteller's exaggeration. The Old Nichol Street rookery was bordered by the common sewer and had been spared by the Great Fire, but the area had not seen refurbishment for its pauper residents since that time. A true cesspit. A great ditch of putrefaction, dotted with sties, hovels, and dung heaps, where the air sang with the sharp tang of industry and the lusty howls of hungry babes.

Hell on earth.

As Albert Garrick hummed, the words fluttered from the dark shadows of his past and the assassin sang them in a sweet tenor:

> One little babby, ten, twenty,
> Only last week I had wages plenty
> Then Nick came a-stealin' my babbies away
> Now I begs for me supper every bloomin' day.

Garrick gave a dour chuckle. A cholera nursery rhyme, hardly the subject to soothe a little one's fears, and more often it would keep him awake than send him to sleep, but then Garrick had lost a family of nine to the disease, and it would have claimed him and his father had clever Da not slit the Adelphi Theatre caretaker's throat in an alley one night, then turned up to claim his place the following morning. The caretaker had been Father's bully chum; but it was life or death, and the Thames was chock-full of best friends. Barely a tide passed without someone's bosom pal washing up on the mud banks at Battersea.

For over a year the father and son slept in a secret space behind the Adelphi's green room, until they could afford digs far away from the Old Nichol.

Garrick knelt on the elaborate fleur-de-lis rug in front of

him, banishing memories of his past and concentrating on this night's business. Carefully he placed the tips of his blades on the central petal of the pattern. Six knives in total, from stiletto to shiv and four-sided bo-shuriken throwing knives; but Garrick's favorite was the serrated fish knife that had lived under his pillow since childhood.

He tapped the wooden hilt fondly. It was true to say that Garrick held this blade in higher regard than any person of his acquaintance. Indeed, the magician had once risked prison by dallying to reclaim the blade from a mark who had snarled the knife in the farrago of his entrails.

*But I would sacrifice even you for a taste of magic*, he admitted to the knife. *In a heartbeat and gladly.*

Garrick knew that men would come to this place when their own magician was returned to them a cold corpse. The old man had promised as much—*if you harm me, men will come to make sure you didn't take my secrets*—and Garrick believed those words to be true. The old man's secrets were magical ones, and the men would come, because magic was power, which in turn was knowledge. And he who controlled knowledge controlled the world. Knowledge was a dangerous thing to have skittering around loose, and so men would come.

A hanging circle of bats clattered in the broad chimney flue, wings slapping like a tanner's brush.

Perhaps they sensed something? Perhaps the great moment was upon them?

*Come, gods of magic. Come and meet Albert Garrick's steel, and we shall see if you die like men.*

Garrick pocketed his blades and melted into the basement shadows by the grandfather clock.

When a traveler emerges from a wormhole and the quantum foam solidifies, there are quickly forgotten moments of clarity when the time traveler feels at one with the world.

*Everything is all right and outta sight,* as Charles Smart quipped in the famous talk at Columbia University during his U.S. lecture tour. *When those little virtual particles annihilate, a person gets literally plugged into the universe.*

Of course this was just quantum-jecture, another of Professor Smart's terms. There could never be any proof of these brief moments of oneness, as they dissipated almost instantly and were all but impossible to record. Nevertheless, Professor Smart was correct: the "Zen Ten" does exist and was being experienced by the hazmat team as their bodies solidified and left them standing in short-lived awe, like kids at a fireworks display.

The team stood on the bed, which Charles Smart had rigged as a receiver, wreathed in a wispy curtain of orange light that jerked back toward the wormhole that hovered behind them like a floating diamond.

"Hey," said the point man, crossbow dangling loosely from his fingers. "Do you guys see the parallels between Einstein and Daffy Duck now? That duck knew what he was talking about."

There would have followed another eight seconds or so of cosmic wisdom had not Garrick realized intuitively that fate would never again drop such a ripe opportunity in his lap. He attacked like a death-dealing dervish, springing from his hiding place onto the four-poster bed, where his opponents stood like cattle in a slaughterhouse pen.

*Use yer bows now, my boys*, he thought.

Garrick's arrival on the receiver bed smashed the cocoon of bliss, and the hazmat team was instantly vigilant—all but Smart, who was still shrouded in quantum particles, which caused his extremities to warp and shudder as though underwater.

Garrick's first strike was the sweetest, as it drew hot red blood. He had been anxious that his steel might encounter armor of some kind, but though the material was exceptionally hardy, it could not resist the singing sharpness of his trusty fish knife. The man who had spoken of ducks sank to the sheets, his heart popped in his chest. A second black-clad newcomer arranged his fists in an approximation of a boxer's stance and delivered a lightning hook to Garrick's solar plexus.

The assassin grunted in surprise, not pain. These dark demons were fast, but not magically so, and it would take a sight more gumption in a blow to penetrate the flat boards of muscle on Garrick's torso.

Garrick had studied many of the fighting arts, from Cornish wrestling to Okinawan karate, and chosen what he wanted from each one. These skills he augmented with his own speciality: sleight of hand. His was a style that could not be clinically recognized and defended against, as there was only one master and only one pupil.

The magician engaged his unique skill and palmed the blade across to his left hand. The second man in black followed this move with a tilt of his head, but he did not cotton to the throwing spike that sprouted in Garrick's right hand as though growing from the vein.

By the time the man in black caught the deadly glint from the corner of his eye, the spike had already begun its flashing flight toward its target. Not toward the second man, but toward a third while the second was distracted by Garrick's left hand, which held the fish knife.

The second man realized this too late and had barely time to watch the throwing spike puncture his comrade's chest before the fish knife slashed across his own jugular.

*So much blood*, thought Garrick. *An ocean of blood.*

Three of the hazmat team were down. The fourth opted to attack rather than be slaughtered where he stood. This guy was a real bruiser, who was famous in the FBI for having punched out a world boxing champion in a Vegas bar fight. He sent out a lightning right cross that would have floored an elephant and mentally mapped out his next three punches.

He would not need them. Garrick ducked under the punch, rolled the man across his back, and met him on the other side with a prison shiv. The agent did not die immediately, but he would not tarry long.

One left now, the one clothed in magical light. The man with true power. Garrick felt himself salivate.

How to steal the magic? What was the technique? An incantation, perhaps? Or did they need a pentagram? Everything

Garrick had tried in the past to suck even a spark of power from the ether now seemed garishly jokish. Candles and weeds, animal sacrifices. He had been a mere child scrabbling around in the dark. Here was true power in front of his eyes, if he could take it.

Garrick pocketed the blade and dipped his icicle fingers into the orange light until he found the man's neck. The tendons looked taut as gibbet ropes, but to the touch they were softer than butter. Garrick saw his own fingers somehow merge with the stranger's body, and with the merging came a sharing of souls.

I know this man, he realized. And he knows me.

With his free hand Garrick ripped off the man's mask, to demand the knowledge that he could not find in the man's mind.

"Tell me how to take your magic," he demanded. "Give me your secrets."

The man seemed in a stupor. He saw but did not see, his gaze soft and blotted, a look Garrick had seen on the faces of soldiers emerging from chloroform.

*I know you, Albert Garrick*, said the man, though his mouth did not move. *I know what you are.*

It seemed to Garrick, as he listened to Felix Smart's thoughts, that he had joined utterly with this man. Smart's entire life was compressed into a bitter capsule and shoved down his throat. Memories exploded inside him, more vivid than his own. He tasted blood and sweat, smelled gunpowder and rotten flesh, and felt his own secret shames and regrets that he had never dared acknowledge.

This is the magic, he realized, even as his past life crawled into his gut like a worm. To see, to know.

"Give it to me," he said, tightening his grip around the man's neck. "I want it all, d'you hear?"

"They sent you to Afghanistan," gasped the man, the words grunting out of him.

So surprised was Garrick to hear this that he actually engaged.

"Not many know that, Scotsman. I took up the queen's rifle, killed my share, and came back a hero." Garrick shook his head to dislodge the orange man's probing. "Quiet with your talk, man, unless it is to divulge secrets."

The man closed his eyes—sadly, it seemed to Garrick. "I can't. And I know what you intend to do, so . . ." His hand moved toward a red button on his belt, and Garrick gripped the wrist in his fingers.

A quantum circuit was completed and information exchanged on every level. Knowledge, secrets, and the very essence of being—all whipped between the two men locked in grim combat. Garrick struggled to hold on to himself in this blizzard of awareness. He saw and understood everything, from amoebas to microwaves. He felt his own self as a collection of jittering neutrons and understood the concept. He saw the surface of the moon, an earth ruled by dinosaurs, matchbox-sized computers, the Scottish man of science, the little Shawnee lass, and the boy Riley.

Riley, he thought, and the thought skittered away from him on a tide of quantum foam. He cocked his head to follow it, and the Scotsman used the distraction to press the red button on his belt.

Garrick felt mercury shift and smelled the explosives and knew that there was only one way to perhaps escape death. He crushed Felix Smart's barely solid windpipe in his fist, then tumbled them both into the tiny pulsing circle of light that lay in the center of the mattress.

It did not seem possible that two grown men could fit into that tiny space, but the wormhole was pure physics and so did its work, dematerializing the battling pair just as the tiny suit-bomb exploded.

Charles Smart, the godfather of time travel, had speculated in his famous Columbia lecture that if a spontaneous energy shift were to be introduced into the quantum stream, then the effects on local travelers could be spectacular, producing, in theory, a being imbued with all the powers not yet granted to humanity by evolution. Or, as he put it, *Clark Kent could indeed become Superman.*

The world could see superheroes.

Or supervillains.

BEDFORD SQUARE, BLOOMSBURY, LONDON, NOW

Chevie Savano plugged Charles Smart's Timekey into the weirdly pronged socket on the bank of antique computers in the pod room.

A message appeared on the screen: WARMING UP.

*Warming up?* What was this? *A photocopier?*

*Alt-tech* was a term Felix liked to bandy about. Alternative technology. What he meant was old junk that didn't work properly anymore.

*Warming up?* The next thing you knew, this contraption would ask for more gas.

Eventually a menu shuddered into life on the small convex screen. The kind of screen nerd grandpas collected to play Pac-Man. The operating system was unfamiliar to her: a set of consecutive menus that reminded her of a family tree.

*Well, I guess even Apple and Microsoft can't control the past,* she thought, smiling.

It did seem as though everything was on this Timekey. The entire history of the project, including previous jumps, personnel files, pod locations, and, of course, Professor Smart's video diary.

Chevie selected the proximity-alert recordings with an honest-to-God wooden mouse, and scrolled through to the last couple of minutes.

It was a grainy picture, colors muted by the darkness, but she could clearly see the boy Riley approach stealthily, eyes and teeth shining out of his blackened face. The blade in his hand was visible too, just the top edge where the soot failed to cover it.

Suddenly the screen glowed green, and Riley's features were underlit like a Halloween storyteller. The boy looked pretty guilty, it had to be said: sneaking into an old man's house in the dead of night, armed with a wicked-looking blade. The alert changed from green to red as Riley drew closer, and the view flipped as Professor Smart sat up.

There was a little chitchat, which was impossible to make out, then Riley struck and everything went orange. End of story. QED, the check's in the mail, the prosecution rests.

*Or does it?*

Chevie freeze-framed the moment when Riley lunged. It seemed a little weird. Chevie knew all about knife fights, and the boy's stance seemed off to her. He was leaning backward while moving forward. This was not an easy thing to do. Also, the look on his face was pure horror.

*Either this kid is schizophrenic, or he had a little help.*

But there was no one else in the dark room. No one that she could see, at any rate.

Chevie was tempted to pound the ancient hardware.

*Alt-tech, my butt. I can't even clean up the image a little.*

Then Chevie had an idea: maybe she couldn't clean up the image on this box of bolts, but if she could transfer it . . .

Chevie pulled her smartphone from her waistband and took an HD shot of the screen. Simply transferring the image to her phone seemed to sharpen it up a bit, but it was still dark and fuzzy.

*Dark and fuzzy, not a problem.*

Chevie had no fewer than four photo manipulation apps on her phone, and she selected one to run the picture through.

In a way it was therapeutic to have such a mundane task to

perform, which could momentarily help her to pretend she was working on a normal case.

She ordered the phone to sharpen, lighten, and boost color.

It took a few seconds, then another person appeared from the shadows, behind Riley to the right. A tall man, slightly bent, with dark, close-set eyes that were devoid of expression, like those of a corpse. The face was bland, made more so by the soot smeared across his features, and Chevie couldn't imagine ladies ever swooning before this guy, but the eyes gave him away. Chevie had seen those dead eyes before, on the faces of serial killers in the Quantico files.

Chevie shivered.

So that's what it feels like when your blood runs cold, she thought. I've heard the expression but never understood it.

This was the man Riley had spoken of, no doubt about it. Death, the magician. This guy looked capable of anything.

*Yet it was Riley holding the knife. The boy was still guilty.*

But . . .

Chevie double-tapped the image to enlarge it, then centered the crosshairs on Riley's knife arm, enlarging again. It seemed conclusive. A hand holding a knife, a forearm, wrinkle shadows at the elbow.

*Wrinkle shadows . . .*

Chevie enlarged again until the pixels blurred and saw that the shadows were not shadows.

*Not unless shadows have knuckles.*

There were four long fingers gripping Riley's arm, forcing his hand.

The boy is innocent! she thought, releasing a breath that she'd not realized she was holding.

Looking into that blackened face, with those flat eyes, Chevie was glad that this man could not, contrary to what Riley believed, make his way into the future.

All the same, she thought. Maybe I will stand guard over the pod with a round in the chamber. Just in case.

Chevie tugged the Timekey from its socket and hung it around her neck for safekeeping.

*Just in case.*

Special Agent Lawrence Witmeyer, her boss in the L.A. office, was a man with a parable for every occasion. Many involved a made-up Fed called Agent Justin Casey, who was always prepared and never got himself shot because he forgot to follow protocol.

Chevie snorted. *Agent Justin Casey. A helluva guy.*

And if she hadn't been a little distracted by her reminiscing, she might have noticed an angry blister of red energy boiling at the heart of the WARP pod and had time to duck before the explosion.

Unfortunately she *was* distracted and didn't see anything until the computers set off a warning alarm. By then it was already too late.

Garrick and Smart tumbled into the wormhole together, but as separate people. Once inside, Garrick held on to his consciousness, but Smart's heart had already stopped beating and his brain was winding down. The effect of the self-destruct bomb was to excite some particles that were not meant to be excited and corrupt the transition, in effect merging Smart's last neurons of consciousness with Garrick's and some of his physical characteristics too, which the WARP pod would rebuild around his altered DNA.

A new being with accelerated evolution. All the gifts that millennia of adaptation would bring.

For a length of time that was immeasurable and yet instant, Garrick felt himself disembodied in the wormhole. He could not see anything and spent the time flicking through Smart's memories.

I have killed both father and son, he realized, and wished that he had received payment for the second murder.

This thought of payment set Garrick thinking about the shady cove who had contracted him for the murder of Charles Smart.

Did he know, Garrick wondered, about all of this magic?

On a normal outing there would have been no complications. Garrick would have slid in and out like a gust of wind, but Riley had been along for his first kill. It had been a trial run for the lad, plain and simple. Garrick had kept an eye on the comings and goings for a few days, then sent Riley in through an upstairs window. He would never have risked his reputation or purse taking the boy along had there been even a smell of peril.

*All of these magical happenings are luck or fate.*

Though Garrick could not now believe in either magic or fate. Atoms collided or they did not, simple as that.

Atoms, thought Garrick, delighted with the new understanding that the merge with Felix Smart had brought him. I can see their systems in my mind's eye.

Garrick was not anxious or ill at ease over this curious transition. He knew now exactly what was happening and what awaited him in the future. Nor was he disappointed over the absence of "real magic," for was this not magic all around him now? Wasn't this new knowledge power without measure? Garrick was too enchanted by his new state to take to brooding.

*The future awaits and, with my new awareness, I will be master of it.*

These were issues to be decided in a future Garrick knew well.

*Three-D movies and pocket-sized computers. Automatic weapons and Japanese robots. My oh my.*

On this occasion there was no gentle materialization in the house on Bedford Square, no wisps of ethereal mist or shuddering passengers in the pod. This time a red ball of liquid appeared, maybe the size of an apple, and then it exploded in a grisly mess, vomiting sheets of blood into the basement, accompanied by a sonic boom and wave of concussive force. The ring of dampers set around the pod exploded like fireworks at a rock concert.

Chevie was lifted like a leaf before a hurricane and tossed backward the length of the basement corridor. She touched down a couple of times before crashing into a stack of her own packing boxes under the stairs, which she had been meaning to fold flat since she'd arrived. The boxes tumbled on top of her, leaving a triangular tunnel for her to keep an eye on the pod. And it was only one eye; Chevie's left eye closed on impact and her senses longed to desert her, but she held on long enough to see what else came out of the pod.

What came out was a sac of flesh and bone, lurching across the blood-slick floor, fighting with itself. Chevie saw a hand punching through the membrane and a face pressing against the viscous surface.

"Smart," called Chevie weakly.

Then the face bubbled and changed, becoming that of the man on the screen.

*I am in a nightmare. Wake up, Chevron Savano. On your feet.*

If this was a dream, it was incredibly realistic, engaging all of her senses, even smell.

*I can't remember smelling in a dream before.*

Chevie knew it was no dream. The tiles that smooshed her jaw and cheek were too slick with lumpy blood and ichor.

The jumble of body parts clicked and rattled with labored breaths, drawing bolts of energy from the pod. It shook like a wet dog, shaking off globs of its cocoon until the figure of a man emerged. The man oozed into a standing position, then spread his arms wide, flexing his fingers as though they were wondrous inventions.

Chevie felt her legs piston feebly as they sought traction on the floor, but even that effort made her head spin.

*Riley. I need to save that boy.*

The figure seemed to hear the thought and shrugged off the

remains of the distended bubble of sloppy substance, transitioning from solid to gas and floating in clouds toward the ceiling.

Clothes grew on the man, literally appearing stitch by stitch, crawling like worms along his solidifying skin. The garments were a curious blend of hemp, hazmat leggings, and a Victorian gent's overcoat, topped off by a bowler hat that seemed as out of place as a bow tie on a shark.

"Riley," said the man, as if testing his mouth. "Riley, my son. I have come for you. I know where you are incarcerated. The futurist Smart showed me."

Smart showed him, thought Chevie, and she knew in her gut that the hazmat team was gone.

Chevie remembered having a gun, which was possibly in its holster at her side, but that seemed like an impossible distance for her hand to travel. It was all she could do to keep one eye open. She saw the magician fondly tap the keyboard on one of the old computers, then his gaze turned on her.

He sees me, Chevie realized, feeling the cold from the basement's floor seep into her body.

His gaze lingered on her a moment, then the magician made his way with determined strides toward the lockup door.

It's okay, she thought. That door is reinforced steel. The devil himself is not getting in without a card or a code.

The demonic figure came to a halt in front of the security keypad, cracked his knuckles theatrically, then punched in the code.

"Abracadabra," he said as the holding-cell door yawned open.

*I am sorry, Riley*, thought Chevie. *You told me the truth, and I left you there to die. Forgive me.*

Garrick doffed his hat, as though entering a church, then ducked inside the cell.

Chevie closed her eye. She did not want to see what happened next.

Albert Garrick had literally become a new man when he emerged from the sac and stepped into the future.

Everything was different: his DNA, his vocabulary, his range of expertise, his stance, muscle development, comprehension. He had even studied Shakespeare, or at least Felix Smart had.

*To be or not to be, my little Riley. In your case, I am undecided.*

It occurred to Garrick that there might be some danger lurking in this *facility* in which he had materialized, though Smart's memories assured him that the sole sentry was a young girl, a slip of a thing who one would imagine to be relatively harmless. And yet Smart's memories told him that she was an accomplished combatant who had performed most admirably in the City of Angels.

*And she wears the last Timekey in this century,* he remembered. Even though Smart's memories had emerged from the wormhole intact, his Timekey lay like a cinder on his chest.

*Do not underestimate the girl,* Garrick told himself, *or unto dust will be your own destination.*

Garrick planted himself firmly in the real world and cast his eyes around. This was a strange place; windowless walls were lined with colored ropes and wall-mounted machinery.

*Cables and servers*, the electricity flowing between his new nerve endings informed him.

The gory evidence of Garrick's passage from the past was evident: blood striped the walls and lay in congealing splashes on tabletop machinery.

"Riley," he said, testing his voice. "Riley, my son. I have come for you. I know where you are incarcerated. The futurist Smart showed me."

Garrick headed toward the machinery. This is a laptop, he thought, tip-tapping the keyboard. How charming.

There would be time for such fancies later, but for now he must release Riley, retire to a safe crib, then let the boy bask in his master's new glory.

There was no obvious sign of Miss Savano. Perhaps the violence of his arrival had done her in?

*Or perhaps she lies in wait?*

Garrick forced himself to concentrate. He moved to the wall, squinting through the smoke and flashing lights down the red-bricked hallway to the jumble of containers.

*There. Look!*

An arm was sticking out from below the boxes. The fingers twitched spasmodically and the head resting on that arm wasn't moving. One eye was fully closed, the other glazed and swollen.

*That little periwinkle is a shade from death. I will nab my boy, then extinguish her final spark on the way out.*

Garrick moved quickly down the corridor, feeling better

than he had in decades. The trip through the wormhole had purged his system. He felt like a giddy whelp about to shinny his first drainpipe.

Another challenge lay before him, a challenge for the old Albert Garrick that was. Not the new model.

Version 2.0, he thought, then pinched the skin on his own forearm to force concentration.

The challenge was a keypad for the electronic lock.

*This machine can be fed with numbers or cards. I don't have the card, but the codes to everything in this house are in my head somewhere.*

Garrick cocked his head while his brain supplied the numbers. He cracked his knuckles, then tapped the code into the pad. The light winked green and the door popped open.

"Abracadabra," he said with satisfaction.

Garrick doffed his hat and ducked inside, smiling at the thought of Riley's amazement.

*Oh, my son. We have much to share. So much.*

The cell was spartan, with only a narrow cot, a single chair and, of course, a camera crouched like a spider on the ceiling. But that was all.

No boy.

Riley had gone. His son.

Garrick would not allow himself to roar the boy's name. He had once been a celebrated illusionist, after all, not a simple player of dreadful melodrama. Instead he contented himself with a resounding slam of the door on his way to interview Miss Savano.

How fortunate that I did not kill her before, he mused. Now she may help me find Riley before she dies.

Chevie's world was spinning in a kaleidoscope of dull colors. Concrete gray and streaked brown. She had been thinking, The boy is dead, over and over, but now she couldn't remember if that was a snatch of a song lyric or an actual thought she should be concerned about.

Something was happening outside her head to one of her body parts. A shoulder, maybe? Yes, her shoulder. Why was someone shaking her shoulder when all she wanted to do was sleep?

"Miss, wake up," said a voice urgently. "He's coming."

Wake up? No, thanks. This was her day off. Maybe a little surfing later on down at Malibu.

"Miss, on your feet now, or Garrick will kill both of us."

Garrick.

An image flashed through Chevie's mind of a bloody body emerging from some kind of cocoon.

One of her eyes fluttered open; the other was still swollen like a pink beetle in her eye socket. The boy leaned over her, hoisting her by the lapels.

"Riley?"

"The one and only, Miss Savano. We have to quit this place right now."

Leaving? But I thought you were dead. I'm just going to close my eyes for a second.

Riley grabbed the agent under her armpits, and hauled her upright.

"Come along now," he grunted. "Upsy-daisy."

Chevie's good eye flicked open. "I am not a child."

At this moment Garrick appeared in the corridor, his face set like alabaster and streaked with blood.

He is angry, Riley realized, and the sight of his master's cold expression nearly paralyzed him with fear.

His survival instincts took over. He grabbed Chevie's pistol, placed it in her fingers, and, clasping her hand in both of his, he aimed the gun at Garrick's chest.

"Shoot, miss," he said. "Now!"

With Riley's help, Chevie managed to squeeze off not one but two shots, both pulling high, but the second slug struck close enough to give Garrick pause. The magician snarled like a cornered street mutt and changed his pattern of movement entirely, becoming fluid, but also erratic, never arriving where his body language forecast he would be. When it seemed as though he was committed to a side step, his body would make an impossible diagonal lunge forward.

The gunshots jarred Chevie back to reality, and she noted that this Garrick person moved in a way she had never seen. She blinked her good eye.

"What? This guy is like a cat."

"Misdirection, a magician's ploy," said Riley, grunting as he hauled Chevie backward up the stairs. He could explain more about Garrick's unique style later, when they had escaped this death house, if escape was possible.

Chevie backed up the stairs, keeping her gun trained as much as possible on Garrick. The magician hissed now, like a vampire, and jammed his bowler hat down to his brows so he would not lose it.

He's getting ready to spring, thought Chevie.

"Yeah, that's right, fella," she called down to the magician. "You come a little closer. Let's see how well your disco moves work in a narrow stairwell. I will drill you right through your eyeball."

The warning seemed to work, possibly because there was a lot of truth in it. If Garrick set foot on the stairs, he would be boxed in by the wall and banister. But if Chevie thought the nineteenth-century man would be cowed by her futuristic weapon, she was wrong.

"You cannot escape me, Chevron Savano," he said, head cocked to one side. "I will have my boy back and the secrets of the Timekey."

Chevie's blood ran cold. This guy knew an awful lot for a Victorian.

"Take one more step," she said, keeping her weapon as steady as possible, "and we'll see who escapes."

All this time Riley muttered into Chevie's ear and dragged her backward toward street level.

"Step and retreat," he said, trying not to catch Garrick's eye, for that glacial gaze would freeze and shatter his resolve. "Step and retreat."

They were near the top step now, while Garrick lurked at the bottom, flexing his fingers in frustration, wishing for a throwing knife. Chevie had an idea.

*I have this guy pinned down. Backup can be here in two minutes.*

"It's okay," she told Riley. "We've got him now. He's going nowhere. There's a phone in my waistband—pass it to me."

Garrick also had an idea. The magician suddenly withdrew from the foot of the stairs and hurried along the subterranean corridor to the computer banks.

That's okay. That's fine. All he can do with the computers is slap the keyboards. No password, no access, Chevie thought. Then: Really? The holding-cell door didn't slow him down much, remember?

"Phone, Riley. Get my phone."

"Unless it's a weapon, Agent, forget your bloomin' *phone.* Aim your gun and fire off another shot."

"No, don't worry. He's contained down there."

Riley understood that Miss Savano believed she had gained the upper hand, and his eyes watered with frustration.

"You don't understand, miss. Garrick is a devil. He ain't no bludger nor simple broadsman. Didn't you see him delivered from the pit with your own two gawpers?"

Chevie had seen it, but she refused to relinquish the rules of her world entirely. "Maybe, if he could get into the weapons locker, he could do something, but that's protected by a code."

From below came a double bleep, which Chevie recognized as the weapons locker keypad turning off its alarm.

Riley knew without being told what the noises were. "That was your locker, wasn't it, miss? That was Garrick outfoxing your code?"

Again, thought Chevie.

"That was our cue to go," she admitted, hitching herself over the top step and into the hallway. "What you said about leaving? You were right."

"Praise the Lord for good sense," said Riley, and he ducked under Chevie's arm so he could drag her more efficiently.

Garrick appeared, cradling an AK-47 assault rifle, which had probably been new when Chevie was in grade school.

*The gun's age won't slow down the bullets,* thought Chevie, forcing Garrick to duck as she sent three more rounds humming down the stairwell. *That should buy us five seconds at least.*

Five seconds was about three seconds more than she got. Before the echo of her final shot had faded, Garrick's head appeared once more around the corner of the first flight of stairs. This time he had the AK's stock expertly wedged between cheek and shoulder.

Riley knew then that Garrick had come out of the metal transporting machine with knowledge and abilities he had not previously possessed. He was somehow improved.

"Now, little girlie," Garrick called, "let us see if what I dreamed about this contraption is true."

Garrick pulled the trigger, sending a stream of bullets into the ceiling over Chevie's head. The kickback got away from him for a second, but he soon recovered. The noise was deafening in the confined space, like overlapping thunderclaps. Riley and Chevie hunkered on the floorboards, unable to tell if they had been shot or if they were screaming.

Riley had no combat experience like Chevie's, but his entire life had been one long trauma, so he was accustomed to getting on with living even when death was close at hand. He grabbed Agent Savano by the collar and dragged her backward like a sack of coal.

"Come on," he cried. "We must get to the streets."

They stumbled along together, with the threat of Garrick like a wind at their backs; and in a ragged moment they were at the front door, which was secured by three bolts set into a steel frame.

Swipe the security card and we're out, thought Chevie.

Chevie felt for the tiny reel clipped to a pant loop where her card normally hung.

*No card. Must have lost it in the explosion. Unless . . .*

Chevie glared at Riley. "Give me my card, thief."

Riley already had it out. "You leaned a fraction close doing the manacles. And I opened them with a pick from me sock that came out of the machine with me. Sorry, Agent. Life or death."

They could talk about this later. Chevie swiped the card as bullets bounced around the hallway, shattering glass and blasting a crystal chandelier. It crashed to the ground, showering Riley with glass shards and blocking the stairwell.

"Riley!" called Garrick. "Kill her, boy. I know it's in you. I will wipe the slate, my word on it." All this while climbing the stairs and changing magazines.

The door popped open a slice, and Chevie put her final bullet into the control pad.

A red light flashed on the alarm pad and a peeved voice said: "CONTROL PAD TAMPERED WITH. LOCKDOWN IN FIVE SECONDS. LOCKDOWN IN FOUR SECONDS."

Garrick hopped nimbly over the twisted remains of the chandelier, raising his knees unfeasibly high to the level of his ears, carrying the automatic weapon overhead.

"Strike, Riley."

In case Riley chose not to strike as ordered, Garrick fired another burst at Agent Savano, but he was too late. The door had closed behind his quarry, all three bolts engaging automatically. Simultaneously the rear entrance locked itself, and bars dropped over every window in the house. The security system was the best federal dollars could buy, and in under three seconds the house on Bedford Street was locked down tighter than the average Swiss bank.

Chevie rested with her back against the door, feeling her pulse drumming inside her swollen eyelid.

"Okay, we have a breather now. That monster may have beaten the weapons code out of Smart, but he's not getting out of that house without FBI clearance."

Riley tugged Chevie away from the door.

"We must keep moving, miss. No building can hold Albert Garrick for long," he said.

Chevie allowed herself to be tugged through the cordon of emergency tape tied across the railing. She was starting to believe that maybe this Garrick character was just as dangerous as Riley claimed him to be.

# 5 » A VISIT TO THE OUTHOUSE

RILEY AND CHEVIE STUMBLED INTO THE ORANGE glow of evening streetlamps on the square lined with Georgian four-story houses bordering a small park like something from *Peter Pan*.

"This at least is familiar," panted Riley, gazing at the square, purposefully ignoring the sounds and sights beyond. "I was terribly afraid that modern wonders would be too much for my poor nut."

*Wait until you see Piccadilly Circus*, thought Chevie.

Riley drew in a huge shuddering breath. "Garrick is always telling me to breathe. It calms a body, if a body needs calming." Riley stopped talking as his nose took stock of the air that had just gone into it.

"How curious," he said, then threw up all over the pavement.

"That's great," said Chevie. "We'll never get a black cab to pick us up now."

But she did manage to flag down a cab outside a boutique hotel on Bayley Street, and soon they were lost in traffic, heading toward Leicester Square.

Riley kept his head between his knees, drawing sticky breaths until he could make himself stop shaking. "The smell, miss. It's like the inside of an apothecary's pocket. I can't smell the city."

Chevie patted him on the back. "I guess it's a bit cleaner these days. No one empties chamber pots out the window anymore."

"I can't smell the people. Are there fewer people now?"

Chevie looked out at the teeming metropolis rolling past the window. "Not really."

Riley clasped his knees tightly and raised his eyes.

"I don't smell any horses," he croaked.

"Nope, no horses. Except outside Buckingham Palace on occasion."

Riley straightened and pressed his face to the window. "Generally, we have horses. But I've seen automobiles, so this ain't so terrifying." Then a double-decker bus loomed alongside.

Riley flinched. Perhaps he could handle a carriage-sized automobile, but this craft was bigger than a cargo barge.

His eyes took in one modern wonder after another. Neon

signs. Computer shops. Skyscrapers. Eventually he saw something familiar.

"There's an honest-to-god Blighty pub," Riley gasped. "Can we go in, Agent? A quick dram of brandy for my nerves?"

Chevie snorted. "You are not drinking, Riley."

"Why not? Is it outlawed entirely?"

"Yeah, that's right. Totally illegal. You touch one *dram* and I'll have to shoot you."

Riley sighed a spot of condensation on the window, then lifted his gaze skyward, and his breath came in sudden shallow bursts, clouding the glass.

"A-a-agent Savano?"

Chevie was halfway through dialing a number. "In a second, kid."

Riley touched her arm with one finger, and Chevie could feel it tap-tapping with fear.

"It ain't the Martians, miss, is it? Like in Mr. Wells's new story, *War of the Worlds*?"

Chevie followed the boy's troubled gaze and saw the silhouette of a passenger plane overhead.

"Don't worry, kid. It's just Ryanair, not aliens, though it's a reasonable assumption. I think I'd better get you off the street before your head explodes."

"Oh my God. A person's head is likely to explode these days? Is it heat rays? I need a brandy, miss, upon my life."

Chevie punched the last three numbers into her keypad. "You don't need a brandy, Riley, you need an outhouse."

"You are not in the wrong there," agreed the boy. "It seems like a hundred years since I last went."

Chevie held the phone to her ear. "Not that kind of outhouse."

The FBI had several safe houses, apartments, and hotel rooms spread across London in case one of their agents got into hot water during an operation and needed a place to lie low and wait for the cavalry to gallop across from the U.S. embassy.

These safe houses were officially known as *secure facilities*, but the agents had referred to them as *outhouses* (*out* as in *Officer Under Threat*) since the term was popularized by a seventies spy series *Double Trouble*, starring the English actor Sir Olivier Gamgud and his faithful Yorkshire terrier.

The closest outhouse to Chevie's location was a suite in the Garden Hotel, an understated boutique hotel on Monmouth Street where movie stars and models could be found enjoying the famous breakfast on any given morning. Bureau rumor had it that the section chief chose the Garden because of its proximity to the Monmouth Coffee Company café, which served arguably the best espresso outside São Paulo.

Chevie called the desk and asked for Waldo.

"Hello, this is Waldo," said a deep voice. "How can I help you?"

Chevie spoke slowly, sticking to the code. Waldo was a notorious stickler for protocol and would hang up if she strayed from the correct wording.

"I would like to speak with my Uncle Sam, Waldo," she said. "He's in room one-seven-seven-six."

Waldo was silent for so long that Chevie thought he might have disconnected.

"I'm sorry. *What* room did you say your Uncle Sam was in?"

Chevie fumed, and silently vowed to kick Waldo really hard somewhere soft at a later date. "I'm sorry, Waldo. My Uncle Sam is in room seventeen seventy-six."

Another pause, but this time Chevie could hear a keyboard being tapped. "And what did you say your name was, miss?"

"My name is Chevron, but Uncle Sam has always called me . . ." Chevie crossed two fingers, hoping she had the right code name for today. "Spiderwick."

"Spiderwick. Yes, I *do* have you on the visitors list."

"Good. Great."

"Your Uncle Sam is not in residence at the moment. Perhaps you would like to wait for him in the suite?"

"I would like to wait. We both would."

More tapping. "Ah . . . both. The hotel has excellent facilities; would you care to make use of them while you are waiting?"

Chevie looked at Riley. "I think a wardrobe and some first aid are definitely needed."

"Very good, Spiderwick. How soon can we expect you?"

Chevie checked the street. "ETA two minutes, Waldo."

Waldo hung up without another word. He only had two minutes; there was no time for chitchat.

• • •

The cab pulled up outside the Garden Hotel slightly more than three minutes later and disgorged a very unlikely couple onto the street.

One seventeen-year-old FBI agent in Lycra, and an assassin's apprentice from the nineteenth century, thought Chevie. We must be quite a sight. At least both of my eyes are open now.

Monmouth Street itself was quiet, in spite of its proximity to Covent Garden, with only a few tourists cutting through to Seven Dials or Leicester Square and the faint echo of carnival music. Most of the street was fenced off for street repairs, and the taxi driver was forced to reverse and go out the way he had come in.

The Garden Hotel was one of those establishments that prided itself on the discretion it guaranteed its very select clientele. There was no sign, no doorman in a top hat, and only a tasteful awning to show taxi drivers where to stop. Chevie had stayed here once before, when Orange had commandeered her apartment during a routine pod service, and she had treated herself to a massage that had worked out muscle pains she'd suffered from overstrenuous exercise routines.

Chevie tucked her holstered Glock under her arm and hustled Riley into the lobby before he had time to throw up again. Special Agent Waldo Gunn was waiting for them by the reception desk.

"Two minutes?" he said testily. "That was closer to four."

Waldo was not anybody's idea of an FBI operative, which was probably why he had survived so long in his semi-undercover capacity as liaison at the Garden. Waldo stood five feet four in Cuban heels and had a bushy gray beard that made him seem about a thousand years old, a look that had earned him the nickname *Gimli* in the Bureau. If Waldo was aware of this nickname, he was not sufficiently bothered by it to invest in a razor.

"Hey, Waldo," said Chevie. "What's up?"

Waldo scowled. "What's up, Agent Savano? What's up is that you should have requested an escort through the service entrance. We try to maintain a low profile here in order to avoid raising suspicion, and yet here you stand in tattered training gear with a chimney-cleaning midget in tow. Hardly low profile. That is what is up, Agent."

At least he called me Agent, thought Chevie.

Waldo turned on his heel and strode through the small lobby furnished in late Victorian style, which was a huge relief to Riley, whose head was bursting with revelations.

"Should we follow the elf?" he asked Chevie.

Chevie smiled. "We should, or he gets really annoyed."

Waldo translated his irritation into a quickstep, so Chevie and Riley had to hustle to keep on his tail. He led them around the front desk and into a small steel elevator, which he summoned with a remote control fob on his waistcoat.

Riley tried to appear blasé. "It's an ascending room, no great shakes. I saw 'em at the Savoy years ago when Garrick sent me to suss out some swell's gaff."

Waldo raised an eyebrow at Chevie, who knew exactly

what the unasked question was. "Yes, he talks like that all the time. It's all *Strike me blind* or *Cor, luv a duck* with this little gent."

Waldo took a smartphone from his pocket and typed a note. Chevie would be willing to bet that the word *delusional* was in the note somewhere.

They took the elevator to the fourth floor, with Riley holding grimly on to the rail.

"You can't be overcautious," he told Chevie. "I heard about one of these things snapping its cable in New York City. It dropped quicker than a shirkster at closing time. Made jam of the passengers."

"I'm getting a headache listening to this cockney speak," said Waldo. "Please God there won't be any rhyming slang."

Riley literally jumped from the elevator when the door opened, then they pushed through a fire door and climbed some back stairs up two more flights.

"Here we are," said Waldo, indicating a nondescript gray door with the sweep of his arm, as though it were the gateway to a palace of wonder. "Room seventeen seventy-six."

He pressed another button on his remote and the door swung smoothly open.

"In you go, Agent. You can hole up here until a field team arrives. It shouldn't be too long, though head office tells me that our team has already been deployed to deal with a sus-pected terrorist hive, in Devon, of all places. False alarm, as it turned out. So I'm guessing it'll take an hour for them to make it back here. Plenty of time for *you* to get some clothes on, and for the Artful Dodger to take a bath."

"Cheers, guv'nor, you is a proper swell," said Riley innocently, and Chevie guessed that he knew exactly who the Artful Dodger was.

Waldo frowned suspiciously but continued his briefing. "We have a range of clothes in the closet, so you should find something to fit. And there is a fridge with cold food. Don't open the door to anyone but me, and if someone comes through that door who is not me, then feel free to shoot them. While we are not in the embassy and so technically not on American soil, this suite is attached to the embassy, and so a strong case can be made. In any event, jurisdiction over these rooms is a gray area, which should be enough to get you back Stateside if anything goes wrong." Waldo opened a drawer in a writing desk. "In the event you are out of ammunition, we have a selection here, behind the stationery."

"Ooh," said Chevie. "Stationery. Cool."

Waldo bristled. "I would have thought, Agent Savano, that after the Los Angeles foul-up, you would take this job a little more seriously."

"I am being serious," said Chevie. "One of my foster moms collects stationery."

"I shall be writing a full report," continued Waldo, "and your attitude will be both underlined and in italics."

Chevie selected a clip for her Glock. "Sorry, Waldo. I get a little giddy under pressure. There's someone after us. Someone a little out of the ordinary."

Waldo was not impressed. "Well, your *someone* won't be coming in here without an assault team behind him. And even then he'd need the door remote, which is paired to my biometric readings."

Riley took his nose out of the fruit bowl. "Thanks for the grub and everything, mate, but none of you Yankees knows what you're talking about. Garrick will come for me."

Chevie opened her mouth to disagree, but all that came out was a soft sigh. Garrick had come through a wormhole to find Riley. He had overcome Smart's ninja hazmat team. It seemed unlikely that a hobbit and a locked door would keep him out.

She checked her watch. "So, Gim— Waldo. Fifty-nine minutes, right?"

Waldo made a sound that was very close to an actual *harrumph*, then composed himself and smiled sweetly before extending his left hand, palm up.

"Tell me you are not looking for a tip," said Chevie in disbelief.

Waldo's smile disappeared and he closed his fingers tightly, as though crushing the soul of an enemy.

"Force of habit," he said, and beeped himself out of the door.

Chevie and Riley spent the next half hour trying to relax, but neither of them could shake a feeling of frosty foreboding. And it wasn't one of those vague feelings that something bad was on the way; it was the very specific belief that any second Albert Garrick was going to burst in through the reinforced door and shoot them both in the head.

Chevie wondered if she should call someone, and if she did call someone, what would she tell them?

*The FBI have a set of secret time machines that we use to hide witnesses in the past.*

Or, *A death-dealing magician has come from the nineteenth century to kill an urchin.*

Or, *The world's greatest scientist has been turned into a dead monkey by a wormhole.*

It sounded pretty insane, whatever way you presented it. Better to wait until reinforcements arrived and hope that the agent in charge would have some knowledge of what was going on—otherwise Chevie was going to look guilty of something.

Riley emerged from the bedroom all dickied up in what looked like a school uniform, taken from Waldo's stash. He caught a glimpse of himself in the mirror and seemed surprised by his own features.

"That's an excellent looking glass, Agent. I never saw myself so clear. Look, my hair has both brown and black in it. There's a turn-up for the books."

The boy studied himself for a long moment, pulling at the skin of his pale face, sweeping his long dark hair back from his forehead. In the mirror he caught sight of the flat-screen television on its bracket.

"What is that device bolted to the wall? Is it a work of art, perhaps? A cloudy night, or some such? Toffs will buy any old rubbish if they believe it was scribbled by a master."

"It's a television, actually, Riley. Moving pictures on a screen."

Riley turned to stare at the TV. "Moving pictures." A thought struck him. "When I woke this morning it was the year of our Lord 1898. How far have I traveled?"

"More than a hundred years," said Chevie softly.

Riley sank deep into a sofa, eyes downcast, and hugged himself.

"A hundred years? That far. Everyone I know is dead, and everything I know is gone."

Chevie didn't know what to say. She tried to imagine herself in the boy's situation, but couldn't. The shock must be incredible.

"I feel lost at sea," Riley admitted. He pondered, then said, "But Garrick doesn't. He is somehow different. Something has changed him. He has knowledge of your weapons and codes. Who's to say he does not already have the codes for this gaff?"

Chevie sat on a low glass coffee table, facing the boy. "Garrick would have to be crazy to come here. He's got all of London to get lost in. Why would he even bother tracking down a kid?"

"His reasoning is difficult to explain," said Riley, frowning. "He calls me his son, to save or drown as he pleases. But I ain't his son, and I hate him. I have bolted before, and he has followed me across the whole of the city." Riley pointed to his right eye. "I ran away to Saint Giles last year. Squared myself away down with the guttersnipes, but Garrick's snouts informed on me. That devil rooted me out and gave me a sound thrashing. The eye was never the same, but I can see out of it clear enough. Now Garrick has even followed me here, like Mr. Wells's Time Traveler."

"Well, Mr. Garrick has no *snouts* here," said Chevie. "And, just for your information, people have been trying to find the outhouse for years. People from *this* century—if they couldn't find it, neither will he. You have no idea how things have changed since your day." Chevie thought of something. "But I can give you an idea. Sit there."

Chevie pointed to the deep purple sofa in front of the flat black TV. She logged on to the Internet and chose a site that had a series of videos documenting major political, scientific, and cultural changes. She selected one and played it.

"Now sit there and learn something," she instructed the Victorian boy.

Riley had been dumbfounded so often already this evening that he did not remark upon the HD graphics, but the site's music almost moved him to tears.

"It's like sitting beside the entire orchestra," he said softly. "A music machine with pictures."

Chevie walked toward the bathroom. "A music machine with pictures. I like that. Okay, you absorb whatever you can while I clean up a little. Just don't touch the screen."

This time Riley did look away from the TV. "Why not? Would I be transported to the land of the magic machine?"

Chevie was tempted to say yes, but the kid had been through enough for one day. "No, this ain't *Tron*. But you would smear the screen, which would freak out the elf."

Riley returned his gaze to the screen. *Freaking out the elf* sounded like a terrible thing indeed. He would look but not touch.

At first Albert Garrick was mightily angered by being trapped in Bedford Square, but such were his new powers that a dozen solutions to his problem soon flowed like a balm across his spiky mood. The magician calmed himself and sat in front of his laptop in the ground floor office.

*No, not my laptop. Felix Smart's laptop.*

Though that more or less amounted to the same thing. Felix Smart's mind was inside his own, leaking information like a cracked gourd.

*And there is more. The explosion inside the wormhole has changed me. I am more than human now. I am the universe's first quantum man. The rules of normal space do not apply to me anymore. My very appearance is fluid, and my mind is chock-full of useful nuggets.*

It took Garrick mere seconds to lift the lockdown from Bedford Square, and he listened with satisfaction as the shutters rolled back from the windows.

The magician cackled aloud.

*Computers! Wonderful machines.*

He was free now to leave and wreak havoc on this new age, with no one to stop him or even understand what they were trying to stop.

*So, why don't I abandon my hunt for Riley and disappear into the multitude?*

Garrick now understood his need to track the boy down. Garrick's father had deserted him in dramatic fashion when he was ten, so he had a deep fear of desertion.

*You is sorted proper now, my son,* his father told him one morning. *And I cannot live sober with what my hand was forced into doing to secure your future. I slit the throat of my best mate and a few more besides to keep you in a bed away from the Old Nichol.*

The ten-year-old Garrick noticed his father's belongings tied in a pillowcase at the foot of their room's small bed.

*Are you leaving me, Da?*

Tears flowed down his father's ruddy cheeks as he answered, *I am, boy. You know I have struggled with a grog habit all my life. And now, with dreams of blood and your poor brothers and sisters occupying my mind, I can't fight no more. So it is my intention to return to the Nichol and drink myself into the grave. Shouldn't take more'n a month. Don't try to find me, as I plan to be drunk and violent. I will shout hello to your mother on my way past the pearlies, and keep an eye on you from the devil's shoulder.*

And he was gone, stumbling through the doorway, half blind with tears. Albert never saw his father again but heard rumors that he had died from a fractured skull following a crack on the head from a peeler outside the Jerusalem Tavern.

*I was deserted and so have a fear of desertion,* concluded the creature that was Albert Garrick. *I know this but still feel it.*

But there was more to this current pursuit than a fear of desertion. Wherever Riley was, there too would be Chevron

Savano. Garrick had an urgent desire to make contact with that young lady, for she possessed the final remaining Timekey, and with that he could return to his own time and be its master.

Garrick knew that in this world he was something of a prodigy; there was much he could achieve, but he would always feel the scrutiny of satellites, crouched like electronic spiders in high Earth orbits. And with enough resources, his enemies could find him and kill him, as there were many with his knowledge in this era. But back in his own time, Albert Garrick could be godlike. In Victorian London, a man with his knowledge and foresight could be a prophet in his own land.

*I could lead a revolution against the government. I could discover antibiotics and invent the solar panel. I could build the first working airplane and drop hydrogen bombs on my enemies. There is nothing I could not do.*

*But first I must open the wormhole. This is where my efforts must be concentrated.*

Given ten years, unlimited funds, and the backing of a large government, Garrick knew that he could possibly construct a Timekey, but there was already a key in existence and it hung around the neck of Special Agent Chevron Savano.

*That strange and stupid girl*, thought Garrick. *She will follow procedure and I will trap her in the Bureau's own red tape. Once I have the key, all I need is five seconds with the WARP pod.*

Garrick quickly posted out a Be On the Lookout report to the Bureau network for Chevron Savano, and tested the extent of his new computer skills by inserting her on the FBI's most wanted list. The hazmat team was gone, so why not make Miss Savano responsible for killing them?

Hazmat, thought Garrick. What a delightful word.

Garrick removed his own bowler, plucked Smart's soft-brimmed hat from the stand by the desk, and, tip-tapping his spidery fingers along the brim, put it on.

*Only six people in the Bureau have met Felix Smart since he came to London. Four are dead, one is on the run, and the last is on assignment in Iraq.*

"Hello, Waldo," he said, trying out Smart's voice. "I've heard a lot about you." He cleared his throat and tried again. "Agent Gunn. At last we meet face-to-face. I believe you've got a couple of fugitives for me in the penthouse?"

It was a fair approximation of the Scottish agent, and perhaps there was more he could do to bolster his impersonation. He was the master of illusion, after all, and the world's first quantum man.

Garrick checked his appearance in the hat-stand mirror. His face had always been plain as tapioca, which was a boon in his line of work, as people tended not to notice him, or to forget him instantly if they did. During his theater days, he would literally paint a personality onto his face, changing it to suit the illusion.

Garrick stared into the mirror and watched as his skin began to bubble.

For Garrick had come by more than knowledge in the

wormhole; he had gained control of his own workings, right down to the smallest particle. Where most men operated on a small slice of brain, Garrick had the choice of the whole pie. This did not lead to telekinesis, but it meant Garrick could communicate with his own fibers more efficiently. He could control the whorls of his own fingerprints, or the balance of his thyroid to turn hair gray. Or, with a little effort, he could communicate with the marrow in his bones or the layers of fat under his epidermis to entirely change his appearance. He could not become just anyone, nor stray too far from his own mass, but he could certainly allow a physicality that was already inside him to emerge.

THE GARDEN HOTEL, MONMOUTH STREET, LONDON, NOW

Chevie took a quick shower, strapped a gel-mask across her eye to bring down the swelling, then checked the closet for something to wear other than the workout gear, which seemed to scandalize Riley. There were numerous outfits to chose from, all draped in plastic, including several pairs of crime-scene overalls, a leopard-skin dress, and a puffy cartoon character mouse costume.

Some of these people were deep, deep undercover, she thought, selecting a women's Armani suit and a pair of black Bally loafers that would have cost her more than a month's pay.

*Finally. A perk.*

The suit fitted well, and after Chevie had checked herself

in the full-length mirror, she sat down to compose a report on the bedroom computer, trying to make the day's events read more like real happenings than an episode of a sci-fi miniseries.

*Found out I was guarding a time machine in case the inventor happened to pop in from the nineteenth century.*

Nope, there was no way to make it sound like a serious report, even by using Bureau buzz terms like *unsub, asset,* and *AO.*

By the time she had pounded out five hundred words on the keyboard, Chevie was developing a headache behind her right eye and was glad to hear the doorbell ring. She pulled off the gel-mask.

*The cavalry, finally.*

Riley was still stuck in front of the TV when she passed him, stuffing his face from a platter of cold meats.

"I hope you're not drinking brandy," said Chevie.

"Absolutely not," said Riley, waving a brown bottle. "Beer only, Agent. I do as I am told, I do."

Chevie deviated from her course to snag the beer bottle. "No alcohol, Riley." She nodded at the screen. "How are you liking the twenty-first century?"

Riley burped. "The Take That are most melodic. And God bless Harry Potter is all I can say. If not for him, all of London would have been consumed by the dark arts."

"Keep eating," said Chevie, thinking that she would have to watch the videos with him next time. "And you can stop worrying, kid. Help is here."

"We need all the help we can get, Agent. You should fill your belly, so we can face the challenges of the day with full bellies and without weevils in our shirts, eh?"

Chevie was not sure what a weevil was, but she was pretty certain that she did not want one in her shirt.

"No weevils," she said. "I'm with you on that one."

She left Riley by the TV and walked to the door, flattening herself to the wall as she had been taught, drawing her weapon, and pointing it at the spyhole. There was a small video intercom mounted on the wall beside the door, and Chevie was relieved to see Waldo on the screen, looking even grumpier than last time, which was somehow reassuring. The security camera showed that the hobbit-like liaison officer was alone in the corridor.

Chevie pressed the TALK button. "Has the Bureau team arrived?" she asked.

"They are on the way," replied Waldo. "I am to debrief you, apparently. Though that is not in my job description. What do they think I am, a secretary?"

"Don't get your baggins in a twist," said Chevie. She holstered her Glock and opened the door. "This is an important case. We need to work together."

Waldo stood in the hallway, hands behind his back, not looking remotely in the mood for cooperation.

"Work together, you say? Like you worked together with the hazmat team?"

Chevie felt her stomach lurch and reached for her pistol. She even managed to get it clear of the holster before Waldo whipped a stun gun from behind his back and fired two needle-tipped darts into Chevie's chest, sending 50,000 volts sizzling through her frame. Chevie felt the shock like a thousand hammers pounding on every inch of her skin, forcing her to her knees and then onto her back.

"I got the BOLO from Agent Orange," she heard Waldo say. His voice was thick and slow, floating from far away. "You killed those men, and one of them owed me money."

*No,* Chevie wanted to say. *It's a trick. You're being tricked.*

But her tongue felt like a pound of raw steak in her mouth, and her limbs were slack, like half-filled water balloons. She saw Waldo loom over her, and the view reminded her of a Godzilla movie when the monster stepped over a bridge.

"I've got one more charge," said the harmless-looking hobbit in that faraway, underwater voice.

*Run, Riley! Run!* Chevie wanted to scream, but all that came from her mouth was a hiss of dry air.

Riley heard the exchange in the hallway, and then that particular rumbling sound of a body falling over.

Garrick! he thought, and sprang to his feet on the sofa. He wanted to help, but that would seal his own fate as well as Chevie's.

I must hide, he realized. But there was no time for such tactics, and Waldo stepped briskly into the living room brandishing a metal tube.

"I will only use this," he said, "if you attempt to flee, if you attack me, or if you insist on speaking in that ridiculous accent."

Riley tested the spring of the cushions underneath his feet.

*With my training, I could jump clear over that little man's head, like Spring-Heeled Jack*, he thought. *That baton of his won't be much use if I stay beyond arm's length.*

Riley bounced twice, then threw himself into the air, arcing over Waldo's head, leaving the FBI agent no choice but to shoot him in the stomach with the second charge from his stun gun.

Riley's head hit the floor with a thump, and in his dream the thump was Albert Garrick rapping him on the forehead with sharp knuckles during a lesson.

"Attention, son," he said. "This is one of the basic principles of stage magic, which is the kind we are stuck with presently."

They were onstage at the Orient, where Riley's lessons were conducted. On these boards he studied fencing, marksmanship, strangulation, and poisons, as well as the more exotic skills of escapism and camouflage.

"Now, I pose the question again: Where is the guinea?"

Riley stared at the three cups on the boards where he knelt and hesitantly pointed to the center cup, already knowing that the coin would not be his.

"No, Riley," said Garrick. "Though you were a step closer this time." He lifted the cup on the left, revealing a shining coin beneath. "I gave your eyes the slip on the second-to-last switch with a tap of my nail on the center cup. Misdirection, you see? I sent you toward what was not there."

I understand, thought Riley, wishing that somehow he could use misdirection to escape from Garrick.

*Someday, I will send you somewhere that I have never been. And then I will give you the slip for good.*


Chevie woke up with plasti-cuffs around her ankles and wrists securing her to the toilet. Her head throbbed with dull pain, and drops of blood plinked into a pool between her feet from the tip of her nose.

She was about to unleash a string of swear words when she noticed Riley in the bath, cuffed to the safety rail.

"Are you hurt?" she asked, the sentence's final *t* stabbing her brain on its way out.

*Waldo! That moron. I will shave him while he sleeps for this!*

"No, miss," said Riley. "Though that lightning rod knocked the stuffing out of me. These cuffs have me baffled. They are slimmer than a shoelace, but I can't even get a stretch on 'em."

Riley talked a little more about the cuffs and their fantastic strength, but Chevie zoned him out. What she needed was a moment or two of quiet time so her mind could settle down a bit after the Tasering Waldo had surprised her with.

*I wasn't expecting that. And how was it possible that Felix Smart had put out a Be On the Lookout for me on the network when he never made it back from the past?*

*Unless he did come back and holds me responsible for all the mayhem?*

It didn't sound likely or plausible.

*Orange was with the hazmat team. He knows I didn't kill them.*

Riley was saying something. His tone was insistent, urgent even.

Chevie blinked the stars from her vision. "What? What is it, kid?"

"Your nose is bleeding, miss. Snort it up and hawk the lot out in one go. That's the best thing for it."

*Snort it up and hawk it out.*

Chevie did as she was told, spitting a ball of blood into the sink, and was surprised to find that the bleeding stopped immediately, though the snorting did make her head hurt a little more.

"Did Waldo shock you?"

"He did," said Riley. "That electric pistol of his had me dancing the dotard's jig on the floor. I woke just before you."

"We need to get out of here, kid. You opened your cuffs back in Bedford Square. You got any more magic tricks down your sock?"

Riley glared at his own tethered wrists as though he could free them with mind power. "Not one, miss. How do you open a set of bracelets that don't have no locks?"

*You don't* was the answer to that question.

Chevie followed the logic of her train of thought, ignoring the waves of pain.

"Okay. We're secured but safe. Waldo has the wrong end of the stick, but the cavalry are on the way, and we can clear things up when they get here. It doesn't matter how long it takes. So long as we're in this room, we stay alive."

Riley frowned. "So this being trussed up like market fowl is a good thing?"

"In a way, yes."

"No offense, miss, but maybe you being a female has clouded your judgment. If we dangle here for much longer, Garrick will slit our throats and watch us bleed. He won't even need to mop up after me, for heaven's sake, seeing as I am already in the tub."

Chevie glanced sharply at the boy, surprised that he would make a joke, even a gruesome one, at such a time, but then she saw the fear in the boy's eyes.

The poor guy lives with terror on a daily basis, she realized.

From the suite came the distinctive clatter of armed men entering a room. Chevie heard footsteps padding across the carpet and the clicks of pistols' safety catches being engaged. Muted orders were issued, and Chevie imagined agents taking up positions at entrances and other possible breach points.

"Hey," she called. "Hey, you guys. In here."

Seconds later an agent appeared at the bathroom door, dressed in the FBI's version of Casual Male, which had been thirty years out of date when they thought of it twenty years ago. Tan chinos, blue Windbreaker, button-down shirt, and rubber-soled shoes. This guy might as well have had FBI written on his back in big yellow letters, which, in fact, he did have if you ripped away the Velcroed patch. The agent could not suppress a smile when he saw Chevie on the toilet. He drew a switchblade from his pocket and pressed the catch, releasing the blade, as if he were about to cut the plasti-cuffs, then retracted the blade with a touch of the button and pocketed the weapon.

"At ease, Savano. Don't get up."

Chevie scowled. She knew this guy from back home. His name was Duff, and he had been tight with Cord Vallicose, her favorite instructor from Quantico. Vallicose had seen potential in his young student and taken Chevie under his wing.

"Hilarious, Duff. You won't be laughing so hard when I get out of here and rearrange your hairdo."

Duff scowled back, obviously proud of his perfect do. "Can it, Savano. You and your little mystery buddy are in serious trouble. I'm hearing talk that our hazmat boys are MIA. The AD is on his way down from a meeting in Scotland, so until he gets here, keep your trap shut."

Chevie swallowed her anger; she'd have words with this guy when this was all over. "Okay, Agent. I realize you're doing your job, and I would probably do the same thing myself if I was in your nineteen-fifties shoes, though possibly with a little more empathy and less jargon. But we have a scared boy here, and with good reason. There's a pretty impressive guy on our tail, who probably took out the entire hazmat team with a musket."

Duff sighed like this crazy talk made him sad. "Yep, the BOLO said you were delusional. London does that to a person. Can't get a decent pizza in the entire city." He snapped his fingers. "Hey, you know who I should tell about this?"

Chevie stiffened. "Don't you dare!"

Duff pulled a phone from his pocket and made a big deal of focusing the camera. "No, no, really. Cord needs to know about this. He said you were his finest student. This is gonna break his heart."

Duff snapped a couple of shots of Chevie cuffed to the toilet and texted it across the Atlantic to Cord Vallicose.

"Take this seriously, Duff!" said Chevie, struggling to keep her voice down. She knew this guy; the moment she shouted at him he would simply walk away and slam the door. "People are dying, and it's not over yet. Take your weapon off safety, tell your guys to look sharp."

Duff seemed on the point of taking her seriously when a text jingled through on his phone. He consulted the screen and smiled broadly.

"It's from Cord. You should read this—he's devastated." And with a nasty chuckle Duff backed out of the room, closing the door behind him.


Albert Garrick arrived at the Garden Hotel seconds after the London team, and could do little but scowl in frustration as he watched them hurry through the entrance. Six agents in Windbreakers, blending in about as effectively as a half dozen penguins would in the chic lobby.

Garrick cursed them for fools, then treated himself to a coffee from a nearby café while he adjusted his plans. His BOLO had yielded an almost immediate callback from Agent

Waldo Gunn, and Garrick had hoped to reach the safe house before the inevitable band of heavy-handed federal overkillers. Except in this case it was not overkill. An entire garrison of agents would not be enough to keep him from Riley and the Timekey.

Had Garrick succeeded in reaching the scene before the away team, he could simply have taken what he wanted and disposed of Waldo Gunn; but with six armed agents keeping watch, improvised violence could not be relied upon. The odds were still in Garrick's favor, but Riley had skill in the martial arts, having been taught by a master, and Garrick had no desire to be felled by a lucky strike from a child.

For a moment he allowed himself to be mildly distracted by the changes that had overhauled Monmouth Street since what he had begun to think of as *his day*. Even though Smart's memories had prepared him for the bright, shiny wonders of the present, it was quite another thing to spy them firsthand.

In *his day* Monmouth Street had been mainly penny digs, and by this time of night it would be lined with residents taking great amusement from the japes of juvenile beggars trying to pry coin from the theater crowds. Now, there were no beggars on the street, but Garrick did spy a scrap of rubbish in the gutter.

I might have something to say about that, thought Garrick. When I am king.

He was, of course, joking. He had no desire to be king. The prime minister held the real power.

Garrick finished the really rather excellent coffee, thanked the waiter, then strolled across the street to the Garden Hotel.

Inside the safe suite, Waldo Gunn was not happy. This place was blown, and he knew it. After nearly two decades of care-taking this wonderful location, with more than two hundred at-risk subjects sheltered, the FBI away team had rolled up in their black SUVs and marched mob-handed into his discreet haven. Discreet no more.

And, though Waldo was slightly miffed that his own cushy posting was jeopardized, his main worry was professional.

*I don't even know for certain who the bad guy is,* he thought. *Agent Orange makes strong claims against Agent Savano, but nothing in her file suggests such a violent nature. There was that infamous incident in Los Angeles, but in my opinion she acted heroically and lives were saved.*

*So now she was a mass murderer?* It didn't make sense. Everything was topsy-turvy today. Instead of protecting fugitives, he was detaining suspects. Even more irritating was the sight of those clodhopping agents tramping all over his beautiful Italian rugs, and now they were even trying on jackets from the closet.

*If one of them even looks at the Zegna suit, I will shoot him myself,* vowed Waldo.

"Oh, for heaven's sake," he called to a lanky agent sprawled on the sofa. "Take your shoes off the furniture. That's a Carl Hansen!"

Waldo's phone buzzed in his pocket, and it was the dedicated buzz that meant the message was on a coded channel and therefore official business. He checked the screen and saw the text was from Agent Orange. Short and sweet: *Coming up.*

Great, thought Waldo, twisting his gray beard to a point. Another fly in our overcrowded ointment.

The doorbell to the suite chimed, and half a dozen agents instantly threw various combat shapes, training their weapons on every flickering shadow.

"At ease, stormtroopers," said Waldo drily, crossing the small lobby to the intercom. "It's one of our own."

Waldo Gunn knew that he would probably choose to retire when this post went belly up. There was no way he could integrate with an office full of gun monkeys after twenty years of culture at Covent Garden.

The intercom screen showed a single figure outside the door.

Waldo pressed the TALK button. "Identification, please."

The man glared at the camera, as though reaching into his pocket was an inconvenience he didn't have time for, then sighed and pulled out his badge, flipping it close to the lens.

It was Agent Orange, all right. Not a great photograph, but definitely the same man.

Maybe so, thought Waldo. But the FBI doesn't operate on mugshots in our own facilities anymore. Why would we, when we have biometrics?

"Thumb on the scanner, please," he ordered curtly.

"Really?" said the man with Agent Orange's FBI badge

and card. "I'm in a hurry here. Don't want to be stuck in the cold just because some bucket of bolts can't read my digit."

"Thumb on the scanner, if you please," insisted Waldo, not bothering to argue. If Orange was in a hurry, he should simply press the glass and be done with it.

"You're the boss for now," said Orange, and he placed his right thumb on the scanner bar, which took about five seconds longer than usual before matching the print to the one on file.

"See?" said Waldo. "That wasn't so difficult. It's just protocol."

Waldo opened the door and shivered as a chill wrapped itself around his legs.

*Must be a window open*, he thought. *I could have sworn I closed them all.*

"The legendary Agent Waldo Gunn," said Agent Orange, extending a hand. "Protector of lost sheep."

"Legendary in certain circles," said Waldo. He shook the offered hand and thought involuntarily, *I don't trust this man's hand.*

Waldo could not help glancing down. He noticed that Orange's fingers were slim as a girl's and the nails were as long.

*Why the instinctive dislike?* wondered Waldo, and then he remembered one of his mother's various long-winded sayings: *Never trust a man with long nails, unless he's a guitar picker. A long-nailed man has never done a day's work in his life, not honest work at any rate.*

Orange relinquished Waldo's hand and stared over his shoulder into the suite.

"Quite a gathering you have here, Waldo," he said, his Scottish accent making the sentence five seconds longer than it would usually be.

That accent would drive me crazy, thought Waldo. It could take all day to finish a conversation.

"What can I do for you, Agent Orange?"

Orange's smile was wide and thin. "Isn't it obvious? I need you to release the suspects into my custody."

Waldo bristled at the idea, which was so outlandish that he initially thought Orange was joking. "Your custody? That's hardly procedure. These are suspects in an investigation. You are not an investigator."

Orange seemed saddened by this attitude. "Perhaps not, but I do outrank you, Waldo."

Suddenly Waldo did not appreciate this man calling him by his first name. "That's Special Agent Gunn, if you please. And for your information, nobody outranks me in this suite. As officer in charge, I can trump the president himself if I deem it necessary. At any rate, the Assistant Director is on his way, and he has ordered that nobody interfere with the subjects until he arrives."

"But they killed my entire hazmat team!" objected Orange. "No quarter was given, though it was asked. I was lucky to escape with my life."

No quarter was given, thought Waldo. Quaint choice of words. "You do seem remarkably *alive*. And unscathed, too. Where are the bodies?"

Orange coughed into his fist. "That's delicate and strictly

*need to know.* It's connected to our operation, which is about fifteen grades above your security clearance. I could tell you, but then . . ."

"You'd have to kill me," said Waldo, completing the hackneyed phrase.

"And your family," added Orange, straight-faced.

Waldo's instinctive dislike of this Scot burned brighter. "There's no call to be rude. We have a procedure in place here, and that's the end of it. You may wait in the lounge if you wish, but there will be no contact with the suspects. After all, we only have your word for it that the detainees are guilty of anything."

Orange's smile never wavered. "That's an excellent point. Unfortunately, I am not in a mood to be detained at the moment, and as you pointed out, you outrank me only inside the suite. And I am outside. So I shall partake of another excellent coffee from the establishment across the street and return later when the big-knob bluebottle has joined the party." Orange stopped suddenly and his eyes brightened as though lit from within. "Can it be?" he cried, his accent suddenly less Scottish. "Why, I swear that it is."

Waldo was reluctantly intrigued. "What is? It is what?"

Orange gazed past the suite's custodian into the room itself. "Blow me if I haven't been here before."

"I think you're mistaken," said Waldo in the most patronizing tone he could muster. "I have a log of every single person who has set foot across this threshold in the past twenty years, and you are not on it."

Orange was so delighted that he actually clapped his hands.

"This was years ago, Waldo. *Many* years ago. If I remember it right, an exceedingly dodgy character answered the landlord's rap in those days."

"Fascinating story, really. But if you won't come in, you must leave. Security and all that."

Orange doffed his cap, revealing a head of hair that seemed gray or black depending on the incline of his head. "And all that, indeed, Waldo. A quick coffee bath for the ivories, and I shall return. Watch for me, won't you?"

Neither man offered his hand upon parting, but Waldo Gunn flicked through different camera views on the security screen so that he could watch Orange all the way to Monmouth Street.

"I will *watch for you*, Agent Orange," he said between his teeth. "You give your ivories their coffee bath, and I will watch for you like a hawk."

Waldo placed a hand on his round stomach, the result of too many fried Cumberland sausages and late night hot chocolates with Chantilly swirls.

What is that feeling? he wondered, trying to match an emotion to the acid churning in his belly.

Waldo Gunn realized that, for the first time in twenty years, he did not feel safe in his own fortress.

Don't be ridiculous, he told himself. Orange is a disconcerting character, that is all. He's not dangerous.

But Waldo Gunn's subconscious was trying to tell him something, and the portly agent really should have listened.

• • •

Garrick ignored the coffee shop and virtually skipped down the Garden's service alley, still hardly crediting his good fortune at having previously cracked this establishment.

He found that he could roll through his memory like a moving-picture show and find each frame as clear as reality, smells and all.

He remembered this house well. In his day, a flourishing bootmaker's shop had stood on the ground floor, with a brass plate in the window claiming Charles Dickens himself as a patron, which was difficult to contest as by then the great novelist had been dead for nigh on a decade.

Above the bootmaker's lived the dodgy character with a curious name. Biltong . . . no . . . Bill*toe*, that was it. George Billtoe had passed a sheaf of homemade pound notes in Barnet Horse Fair and incurred the wrath of a certain gang, who did not appreciate their turf being poached without ask nor license. The gang's wrath was embodied in the form of Albert Garrick.

*Vengeance from above*, thought Garrick. *As I came down the chimney.*

George Billtoe had heard rumors that papers had been passed on him, and he grew increasingly secretive and prudent, barricading himself into the upstairs apartment, paying an urchin to run his errands. Garrick was forced to use all his skills as a contortionist to inch his way down the man's chimney.

Garrick chuckled. On that night he had actually roused Billtoe before slitting his throat, just so the mark would realize that his precautions had counted for nothing.

*Happy days.* How he and Riley had chortled over that faker's folly.

Garrick remembered acting out the entire episode, right down to Billtoe's stunned final plea for mercy before he gave him a close shave across the Adam's apple.

The magician smiled at the memory as he scaled the hotel fire escape to the third floor, sliding silent as a shadow across the cast-iron steps. The top step stood eight feet below a flat copper roof, which offered a wide lip and ample grip for a man of Garrick's abilities. He trusted the strength of his fingers and launched himself upward from the railing, grasping the cold copper rim and swinging himself bodily onto the flat roof.

Across the dull copper he ran, hunched to avoid the prying eyes of curtain twitchers, bent so low that his torso was horizontal and Orange's sharp nose cut the night air like a beagle's.

This is indeed the life of champions, thought Albert Garrick. A fresh breeze from the Thames, preternatural quantum powers, and a room full of Yankee bully boys to test my skills against. Magic is real and lives inside my person.

The chimney was where he remembered it, a red and yellow brick stack bound with crumbling mortar, weather-stained, perhaps, but otherwise virtually unchanged. Even during Billtoe's residency the chimney had been out of service, plastered up at the base with a line of cracked clay pots that had not diffused smoke in many a decade. Garrick brushed the pots aside with a cavalier sweep of his arm and heaved the chimney cap from its perch.

Not even a slap of mortar, he thought, almost disappointed.

These federals are supposed to be the world's finest.

The chimney pipe stretched below him from dark to pitch-dark. There was no comforting smell of soot that would have reminded Garrick of home, but there was the feeling of depth and drop and the sour gust of damp. The magician swung his legs easily over the stack and sat on the rim, peering down.

*It's narrow as I remember.*

Garrick's breadth of shoulder could barely squeeze down that shaft, even on the diagonal.

Last time descending this box took some time and a fifth of nerve, thought Garrick. On this occasion it will be different.

Garrick used his quantum abilities to order his shoulder ligaments to slacken so that the ball of his humerus popped out of his socket.

No pain, he told his sensory neurons. I need my senses sharp, and when I descended through this shaft previously the agony was a chink in my plate.

Garrick had always been a touch shortsighted but enjoyed excellent night vision, which he attributed to boiled vegetable poultices that he molded into his eye sockets two nights a week, then ate for breakfast in the mornings.

Even so, he thought, using his good arm to hoist himself into the black shaft, no harm in opening my pupils a little to trap the ambient light.

Garrick smiled, his teeth shining like candied lemon drops in the gloom.

*Ambient light? Smart, my friend, I cannot thank you enough for educating thyself so thoroughly on your multifarious interests.*

Garrick's pupils zoomed till they filled his irises and he could see black spiders hiding in the black hole of a dark chimney at night.

This is what magic really is, he thought. An open mind.

Garrick cranked his knees apart until they braced his body weight, then lowered himself into the darkness like a demon descending into hell.

Inside the bathroom of the safe house, Riley was wondering if his brain had been somehow etherized by his trip. Or if he had suffered some form of mind malady brought on by a life of continual terror.

*I feel nothing. Even my fear is fading. Perhaps I am in a sanatorium somewhere wearing the lunatic's overalls.*

And yet this futuristic fantasy was particularly detailed. Miss Sav-a-no was plainer to him now than any individual he had ever spied. He could make out the drops of sweat on her brow as she worried the plastic ties on her wrists. He could hear her teeth grind in frustration and see the cords of her long neck stand out like a schooner's rigging.

"Are you looking at something in particular?" said Chevie.

Riley started to mumble a denial, but Chevie interrupted him.

"You want to hear something ironic, kid?"

"Yes, miss. As you please."

She tugged on her cuffs, which held her arms fast around the toilet's plumbing. "I find it ironic that I could really use a bathroom right now."

Riley tried not to smile.

"And this is *ironic* because you are tethered to a bowl and yet cannot use it?"

"Exactly."

"Thank you, Chevie. I have often encountered the term *irony* in my reading but never truly understood it till now."

"To educate and protect," said Chevie. "Though I've been falling down a little on the protecting."

"It was bad luck that you came up against Albert Garrick. Of all the coves you could have scooped out of the past, he is the worst, no doubt about it."

"He's just a man, you know, Riley. Whatever you think about him, that's all he is."

Riley slumped in the bath. "No. There are men who are somehow more than men. Garrick has always been one of these, and now even more so. The trip from the past has given him gifts, I would swear on it."

Gifts, thought Chevie. Or mutations.

"Garrick is truly beyond your experience," continued Riley. "Mine too."

"You make him sound like Jack the Ripper."

This casual reference caused the blood to drain from Riley's face as a memory hit him like a mallet, and while his mind wandered, Chevie shifted her focus to the room beyond. For the last fifteen minutes the only sounds had been typical agents-on-babysitting-duty noises: sharp comments, jock laughter, coffee percolating, and an almost incessant flushing from the second bathroom.

"Hey!" she called. "Waldo! Duff! You want to open the door? We're feeling a bit unloved in here."

In response someone turned up the TV. The loud bass of dance music bounced off the door.

"I hate those guys," muttered Chevie. "I am going to work real hard, get promoted, then fire every last one of them." She noticed Riley's stricken face. "Are you okay, kid? Riley?"

Riley's eyes came back to the present. "Garrick told me a story once about old Leather Apron, Jack the Ripper. He play-acted the whole thing in our digs."

"Don't tell me, Garrick *is* Jack the Ripper." Chevie's tone was sarcastic, but at this point she would not be at all surprised if Albert Garrick and the legendary killer were one and the same.

Riley's head jerked backward as if Garrick would hear this accusation. "No. Certainly not. Garrick *hated* Jack the Ripper."

Chevie kept one ear on the noises outside and the other on Riley's tale.

"He hated the Ripper? Weren't those guys like peas in a pod?"

Riley sat up as far as he could. "No. Oh, no. Old Jack did what Garrick would never do. He courted the bluebottles and the press gentlemen. Sent 'em notes and so forth. Gave himself a nickname. Garrick prided himself on being like a specter with his business, and here was this night slasher leaving kidneys and hearts strewn about all over Whitechapel."

Riley's eyes glazed over as he lost himself in the story.

"The Ripper was busy before Garrick got me, but the case obsessed him for years after. I knew to stay clear if the papers were running a story on Jack. Until one night Garrick comes home, just as the sun hangs between the spires. He shakes me gentle, like we are genuine family, and his touch was so soft that I came out of my dream thinking my father had come and I says, 'Father?'"

Riley paused to spit toward the plughole. "I was barely eight years in the world and knew no better, but the word is magical to Garrick, and he smiles like Alice's cat. 'I suppose I am,' he says. 'That is my responsibility.'

"I am full awake by this point and more than a little afraid. Garrick is covered from head to foot in blood, like he'd been swimming in the slaughterhouse trough. Even his teeth are red. He must've seen how scared I was, for he says then, 'Don't worry, son. This is not my blood. Jack will be ripping no more.' And then he waits for this nugget to sink in.

"It takes me a moment, but I gets it. 'You killed Leather Apron? Ripper Jack himself? But he is from hell,' says I.

"This draws a guffaw from Garrick. 'He's in hell now,' he says. 'His soul, at any rate. His body is sleeping with the rotting corpses of common hoodlums in the sludge on the Thames's bed.'

"I know Garrick doesn't like questions, but one pops out before I can stop it: 'How did you find a demon, sir?' But he isn't angry; he seems to be in a mood for questions.

"'Aha,' says he, tapping his forehead. 'With man's deadliest weapon: the brain. Jack was a creature of habits, and that was his undoing. The first five girls were done in a frenzy, but after that Jack calmed himself and used the moon as his clock. For three years now I've been patrolling Whitechapel and Spitalfields on the nights of the full moon, and finally he shows outside the Ten Bells.' Garrick laughs then. 'It's barely credible, this so-called genius plans to snatch yet another girl from the Bells. I spotted him right off, a toff in common getup, all twitchy with nerves.'

"Garrick leaned over me then. I remember blood dripping onto my forehead and I thought, That's Leather Apron's blood."

Chevie was so enthralled by the story that she wouldn't have moved even if the plasti-cuffs had miraculously fallen from her wrists.

"'I let him take a girl, just to be sure,' Garrick says. 'And I trail him from the rooftops down to Buck's Row. I can hear them talking and joking about poor Polly Nichols, who was done for at this very spot. Old Jack had a surprisingly feminine giggle on him, something he never boasted about to the papers. And all the time I am looming overhead with my favorite Cinquedea blade all blacked up and ready for blood.' He showed me the short sword then. It had not been washed, and the blood was thick and lumped with gore."

If Chevie had not been so engrossed in the tale, she might have noticed that, while there was still noise coming from outside the bathroom, the sounds of agents joking had ceased and there were thumping sounds that could not be attributed to the music pumping from the television's speakers.

"'As soon as he pulls out his own blade, a common-as-muck scalpel, I leaped down from on high and had him open from neck to nave. It was a clean swipe, like something from the theater. He went down like they all do, no special powers, no memorable last words. The girl was rightly grateful and fell to her knees, calling me Lordship. I should have killed her, I know, me lad. But the street was dark and my face was blacked, and so I simply says, "Tell your friends that London is rid of Bloody Jack," and lets her run off for herself. It was a moment of weakness, but I was feeling well disposed toward the world. And then, what's this? A little moan from the cobbles. My boy Jacky is still breathing. "Not for long," says I, and set to work. Before he goes, Jack confesses to nineteen murders, with something of a gleam in his eye. "Nineteen?" says I to him. "I done twice that last year alone." His heart gave out after that.'"

Riley drew a shuddering breath. "And that was when I realized that Albert Garrick was indeed the devil."

The bathroom door buckled suddenly as a body was hurled forcibly against it. The crash startled Riley from his reverie. Again the door heaved, this time coming away from its hinges entirely, falling into the room, weighed down by the unconscious form of Agent Duff.

A dark figure appeared in the doorway and seemed to glide into the room.

"Orange?" said Chevie, but she saw almost immediately that, while the figure resembled the FBI agent, it was not in fact him.

Riley looked into the man's cruel, dead eyes. "No. No, it's my master. Now do you understand?"

Albert Garrick hammed it up for Chevie, striking a pose, then he gave a deep bow.

"Albert Garrick, West End illusionist and assassin-for-hire at your service, young lady—come down the chimney to introduce myself proper."

As he bowed, a drop of someone else's blood fell from his nose, landing on Chevie's forehead, and she was struck to her core with a terror that she could barely contain.

"Now I understand," she said.

# 6 » VICTORIANA

**A**LBERT GARRICK HAD BEEN APPRENTICED TO the Great Lombardi for more than ten years, and in that time the little Italian became like a second father to the orphan boy. But young Albert never forgot his first father, who had killed for him, and it was years before the nightmares of those cholera days in the Old Nichol faded and he stopped worrying every time a patch of dry skin appeared on his elbow or his eyes seemed a little sunken.

Lombardi worked him hard but was not cruel and never once struck him unless he deserved it. They traveled the length and breadth of England, working the theaters, and once even took the Boulogne ferry for a summer season in Paris's

Théâtre-Italien, where sections of Lombardi's act were woven into a street scene for a Verdi opera. Lombardi wept at the final curtain every night and often told young Albert that he saw working with Verdi as the crowning achievement of his career.

"I have searched all my life for real magic," he said some years later as he lay dying from tuberculosis in their digs in Newcastle upon Tyne. "And I found it in the music of Verdi. An Italian. *Dio lo benedica.*"

Lombardi died that night, forcing his apprentice to appear in his stead at the Journal. The night was not an unqualified success, but many of the doves survived, which encouraged young Albert to adopt the Lombardi name and to fulfill his master's engagements.

Garrick inherited not only his master's bookings but his assistant, too. Sabine was the most exotic and beautiful creature Albert had ever seen, and he'd been in love with her since that first day, when he had watched, slack jawed, as she emerged unscathed from Lombardi's Egyptian saw-box.

THE GARDEN HOTEL, MONMOUTH STREET, LONDON, NOW

And now, Garrick felt an echo of the passion of his youth as he took his first proper look at Chevron Savano.

She looks like Sabine, thought Garrick, gazing down at the girl.

He cupped Chevie's jaw in his hand, tilting it back. *It's uncanny, the resemblance.*

And another part of his brain told him, There's a passing likeness, nothing more. Garrick was shaken, all the same. His resolution to pierce this maid's heart had evaporated like morning mist.

*What is happening to me?*

Garrick bowed once more to Chevie. "Beg pardon, Miss Savano. I need a moment to gather my thoughts."

Garrick ducked out of the bathroom and strode to the kitchenette, where there stood what looked like a squat refrigerator of the American style. Garrick pulled open the door and inside, instead of rows of chilled food and beverages, he saw Agent Waldo Gunn, sitting behind a sheet of bulletproof glass.

Garrick knew from Orange's expertise that this fake fridge was a personal panic pod and was just as secure as the president's bunker under the White House.

Waldo sat shivering behind the glass, as though he were seated in a real refrigerator. He punched numbers into his phone with shaking fingers.

"This pod is not in the system, is it, Waldo?" said Garrick. "You have been augmenting your security."

Garrick slammed the door so hard the catch snapped, and the door swung open. The fact that Waldo had been able to secure himself made Garrick's own escape more urgent. The FBI would be aware of his existence now and would soon be—what was the expression?—*hot on his trail.* This century was becoming a dangerous place. Time to go home.

*No more dallying!* he told himself. *In there you go, mate. And kill her. She is puny and helpless. One slice across the windpipe will more than do the trick. The noise will be distasteful, but there it is—too late now to be letting your qualms get in the way.*

Garrick froze in mid-pace.

*My qualms? But I don't have qualms.*

And, in a bolt of self-awareness, it came to him.

*These are Smart's qualms. He was fond of this Savano girl, and this fondness bleeds across my neurons, reinforcing this false identification with Sabine. This young woman is no more a reincarnation of Sabine than she is of Her Majesty, Queen Vic. I shall kill her and be well rid of an adversary.*

Garrick stocked up on weaponry from the FBI arsenal, including Duff's switchblade, which he had casually knocked from the agent's grasp.

*How charming,* thought Garrick. *The standard of weaponry has really improved. Killing in this time will be so much easier.*

This notion cheered him immensely and he reentered the bathroom, bolstered for his grisly work.

Inside the bathroom, Chevie had her foot hooked underneath the unconscious Agent Duff's chin and was trying to haul him toward her when Garrick's frame filled the doorway.

"Most enterprising, Agent. Perhaps he has a blade of some sort on his person? One never knows, eh?"

Chevie glared at the assassin belligerently. "You killed them all, didn't you? Smart, the hazmat team, those officers outside?"

Garrick twirled the blade. "Not all," he said, nodding pointedly at Duff. "Not yet."

Chevie withdrew her foot, hoping that Duff at least would be spared. "Riley was right about you."

"Oh?" said Garrick, prepared to listen to this before silencing this girl forever. "And what did my wayward assistant say?"

"He said that we could never stop you. That you would cross heaven and hell to find him."

Garrick tousled Riley's hair, and the boy forced himself not to jerk his head away from the touch.

"Time and space, to be precise," said Garrick. "And I picked up a few valuable tidbits on my travels." As he was saying this, Garrick knelt and placed the tip of the switchblade over Duff's chest. "But one lesson I learned long before this particular jaunt was not to leave any witnesses. Not unless I want to swing for the kindness."

"Let me do it, master," blurted Riley. "To make it up to you for all the blundering and trouble I've put you to."

Garrick was touched, but wary. "You would make your bones? Now?"

"Your way is the only way," said Riley. "I see that now. The time has come for me to embrace my destiny. To back the winning horse."

Garrick tapped his own chin with the blade, then leaned forward to slice Riley's cuffs.

"I have no patience for tomfoolery or hesitations, Riley. Strike quickly and earn yourself a footnote in my good books. Otherwise I will be treating you as a hostile."

Riley took the offered blade. "I am grateful for the chance, master. You can count on me."

Chevie could only hope that Riley was making a play; otherwise, if he actually intended to do whatever it took to keep himself alive, that might include killing her and Duff both. In any case, she had to appear outraged.

"Don't do it, kid," she warned. "You kill a Fed, and there will be nowhere to hide."

Garrick smiled slyly. "Oh, but there is a place, isn't there, Agent? Or perhaps a *time*?"

Riley held the blade in his fist and then moved so fast that even Garrick's eyebrows lifted. He twirled the knife a full revolution and then slid it cleanly between Duff's third and fourth ribs, directly above the heart. A poppy-shaped bloodstain blossomed at the spot and quickly soaked the material of the agent's crisp shirt.

"There," said Riley, his voice quavering slightly. "It is done. And no big deal either. Shall I send the other one off also? Unto dust, as you always say, master."

"Murderer!" cried Chevie, aiming a kick at Riley, which Garrick deflected with the heel of one hand.

"All credit to you, boy. That was a clean puncture. In like a hot poker through snow."

"The girl, master?"

"No," said Garrick, taking back the switchblade. "Though every strike binds you to me with blood, I must do this one myself."

Garrick grasped Chevie's chin with his fingers. They felt like steel pincers along her jawline. He ratcheted her head backward, carefully removed the Timekey from her neck, and laid the blade along her windpipe.

Chevie flinched as her life flashed before her eyes, just as the movies had told her it would.

She saw her teacher's face, kind and worried, as she rescued her student from the clutches of a briar patch on the Topanga Canyon trail. She saw her father's motorbike accelerate around a bend on the Pacific Coast Highway, and she knew now he would never return, that his fuel tank would explode as he passed through Venice Beach. She saw her friend Nikki riding a big wave on Cross Creek beach, her hands reaching toward the sky as though she could grab on to a cloud.

The images faded, and Chevie discovered to her surprise that she was still alive. Garrick crouched over her, spine curved, a grimace dragging at the corners of his mouth. A man at war with his demons.

*You must prevail, Albert Garrick*, he thought. *Your mind is your own.*

Chevie was afraid to breathe. The tiniest movement would press her tender throat against the razor-sharp blade.

*Do it*, Garrick told himself. *Make the cut. Unto dust.*

Riley tried to take advantage of Garrick's hesitation. "Master, leave the lass be. It's me you're after. Leave her, and let's away."

Garrick rounded on the boy, pointing the switchblade at his eye. "You are plum correct there, my lad. I have come for you, and you proved yourself worthy. Now make yourself useful and check the gentlemen beyond for heartbeats."

Riley hesitated at the door. "We are not clear of this yet, master. Perhaps a hostage would be useful?"

Garrick seized upon this notion. It gave him a legitimate reason for not harming the girl.

"Perhaps a hostage would be of use. But I fear this one will rebel when an opportunity presents itself."

"I will vouch for her," said Riley.

"Do you understand what you are saying?" asked Garrick. "You are offering yourself to pay for her crimes? Her punishment will be yours? And you yourself are teetering on the edge of the abyss after your escape attempt, even with that kill. I will brook not one more scrap of insubordination."

"I understand, master. Perhaps she can help us."

Garrick closed one eye and the other glittered. "Us, is it? There's an *us* now?"

Riley waited for his master's response with held breath. He knew that Garrick would not hesitate to kill Chevie simply to make his argument clear, but something held him back.

I was right. Garrick has changed, Riley observed. His posture, the meat on his bones. Even his tone seems different.

"Very well," said Garrick, after a tantalizing silence. "We take the girl. But if she does betray me . . . you *both* pay the price."

Riley sighed, relieved that Chevie would live, even though she would probably kill him given the chance.

Garrick gazed down at her. "You are as transparent as a window at Fortnum and Mason's to me, girl. You are thinking at this instant that so long as you are alive, then there is a chance of escape."

Garrick bent low over Chevie, tracing her eyebrow with the tip of his blade. "Abandon all hope," he whispered. "For hope has abandoned ye."

Chevie believed him, and so did the boy.


Garrick was positively ebullient to have Riley back. He had an audience again, swelled to twice its size.

"Numbers in the stalls are up by a hundred percent," he commented to Riley as they rode in the black cab toward Bedford Square. "It must be a good show."

Chevie and Riley sat opposite him on the fold-down seats. Chevie was traumatized from stepping over the half dozen federal corpses in the safe suite.

Duff was a jerk, thought Chevie. But he was a human jerk.

Chevie had never seen so much death and was more shaken than she had imagined she would be in a combat situation. Her only consolation had been the sight of Waldo Gunn safe inside his panic pod.

*At least Waldo knows I am not a murderer.*

But this scrap of comfort did little to dispel the shock that crushed her spirit.

Riley, on the other hand, had lived his life in Victorian London, where murder was rare but life was cheap. Many poor children died at birth; if they did survive that first day, the odds were that cholera, smallpox, scarlet fever, or whooping cough would do them in before their fifth birthday. Riley had seen the grim reaper's handiwork more times than he could count.

*Life and death are two ends of the same ride,* Garrick had once told him. *Nothing to celebrate or mourn.*

And so Riley told himself to stay sharp, or he and Miss Savano could be coming to the end of their own rides.

Someday I may mourn all the souls Albert Garrick has done in, he thought. But not this day. This day is for fighting.

It was the early hours of the morning, and the streets were alive with die-hard revelers and city workers, winding along Tottenham Court Road under the eyes of coppers who walked the beat in pairs. Motorized street sweepers scoured the road with their bristled brushes, throwing up wakes of muddied water; and in the shop windows, employees of a dozen electronics stores switched on a thousand television and computer screens.

"Pleasantly warm," noted Garrick, tapping the knife in his breast pocket, so that Chevie would not forget that it was there or what it could do. "What is the season?"

"Summer," said Chevie sullenly.

Garrick sighed, and his face seemed to slide like melting butter until the features were his own again.

The face of an accountant, thought Chevie. Or a geography teacher. Not a merciless assassin.

Garrick punched Riley's shoulder playfully. "Ah . . . summer in London, without the stench of decay in our nostrils, and the two of us finally brothers in enterprise. Could there be anything finer? Almost a pity we have to go home, eh, boy?"

"Why *do* you want to go back?" asked Chevie.

Garrick tugged at the Timekey around his neck. "In spite of my new abilities, this world is new to me. I am at a disadvantage here, and a fugitive to boot. When I return to my own time, London town will be my oyster. Can you imagine what I could achieve with my understanding of the future? In the field of armaments alone, I could change the world."

"A psychopath who wants to take over the planet. How original."

Riley drew a sharp breath, anticipating swift punishment for such an impudent comment, but to his surprise Garrick almost seemed to be enjoying the exchange.

Garrick slapped his thigh. "Oh, Chevron, you are a tonic. The odds are stacked against you higher than the Tower of London and *still* you are full to the gills with pluck. I see now why Felix was fond of you."

Chevie snorted. "Felix? Fond of me? You've been misinformed."

"Felix and I were . . . *close* before he died," said Garrick cryptically. "Felix was fond of you, even if he was not fully aware of it."

"So you knew, but he didn't?"

Garrick half hid a smug smile behind his hand. "In a way, yes."

The magician's smile evaporated when the cab turned the corner onto Bedford Square and the house on Bayley Street came into view. The railings were crisscrossed with police tape, and two FBI agents in blue Windbreakers stood out front, flanked by Metropolitan police officers with machine guns slung across their chests. Obviously Waldo had redirected some of the FBI response team to Bedford Square and called in the locals to boot.

"We should have walked," said Chevie. "We might have gotten here quicker."

Garrick gnawed on a knuckle. "Quiet, girl. Do not force me to commit murder for the sake of a moment's silence."

Garrick considered the heavily armed officers.

Even an individual of my expertise could not be expected to take on the entire police force, he concluded, especially not ones with machine guns. Though according to Smart's experiences, the bobbies are much hampered by their own constitution. Apparently they cannot even dump vagrants into the Thames anymore. But even so, they would have no qualms about cutting down an assassin attempting to gain access to the building.

While Garrick was thinking, Riley stole a glance at Chevie. Her face was tight and her muscles coiled, though she tried to appear at ease; and it was clear to Riley that she intended to try her luck with Garrick in this confined space.

She thinks I'm on his side, he thought. And I cannot let her know the truth without also alerting Garrick.

Garrick had obviously noticed Chevie's attitude, for he pointed a finger at the boy. "Riley, tell your new friend to rethink her strategy. If she takes aggressive action, I will gut her before the seat belt is off, and knife the cabbie for spite."

Luckily the cabbie was separated from them by a plastic screen and did not realize his life was a tool for barter.

"Here we are, mate," he called, sliding open the screen's small window. "Bayley Street. You might spot a few celebs up around here. House on the corner went for forty million pounds last month. There's no recession in this manor, I'll tell you that."

Garrick rolled his eyes. "Apparently the verbosity of London cabbies is constant through the ages." He knocked on the plastic. "I have a new destination for you, driver. Take us to the Wolseley. A *friend* told me about this café, and I feel it would be just the ticket for our ravenous group. Down Piccadilly, if you please, I do not wish to take the tourists' route."

"No worries," said the cabbie. "I know this city better than the wife knows the inside of my wallet. Strike me dead if I try to cheat you."

Garrick hid his face as they passed the armed police.

"That is exactly what I shall do," he said.

By the time the cabbie drew in front of the Wolseley, the restaurant was open for early breakfast. Garrick selected a booth in the window and studied the menu with coos of delight that drew attention from other diners.

"What say you, son? Kedgeree or kippers? Why not both, eh? It is a special occasion, after all."

Chevie sat by the window, hemmed in between the glass and the magician's apprentice, hampered by the table.

I need to make a move, she thought. Orange's last instruction to me was to guard the Timekey. I will not botch another mission. I must get that key back. And I can't rely on Riley to help me.

All traces of Smart were gone now. The person sitting opposite her was a genuine magician from the past, and as if to prove it, he charmed the waitress, pulling a salt shaker from behind her ear and Felix Smart's platinum MasterCard from behind his own.

"I believe this is what passes for money these days," he said, his accent like something from an old black-and-white Sherlock Holmes movie. "Make sure to add a ten percent gratuity for yourself, my dear, pretty as you are."

The girl was used to big tippers. "I think I'm pretty enough for twenty percent," she said, not even bothering to smile.

Garrick waved a magnanimous hand. "Why not take thirty?" he said. "We Smarts are a generous breed."

The waitress pulled a pen from the belt of her apron and took Garrick's order. The magician selected three kinds of eggs: poached, fried, and scrambled. Kedgeree and kippers. Toast, muffins, and American pancakes with syrup. Sausages, bacon, and potato cakes. Oatmeal and granola. Orange juice, grapefruit juice, and a large pot of coffee. Riley opted for hot chocolate and a full English breakfast, while Chevie asked for a glass of water.

Obviously murder gives a person an appetite, she thought.

"Not hungry, Agent?" Garrick asked her.

Chevie smiled tightly. "I'm feeling a bit off. Must be all the corpses."

Garrick winked at Riley. "You grow accustomed to that. Look at my partner here, an apprentice no more. He'll be tucking into his bacon like the hangman's waiting for him in the square."

"Yeah," said Chevie. "Maybe he is. That's what happens when you kill everyone you meet."

"I haven't killed you yet, Miss Savano. Perhaps after breakfast, eh?"

Riley was silent throughout this exchange. He wished only to sleep and perhaps dream of a beach and the red-haired boy.

*Beware the undertow—it'll have yer legs out from under you.*

Had the boy really said that, or was his mind inventing a past for himself? Riley shook his head to dislodge the familiar fog that settled over his brain when he was in Garrick's company. He generally let his mind float away, but today was different. Chevie's life was at stake as well as his own.

The last thing Riley wanted was a fry-up, but his body was hungry and, as Garrick always said, *Eat up, boy. Your next meal will probably be your last.*

"You should eat, Chevie."

Garrick's hand darted across the table and clipped Riley's ear. "*Chevie?* Who are you now, son? The Prince of Wales? Ladies will be referred to by their titles. This is *Agent Savano* or *miss* to you."

Chevie was unimpressed. "Wow, manners. Cool. I had thought you were a murdering psycho, but now you've won me over."

Garrick sighed, weary now of the girl's comments. "This

constant melodrama is so wearing. Isn't there anything I can do to persuade you to be civil, at least while we are at table?"

Psychology 101: get the subject to talk about himself. Any information learned might come in useful later, if there was a later.

"You could tell me what you are, exactly."

Garrick seriously considered this. It would be nice to share the details of his transformation; but then again, too much knowledge was too much power, so perhaps he would sketch in broad strokes. "I know that Felix went over the basics with you. Wormholes through time, and so forth. When Felix and I traveled the time tunnel together, we merged. I am still in control, but Felix is definitely a part of me."

"You killed him?"

"I killed most of him. And it was self-defense: he did detonate a bomb."

"So you can do stuff with what's left of Felix? Tricks?"

"Ah, yes, of course. A trick. Ladies love the magic tricks. Think of a card."

Chevie rolled her eyes. "Oh, please."

"No, seriously now, mademoiselle. Picture a card. *Visualize it*, as you Americans are fond of saying."

Chevie couldn't help it. The Queen of Hearts popped into her mind. It had been her father's favorite bar on the Pacific Coast Highway.

Garrick clicked his fingers. "I have it. You were picturing the Ace of Spades. The card that signifies imminent and painful death."

"No, I wasn't," argued Chevie.

Garrick twirled his butter knife. "You are now," he said.

It was an exchange straight out of a penny dreadful, Garrick knew; but he had grown up onstage and had melodrama in his blood.

The food arrived, and Garrick tucked in with obvious delight, laughing as he ate, plucking morsels from several different plates—he ate sausages dipped in syrup and potato cakes smothered in hot chocolate. He was like a child at a party.

"There is no dirt, not a speck of grit," he declared. "The odors are uniformly pleasant, and what is supposed to be hot is hot."

Chevie watched the magician closely, mentally going over every detail of his face and mannerisms in order to commit it all to memory.

*Middle-aged. Maybe early forties, hard to tell. Pale complexion. Teeth seem a little long. Yellowed. Dark eyes. Blue, maybe, deep-set, with a bulbous brow. Black hair starting to gray. Long and straight. Slim build, but wiry. Nothing obviously threatening about him. This guy would never get the part of a Victorian villain in a movie about himself.*

Surely my chance will come, thought Chevie, but every time she was on the verge of launching herself at the magician, he saw the intent in her face. It was almost as if Garrick could read her thoughts.

"You are wondering if I can read your thoughts," said Garrick suddenly, waving a nub of sausage at her. "I confess that I cannot, but I do have a certain expertise in the science of movement, what you might term kinesics or body language. Your violent intentions are as clear to me as the *Times*'s banner headline."

Chevie glared at him. "Yeah? What's my face telling you now?"

"The FBI often employ the term *acceptable collateral damage*," continued Garrick calmly. "If we were to engage here, I can guarantee that at least half a dozen members of the public would be killed; the number could be as high as ten, if you really inconvenienced me. Felix assures me that you have a certain competence in the martial arts, but you are unarmed, and I have three pistols and a blade on my person. Do you think the Bureau would reward you for provoking me in a restaurant?"

Garrick was right, and Chevie knew it. She could not afford to be aggressive in such a public area.

Again, Garrick read her face. "You have come to the right decision, Agent. After all, these are real people all around us. People with families and loved ones."

Garrick flinched as if struck, as his own words connected him to a memory of Smart's.

"Loved ones," he repeated, pulling the Timekey from under his shirt. "Felix knew that his father had taken a female companion somewhere in London after his mother died. Charles Smart never revealed whom, and Felix presumed that once his father disappeared into the past that was the end of that. But I have spied on many a lovesick mark, and passion will drive a man to almost any lengths." Garrick paused, flipping the Timekey with his agile fingers. "His father built a second pod in London, but Felix could never track it down. And it occurs to me, as a student of human foibles and failings, what better reason to construct a backup pod than to sneak back to this century and visit a secret flame?" Garrick activated the key's small screen and clicked though the menus until he came to a trip log.

"We have several jumps from Bedford Square, as one would expect, the last one in the early 1980s. And that should be the end of it—but, no, I have some coordinates here. More than a dozen more jaunts logged to and from the same spot. Smart, you amorous old dog. Whoever this woman is, you could not stay away."

Garrick stuffed the Timekey inside his shirt. "Riley, my son. We have found our way home."

Riley did not speak, but his eyes spoke for him: *I am not your son.*

Surprising that Garrick could not decipher that.


Garrick used the GPS on Smart's phone to navigate to the coordinates on the Timekey. Felix Smart's memories acted like a living tutorial. Whenever Garrick arrived at a new screen, he simply concentrated for a moment until its workings came to him.

They walked from the Wolseley side by side, like family, past the Ritz and onto Piccadilly. Garrick enjoyed the early morning sun on his face, while Chevie's strides were stiff with tension and Riley walked as though dazed with exhaustion; in reality he was overplaying his fatigue so that Garrick would not press him into conversation, and he could steal a moment to think.

I wish there was some way to signal to Agent Savano, he thought. We can only escape by paddling in the same direction.

He tried to catch Chevie's eye, but she was lost in her own thoughts.

Surely there is an alert out for Garrick at this point, Chevie was thinking. Maybe he will be recognized.

It was doubtful, as Garrick no longer looked like Agent Orange. The only people who had Garrick's true description were walking beside him, and it seemed as though Riley had chosen which side he was on. And she would not have held the boy's choice against him had it not been for the murder of her colleague.

The city center was becoming busy as shops opened for business. In spite of the congestion fee, the streets were soon jammed bumper to bumper with vehicles. The day was shaping up nicely, clear silver skies that would soon turn blue, and a brisk breeze that could stir even the most jaded time traveler. The unlikely trio strolled together through Mayfair, Chevie hoping against hope that somehow the Bureau had tracked them and there was a sniper drawing a bead on Garrick's crown even as they walked.

*Wishful thinking. And, even if somebody does shoot this Garrick creature, it might not even harm him. It could just make him angry. Who knows what this guy is capable of?*

Chevie told herself not to give up. One of Cord Vallicose's maxims was that there was always an opportunity waiting to be noticed; an agent had to be ready when it presented itself.

Whatever it takes to stay out of the past, she thought. I am not going into the past.

But Chevie's subconscious knew, even if her conscious mind didn't yet realize it, that she would hop, skip, and jump into the past whistling "The Star-Spangled Banner" if it meant getting away from this lunatic magician.

They arrived at the coordinates programmed into the Timekey without any sniper fire or indeed incident of any kind. Garrick held his two hostages tightly by their necks, long nails digging into their collars.

"Do you know, Agent Savano," he said conversationally, "that I could kill you now with any one of these fingers?" To demonstrate *which* fingers, he drummed them in a creepy fashion on Chevie's flesh. "One of my trade secrets is that for the last ten years I have been coating my nails with furniture lacquer. They are hard as steel and sharper than a barber's cutthroat. I can slit any package with my thumbnail and explore its contents behind my back for my famous second-sight trick. I have never revealed that to a living soul, but something about you makes a person want to unburden."

Chevie did not appreciate being told a magician's secrets; it made her think that she might not live much longer.

Riley gazed down the length of the street. "Are we here, master? Is this the way home?"

They had arrived at Half Moon Street, and it looked just like the movies said a Mayfair street should look in the summer, with a row of fine old five-story buildings that had been converted into small businesses with a few cafés and pubs. The street was still quiet at this time of the morning, and the sidewalk was barricaded by stacks of cardboard and trash that had yet to be collected by the garbage truck. An old lady in boots was hosing the night's detritus from the entrance to an antiques shop.

"Now, where would be a good place to pick up antiques?" wondered Garrick.

In the past, thought Chevie, and she was suddenly afraid for the old lady.

Chevie felt Garrick's grip loosen slightly as his fingers seemed to grow a little shorter. She glanced up and saw that Garrick was hunched now. He spasmed as though racked by a silent fit of coughing. With every retch, his physical self altered until he resembled Felix Smart once more.

That was my chance, Chevie realized, and I stood here gawking.

Garrick's fingers tightened on her shoulder once more. "You should have had a go there, Agent," he said, sweat pasted across his brow. "Those transmogrifications take it out of a fellow, yes, they do."

"Excuse me, ma'am," he called to the elderly lady. "Perhaps you can assist me?"

The lady did not look up from her labor. "I can assist you at nine. Shop opens at nine. Most of the stuff I have is really old, so another thirty minutes won't matter."

Garrick tapped her window. "I see you specialize in Victorian."

The lady released the hose trigger and swiveled her head upward to take in Garrick.

"Yes, and I will still specialize in Victorian at nine." There was probably more British sarcasm in the tank, but the lady changed her tune once Garrick's adopted face registered.

"Wait a moment. Don't I . . ." And her eyes drifted as though trying to locate an elusive memory. "Your face. It seems so familiar."

Garrick's smile seemed utterly genuine. "People tell me I look like my father."

The lady dropped the hose. "Oh . . . Oh, my. Felix? You are Felix, aren't you?"

"Yes, I am Felix," said Garrick, making it sound like he was the new messiah.

"Oh, goodness. Oh, dear me. Felix." The woman's face was transformed utterly. Gone was the cynical tradeswoman of moments before, and in her place stood a wide-eyed, flustered lady. "Your father said you might find me someday."

Garrick placed a hand on her shoulder. "And here I am."

"Yes, you are here. Plain as day." She drew a worried breath. "Oh, are you hungry? You must be thirsty? And your young friends? They're probably hungry and thirsty."

Garrick shrugged as if to say, *We are terribly hungry and thirsty, but I am too polite to mention it.*

"You must come in. Please come inside." The lady fished a

door key on a chain from under her blouse, then jabbed it into antiques shop's front door.

"But, madam," said Garrick, smiling, "it is not yet nine o'clock."

The lady knew very well she was being ribbed. "Oh, it's always a question of time with you Smart boys." She offered a gloved hand. "I'm Victoria. Your father's . . . friend."

For a moment Garrick's eyes glittered in Felix Smart's face.

"I believe we have come to the right place," he said, bending to kiss Victoria's cheek.

Not only was the lady named Victoria, but the antiques shop was called Victoriana. When she led them through the doorway and into the shop itself, Riley could not stifle a gasp, for it was like stepping back into his own time, without the usual stink of animals, sewage, and nearby death, which in truth he did not hanker for, in spite of his current circumstances.

I have always lived in the shadow of death, he thought, feeling his heart pump like a steam piston as he spied a set of brass andirons that were almost identical to the ones flanking his and Garrick's own hearth in Holborn.

*And somewhere in this place is the gateway back.*

Unlike his master, Riley was in no hurry to return to the nineteenth century's Great Oven. He had experienced wonders during the night and also freedom, however fleetingly, and now had a taste for it.

*I could exist here in this future of marvels, if only Garrick would release me.*

But Riley knew that there was only one way his master would ever release him.

The lady led them through a showroom that glowed softly with the amber warmth of sunlight on wood. Her small shop was presented as a Victorian drawing room, but in this drawing room everything was for sale. There were discreet tags on each item but no prices. If you asked for the price, you were halfway to buying.

What Chevie knew about antiques could be written on the back of a postcard. The oldest thing she'd ever owned was a seventies surfboard that had once belonged to world champion "PT" Townend, but even she could tell that the stuff in this room was expensive. The pieces hummed with history, and it was impossible to look at the bureau without wondering who might have once written letters on its folding lid.

"What a wonderful emporium," said Garrick, all charm and grace. "The pieces are in remarkable condition." He stroked the leather cushion of an angular recliner that was less ornate than the other chairs. "Is this a William Morris, Victoria?"

Victoria retraced her steps to the chair, picking up the cushion and hugging it close as though it were a baby.

"Yes. One of the very first. This was the last thing your father sent to me."

"It seems old," said Garrick, tracing the grain with his finger. "Shouldn't it be almost new?"

Victoria replaced the cushion. "Ah, you see, therein lies your father's genius. The extra power needed to transport this chair from the nineteenth century would be enormous, so

Charles simply bought a field in Greenwich, which he knew would still be under grass, and he buried items there. When he comes to call, he brings a little label with some directions. It is his version of roses and champagne." She flicked the chair's label with a finger. "I still use the labels, as you can see. Anything to keep me going until his next visit."

"You two have something special," said Garrick, and to Chevie's trained ear the assassin sounded sincere, even touched.

Victoria stroked his face, fingers rasping against stubble. "Yes, we do, and the next time he comes I'm going back with him for good. I've been taking the bisphosphonates for six months now. We're to be married." Victoria's eyes were bright with excitement, but she was a decent woman and realized the discomfort her news would cause her beloved's son. "I know this isn't easy for you, Felix, to find out like this. But your father was so lonely—he missed you. He kept an eye on you, but it was too dangerous to make contact. Charles said that if you ever found me it might be because you were ready to understand why he left. He hoped that would be the case."

Victoria led them through a door at the back of the shop floor and into an open-plan apartment with an ultramodern minimalist kitchen and living room. Victoria filled the kettle, then sat them at an oblong table that basked in the latticed rays of sunshine pouring through the blinds. Pictures of Charles Smart and Victoria lined the walls. Apparently they had been having fun all over London for quite a few years.

Chevie checked the apartment for exits and concluded that the best way out was the way they had come in, as long as Garrick did not position himself between her and the door. There was a door at the back that didn't seem to be in use, obstructed as it was by a stack of tea chests, which would take valuable seconds to push aside. Beside the chests a banister poked through from a basement stairway. It was likely that the basement had street level windows or skylights, but Chevie did not relish the idea of charging down into what could easily be a dead end.

Victoria sat at the head of the table and composed herself. Chevie guessed she was about seventy—a petite, striking lady with fine, porcelain features and eyes that were so wide and green they were almost feline. Her hair was mostly dark, but streaked with blond and gray. She wore a period bustier get-up that would not have been out of place in a BBC costume drama.

"So, everyone," she said, "are we all in the loop? The time loop?"

Garrick was getting anxious. His eyes darted around the room, and his brow glistened. Riley couldn't understand it; there was no danger here. Garrick could face down a room full of armed Tartars without a drop of sweat sliding down his beak of a nose. Now here he was, suddenly agitated in the company of one old lady. What was wrong?

Garrick answered for the group. "Yes, yes. We are all aware of Charles Smart's . . . that is, my father's experiments and discoveries. We have reason to believe that he is in serious danger. We need to travel back in time to assist him. So, if there is a WARP pod here, we need to use it."

Victoria pursed her lips. "Hmm. Charles hoped you would find me so we could get to know each other, but he was also afraid that you might come for the secrets of the pod. He said that the FBI were a sneaky bunch, and I should watch out."

"I see," said Garrick, teeth gritted. "But Charles was my . . . father. I am his boy, surely you don't need to watch out for me?"

Victoria wagged two index fingers at him like six-shooters. "Ah, you may be his boy, but Charles said that you were potentially the worst of the bunch. 'Felix is more interested in the government contracts than in the science,' Charles told me. You pushed things forward before they were ready. Your father told me all about the wormhole mutations. He said time travel can give you cancer without the bisphosphonates."

Charles Smart's monkey arm and yellow blood flashed through Chevie's head. *Mutations.*

"But Father is in trouble. We need to save him."

Victoria's eyes were shrewd. You don't keep a business open in central London without being seriously smart. "How do you know Charles is in trouble? He said you can't find him. None of the other pods go to where he is, and you can't just build another pod. Not without Charles."

Garrick frowned and shuddered as if his system were under attack from a virus.

"What about this?" he said, plonking a large handgun on the table. "Now, why don't you tell me where the pod is?"

Victoria pounded the table with delicate hands while the

kettle whistled behind her. "What kind of son are you?" she demanded. "You broke your father's heart, and now you're threatening the woman he loves. You villain."

Garrick covered his eyes, uncomfortable in the light. "Yes, villain, I accept it. Now, where is the pod?"

Victoria rose to her feet. "Never, Judas. You shall get nothing from me."

"Then I shall kill you," said Garrick. "As I killed your beloved Charles."

Victoria paled, then staggered back a step.

"You are not Felix Smart!" she declared.

"No, madam," declared Garrick. "I am not. Felix Smart has gone the way of his father."

Victoria made a noise close to an animal howl and pounced on Garrick with surprising speed.

"Stupid woman!" said Garrick, and slapped her hard on the side of her head. The blow felled them both, for no sooner had Victoria crumpled to the ground than Garrick himself bent double and threw up across the table.

Chevie saw a chance and twisted in her chair, grabbing the back of it and swinging the entire thing at Garrick's head with all the aggression and force she had learned working out in federal gyms.

Garrick managed to get a forearm up, but the chair smashed across his arm and head, driving him to the ground. The assassin went down, blood smearing the floor as he slid on his forehead.

Chevie did not relax for one second. Garrick might be down but he was far from out, and there was his side-swapping, murdering sidekick Riley to worry about.

"Stay out of this, kid!" she warned Riley, who was moving in her direction.

"No, Chevie," said Riley. "You don't understand."

There was no time for understanding now. This situation was all about Garrick and how to neutralize him. There would be plenty of time for understanding stuff later.

Garrick himself reinforced her decision when he rolled over and glanced up at her through a sheet of blood and gasped, in Smart's voice: "Chevie. The Timekey."

"Felix? Is that you?"

He held out the key. "Take it."

Chevie reached out, grabbing the lanyard. She slung it around her neck, but before she could retreat entirely, Smart became Garrick once more.

"No. That is mine," he growled, grabbing the key and yanking it toward him. For a thin man he had a lot of strength, and Chevie was off balance and powerless to stop her tumble.

Riley saved her, tipping the entire table over on his master. The boy, too, was stronger than he seemed. The table's edge landed squarely on Garrick's shin, splintering the bone.

"What?" said Chevie. "You're on my side now?"

Riley held up his left hand and Chevie saw blood congealed on the thumb.

"Always," he said, and Chevie understood. The boy was a

magician's apprentice. He had pierced his own flesh, not Duff's, risking Garrick's wrath to save the agent's life.

"We should go, Agent," said Riley urgently.

"Yeah," said Chevie, then rubbed her throat and coughed. "Yep. Going would be good."

She tucked the Timekey inside her blouse and ushered Riley toward the front door. Shots punched through the table and into the wall, forcing them back the other way. Garrick was still fighting, in spite of the terrible agony he must be feeling.

"We should have killed him," said Riley. "Killing the devil cannot be a sin."

Until quite recently, Chevie would have scoffed at this statement for its superstition and dubious morality, but now she was coming around to the idea.

"Later," she said. "Later."

There was no choice now but to take the rear stairway, and they were close when half a dozen shots ripped into the banister, showering them with wood chips. Chevie grabbed Riley's collar and shunted him behind the sofa.

Riley fell and saw between the sofa legs that the lady was recovering her senses and had rolled onto her elbows. "Victoria is alive."

"Good. I doubt Garrick will spend a bullet on her when we are the ones breaking his bones with furniture."

The broken bone did not hurt Garrick as much as it would a normal person. The quantum magician instructed his nerve endings to hush their messages to the brain, which took a little of the white-hot pain from his injury. He was perfectly aware of the damage done to his limb. His internals were clearer to him than the calcium tungstate photographs those Frost brothers had used to see inside mice. He was suffering from a compound fracture of the tibia inflicted by his own boy. He tried to heal himself, but the process was infuriatingly slow, and he could feel it draining his energies.

Garrick felt the injustice like rising nausea.

"Riley!" he called. "Riley."

Riley ducked low behind the sofa as if the word could harm him.

"We need to be leaving," he whispered to Chevie. "You're the expert in these matters, being some form of agent. Lead on, I says."

Chevie did not feel like much of an expert.

*I am only seventeen*, she wanted to say. *I shouldn't be here. I am not even a legitimate FBI agent, and my program was canceled.*

But she didn't voice these thoughts. Agent Chevron Savano considered herself a teenage professional, and Riley was depending on her.

She wiggled past him, making sure to keep her head down. "We need to help Victoria."

"Draw Garrick away and that will save her life—he don't care a fig for her. It's us and that Timekey he wants. Garrick will follow his target every time."

Riley was right.

"Okay. We go out the back way."

There had to be a yard, or a doorway. If she could make it to a phone, then Garrick was dead and buried, no matter how many faces he had.

*Then I am going home to California, where the sun shines and there are no death-dealing magicians from the past.*

Garrick took a few more shots, but he was firing blind, just trying to corral them to the kitchen.

Chevie squatted on her hunkers, pulling Riley's face close to hers.

"Here's the plan. We run to those back stairs and see where they go."

"Is that a plan?" asked Riley. "Strikes me more as a notion, or a smidge of an idea. Plans have stages and steps. Jinky twists and the likes."

"Zip it, chatterbox. You ready for the plan?"

Riley nodded.

"Right. After three. Run like the devil himself is on your tail."

Which in a way he was.

Chevie counted to three, then hurled a handy vase toward the wall, where she thought it would smash and distract Garrick.

She thought wrong.

Garrick shot the vase out of the air as it twirled, being a practiced marksman from his years in Her Majesty's army.

*Perhaps this is not a brilliant plan,* thought Chevie, but it was too late, as Riley had already bolted for the stairs. Luckily the boy kept himself low and out of Garrick's sight line.

He won't have a restricted sight line for long, she realized. Once he gets that leg free, we're as good as dead.

Chevie raced after Riley, feeling the gunfire impact the wall over her head before she heard it. They ran pell-mell down the stairs, barely managing to stay upright in their haste. The staircase was narrow and dim, but with familiar-looking thick power lines running along the skirting board.

*No*, thought Chevie. *No, no, no.*

The steps led down to a small basement. Chevie and Riley tumbled into the room, instinctively searching for an exit. There was none. The only natural light came from barred windows at pavement level. The legs of pedestrians threw stick shadows on the wall.

Chevie actually stamped her foot. "No way out! I don't believe it."

Riley patted the walls with his palms, hoping for a secret passage.

Chevie cast around the room, searching for something, *anything*, that could be of use to them.

Riley pointed to a blocky shape under a tarp in the corner. "I would wager that if we remove that waterproof sheet . . ."

"I know what it is!" shouted Chevie. "I know. But . . ."

Riley glanced anxiously toward the stairwell. Victorian oaths and grumbling echoed from above.

"My master is not happy."

"I gathered that."

"He is coming."

Chevie paced a little. "Yeah, I know. Death the magician is coming."

"Should I *zip it*?"

"Yeah . . . No." Chevie balled her fists in frustration. "I'm not even a proper agent, kid. I was supposed to keep an ear open in the lunch hall, that's it. No one ever said anything about *time travel*." Chevie slapped her head. "This is insane. I can't do this."

A shot smashed into the banisters, then there was a guttural roar—no words, simply emotion.

Riley twisted a splintered banister free, brandishing it like a stake.

"Chevie. I'll guard the stairs, perhaps even get a lucky blow in. You must activate the machinery."

Chevie knew the boy was right. She dragged the tarp, revealing the WARP pod underneath.

From upstairs: "Riley! You broke my leg."

"That ain't a happy man," said Riley, pointing with his makeshift stake.

He grabbed another corner of the tarp with his free hand, and soon the pod was uncovered. "Make it work, Chevie."

Riley decided to get the show on the road himself and began pounding buttons on the computers rigged up to the pod.

"No, no," said Chevie, elbowing him out of the way. "You need this." She took the Timekey from around her neck and slotted it into a computer drive on a console that was smaller than the one in Bedford Square.

*Perhaps it will be too complicated,* she half hoped. *Maybe I won't be able to fire it up.*

No such luck: as soon as the Timekey clicked into place, the pod shuddered into life, expelling steam from various vents, setting the power lines humming. Damper barrels vibrated on the floor.

This one is smaller, realized Chevie. Version 2.0.

The Timekey activated a tiny screen with yellow graphics that wobbled every few seconds. The screen crackled.

*That sounds like wires burning.*

*No. Don't think about that. It's just warming up.* To confirm this thought, a little cartoon bird appeared on the screen. The bird was without feathers and shivering. A speech bubble popped out of his beak: I'M JUST WARMING UP.

Chevie gave Riley a thumbs-up. "All systems go. No problems."

Slowly the bird sprouted feathers. It seemed as though Charles Smart had had a sense of humor.

From the top of the stairway there came a meaty slap as something lurched across the entrance.

"Riley," cried a rasping voice that seemed full of pain, both emotional and physical. "My son, no longer. My partner, never again."

Four shots blasted chunks from the brick walls of the basement. A series of thumps and curses followed. If Garrick was sliding down the stairs, he would soon be able to take a clear shot at them.

"Get your old battered self down here," called Riley,

attempting bravado. "I have a nice sharp gift waiting for yer organs."

Garrick fired another shot in reply and fragments of brick stung Chevie's cheek.

This is like Star Wars, thought Chevie. We're the Rebel Base and Garrick is the Death Star.

The bird sprouted more feathers.

"Chevron? Agent, hurry," said Riley urgently.

"Coming." Chevie fought the urge to slap the alt-tech computer. "Get into the pod."

"Inside?"

"Yes. Get in."

Riley did not like the idea of backing himself into an even smaller corner, but the only way out was in.

Legs flashed by on the pavement outside. More thumps on the stairs. Chevie thought she saw a scrabbling hand out of the corner of her eye.

"Riley! You cannot escape me."

In the pod, Riley sat on the bench, hands clenched on his knees.

The bird was fully clothed in feathers now, and the speech bubble said: I AM ALL WARMED UP.

Then the bird disappeared, and a menu began loading onscreen.

"Yeah, yeah, what are my options?" shouted Chevie, as though that could speed up the ancient computer.

There were two choices: SYSTEMS CHECK or ACTIVATE WORMHOLE.

She selected ACTIVATE WORMHOLE and, after a few fizzling seconds of nothing much, the familiar corona of orange light bloomed inside the pod.

"No!" came a voice from the stairs. "I forbid it!"

Two shots plowed into the concrete floor, throwing up sharp chips.

Almost in his sights, thought Chevie, and she realized that she would have to run the gauntlet to reach the pod herself. For two seconds Garrick would have a clear shot.

*The longer I wait, the sooner he shoots me.*

Chevie was prompted to remove her key, and the bird reappeared with a countdown in his speech bubble. Thirty seconds. Chevie had half a minute to get herself into the past.

*Thirty seconds. No time to think.*

"Run!" called Riley from inside the orange glow. "Run!"

She did, diving the last few feet into the belly of the pod. She noticed immediately how cold it was in there. Freezing. Her breath burst from her in clouds, then crystallized immediately. There was frost on Riley's hair and brows.

"When do we go?" he asked. "Why are we still here?"

Chevie did not answer, just turned to face the pod's doorway. Through the orange light she could see Garrick dragging himself down the stairs like a corpse that refused to lie down and die.

"Infernal time machine!" declared Riley, striking the bench. "Let us away!"

Garrick's head was cocked and his skeletal face pointed their way. From the depths of sunken sockets, his eyes were locked on them, beaming malevolence into the pod.

Chevie stood and shouted at the top of her lungs, "Wake up, Victoria! Wake up and run."

Garrick raised his weapon to fire but thought better of it, unwilling to risk damaging the WARP pod. Instead he continued his grim crawl.

The pod began to beep. The complicated series of whoops and whistles was matched by small lights on the fuselage.

Chevie suddenly remembered something from Orange's time lecture. *The tests were pretty successful*, he'd said. *There was a small number of aberrations, usually on the return trip, but less than one percent, so acceptable in a scientific sense.*

Oh, my God, she thought. We haven't been taking bisphosphonates. I don't even know what those are. We could come out the other end with monkey parts or dinosaur heads.

But she didn't say anything to Riley, because her voice had been snatched away by the orange light. She didn't lay a warning hand on his shoulder either, because her hand was gone, whisked away as though she were made of sand.

*I am sand in the wind*, she thought.

*As am I*, replied Riley in her mind.

The last thing to go was their sight, so they completed their dematerialization watching Garrick reach the bottom step and begin his lurching hop across the floor.

He's going to make it, thought Chevie. We're not rid of Albert Garrick yet.

She would have closed her eyes and bowed her head, but her head was gone, and now so were her eyes.

# 7 » THE BATTERING RAMS

RILEY FELT HIMSELF GO AND INITIALLY PRESUMED that the *going* would be similar to his previous journey through the tunnel of time. It was not. In fact, this trip was the opposite of his first in almost every way. At the most basic level, he was going back as opposed to traveling forward. Just as a physical journey changed according to a person's direction, so too did a quantum one. Where he had felt propelled, now he felt somehow suctioned into his own past life.

Riley had heard of primal recollection occurring when a subject was under hypnotism—indeed, Garrick had mesmerized him on occasion—but Riley could never remember anything that had happened while in the trances, probably because Garrick had bolstered his own mesmeric talents by swabbing the boy's upper lip with an ether-soaked sponge.

But now vignettes from his life played out before him, projected on the shifting surface of the wormhole.

*The ginger-haired boy. He is Tom. Ginger Tom, Ma always called him. We are half brothers. I remember now.*

Teenage Tom looked down on little Riley, holding out a hand. *Come on, brother. I have a farthing for lemonade. We will share a bottle.*

Tom ran down a beach, and Riley felt himself trot after, following footsteps in the sand. The brothers ran toward a pier, and Riley could hear the plinky-plonk music of a barrel organ.

*Brighton. I live here.*

Tom turned his head and called over his shoulder. *Ma loves 'er bull's-eyes. Shall we bring her a twist?*

The scene flickered, and now little Riley was a baby in the arms of a lady, gazing up into her kind, soft face. His mother wore a plain blouse and her hair in braids.

*Tom is named for his sadly departed da, and will be a heartbreaker like him,* she said, tickling his chin. *But you, my little shillelagh, will carry the name Riley, like your dad. And your Christian name shall be the name of my family, the proudest clan in County Wexford.*

Riley would have cried if he could. She was Irish. I remember now, he thought, and, The name? What is my name?

But then the picture changed, and Riley saw his father looming large and warm above him. The similarity of his face to Riley's own was instantly apparent.

*This is a secret*, his father was saying. *I am only showing this to you because you can't speak yet and you won't remember.* He opened up his hand, and lying on the palm was a golden shield with letters embossed on its face. And the letters were F, B, I.

*Those letters mean I have to protect people. One person in particular. Funny little Mr. Carter. Look, he's outside waiting.*

The infant Riley followed his father's pointing finger to see a man pacing beyond their front door. His legs flashed past, and all Riley could make out were shining black ankle boots and a horseshoe signet ring.

Riley's father shook his head. *This guy is a pain. A royal pain. He's trying to weasel out of testifying after all this time. But no matter how much of a jerk he is, I have to thank him, because, without Carter, I wouldn't have you, or your mother, or your half brother, Tom, for that matter. Without him, and this gadget.*

The gadget Riley's father referred to was a Timekey slung around his neck on a thick cord.

*With this, I can take you to see my home. We will all go one day. It's a new world, my dear son.*

Another scene change, and this time Tom was beside him in the bed they shared, whispering.

"I'm off for a gentleman's engagement on the pier," he said. "Just between us, eh, Riley boy? No need for Mater and Pater to be informed. On my return there will be barley sugar for you, and perhaps tales of a kiss from pretty Annie Birch."

Riley watched his half brother slip through an open window and heard an *oof* and slap of feet as Tom landed on the street below.

Moments later the toddler Riley felt a presence in the room and a low-tide stink of rotten fish wafted through the window. A man stood in the shadows, a blade jutting from his fist. It seemed to the child that the man had simply appeared on the spot.

"Magic," said Riley. "Magic man."

The intruder moved so quickly that the shadow cast by the hall lamp seemed to lag behind.

It was Garrick, come on business, and he leaned over the small boy, knife hand raised overhead, on the point of ensuring his silence, when Riley spoke again.

"Magic man."

Something strange happened to Garrick's face: it warred with itself until a smile broke out. Not a happy smile; rather a momentary relaxing of his features.

"Magic man," he said, repeating the toddler's mumbled words. "Once upon a time . . ."

On hearing this phrase, young Riley burbled happily, certain that a story was forthcoming. And this innocent mumbling saved his life, for Garrick found himself judged a magical storyteller by this little fella and decided not to do away with him until after the main job.

When Garrick returned barely a minute later with blood on his blade, the boy Riley still expected a bedtime story and met him with a broad grin of baby teeth.

"Story, magic man," demanded the three-year-old. "Story."

Garrick sighed, shook his head, and blinked at the fanciful

notion that had popped unbidden into his mind. Then, with only a moment's hesitation, he tucked the boy inside his great-coat and left through the window he had come in by.

In the wormhole, Riley would have cried if he could.

Garrick murdered my parents and stole me away, he realized, and knew it was true. And for all these past years he has been swearing that he saved me from a bunch of street cannibals in the alleys of Bethnal Green. But it was he who orphaned me.

Riley allowed this statement to repeat itself in his consciousness, in case he forgot when he woke.

*Garrick killed my parents. Garrick killed my parents.*

Riley did not want to forget, because remembering this fact would steel his resolve.

*For one day soon I must bring Albert Garrick to justice or be snuffed out me own self.*

Their journey through the wormhole ended gradually as space-time dissipated around them like cloudy fragments of a deep and detailed dream. Riley and Chevron Savano found themselves in a Victorian London basement, both smiling broadly in the grip of what Charles Smart called the Zen Ten.

"Garrick did in my whole family, except my brother, Tom," said Riley. "I am truly an orphan."

Chevie hugged the boy. "Hey, so am I. Two orphans, together against the world."

"And my father was a policeman, like you."

"Like me?"

"An agent in the FBI. He showed me his shining badge and his Timekey."

"I saw that vision too, somehow," said Chevie. "Your dad was a Fed. How did that happen?" This, she decided, was an important detail that she would definitely come back to when her mind was a little sharper.

"He was protecting someone who wore a horseshoe ring," continued Riley.

"Horseshoe ring," repeated Chevie a little dopily, like a patient coming out of anesthetic. "*And neither of us is a monkey.*"

The basement had the same shape as it would in the future, differing only in the bare walls and floor of compacted earth, with brick pillars to support the rooms above.

Chevie stamped her foot and the ground resounded with a hollow bong. "A metal plate. We need that to land in one piece. This plate is specially designed to act as a guide for the wormhole, like a lightning rod."

"I say we dismantle it," said Riley, raising his hand as though voting in the House of Commons. "Perhaps Garrick will find his hands growing out of his backside if he manages to follow us."

Chevie was trying to think beyond the time fugue, and Riley's joking was not helping.

"Stop with the cracks," she said, giggling. "We should check ourselves to make sure nothing is out of place. Sober thinking now."

"I am sober. You won't let me drink, not even beer."

Chevie stepped from the plate. "We should get out of here. Put some space between us and Garrick. I need to get a gun. Do you know anyone? Gun . . . bang bang?"

"Bang," said Riley. "Bang bang."

Chevie pulled Riley from the buried platform and noticed a disk of light hovering in the air, like a spinning silver dollar.

"Silver dollar," she said conversationally, pointing at the dwindling wormhole.

Riley nodded.

"Men with sacks," he said, pointing at two men who had entered the basement and were stealing across the mud floor, holding open the mouths of two flour sacks.

Chevie spotted a third man, emerging from a corner, his mouth full of food.

"Not all of them. That one's got a chicken wing . . . and a blackjack."

"I claim the chicken wing," said Riley.

Chevie was still laughing when the sack went over her head.


HALF MOON STREET, SOHO, LONDON, NOW

Garrick tumbled into the pod less than a minute after his quarry disappeared and no more than ten seconds before the entrance to the quantum tunnel disappeared altogether. Just before his dematerialization, the woman, Victoria, had staggered down the stairs and shot him in the good leg with a small-caliber bullet from an almost dainty rifle, and so focused was Garrick on the diminishing wormhole that he forgot to smother his nerve endings. The sudden hammer blow of agony almost rendered him senseless, which would have been a disaster inside the wormhole. A man needed his senses marshaled and ready for duty inside the time tunnel.

The fault is mine, he thought, for allowing that woman to live.

The last sound he heard from the twenty-first century before he disappeared was the bitter cursing of the old woman, damning him to hell for being a murdering scoundrel.

Garrick had an inkling that sparing Victoria was not all his own doing. The ghost of that Scot muck-snipe, Felix Smart, was making a nuisance of itself in Garrick's own gray matter. The photographs of Smart's father lining the wall and the notion of harming Victoria caused a swelling of phantom emotions that had stayed Garrick's hand twice now.

No more, thought Albert Garrick. I will be a dead man's cat's-paw no longer.

Once the orange energy transmogrified his atoms, enveloping him in the sea of quantum foam, Garrick felt a calm descend over him.

*I am nothing but soul now. Immortal.*

Contentment draped the magician, but then he felt Riley's fear trail ahead of him, and it snapped Garrick back to himself. He followed it to the mouth of the wormhole, borne easily as a corpse in the Thames. As the end of his journey neared, he gathered his bodily parts, reassembling himself, healing his wounds and expelling wisps of Felix Smart's willpower from his thoughts, while retaining his multifarious knowledge. This was a delicate maneuver and Garrick felt that he had not been entirely successful, but certainly he had expunged enough of the Scotsman's foibles that the notion of putting an end to Agent Chevron Savano did not upset him in the slightest.

Killing that girl will cause me no grief whatsoever, he thought, and with a catastrophic loss of energy his particles coalesced, subliming from gas to solid just as Garrick wished them to, relying on his muscle memory to rejuvenate his body.

*My sinews and bones are young, but my mind is full of wisdom.*

His powers were not infinite, he knew. There would be no more healings or transformations for Albert Garrick, but he felt young again, with a brain full of twenty-first-century knowledge, which should be more than sufficient to ensure that his life was a long and comfortable one.

Garrick emerged from the wormhole grinning . . .

HALF MOON STREET, SOHO, LONDON, 1898

. . . to find himself in an empty dungeon. Garrick's grin shriveled, but his disappointment soon burned off like brandy from a pudding.

*I am home.*

There was no doubt that he had returned to his own time. Even below street level, as he was, London's signature blend of smells penetrated the air. The combined excretions of three million souls, and another million beasts besides, created as foul a stench as had ever been known by man. A stench that was breathed in by all, from the queen in her palace to the lunatics in their Broadmoor cells. There was no escape from it.

Garrick inhaled deeply, inflating his lungs with tainted air, and for the second time in his life, gave thanks for London's foul fog, as it was known.

"I am home!" he shouted now to the ceiling, and a savage glee filled his breast.

And *home* would feel Albert Garrick's presence soon enough. No matter that Riley and Agent Savano were in the wind. Where could they run to but the tenement rookeries, and maybe catch a knifing on account of their clean faces? It was true that Riley could lead the bluebottles back to High Holborn and the Orient, the foreclosed theater that Garrick had purchased and turned into digs for him and Riley; but it seemed more likely that the lad would get himself and his protector right out of harm's way and not call any attention to either of them.

I will track him easy as pie, Garrick thought confidently. Riley is leaping in the dark, whereas I know every shadow in this city and every dagger monkey concealed there. I will squeeze my sources and spread the chink if need be, and before the morning slop pails are flung, there will be two more angels in heaven.

There were neither tenants nor squatters in the house on Half Moon Street, though Garrick could smell cooked chicken and found evidence of someone keeping watch. Cigarette ends and beer bottles. Waxed paper and a makeshift toilet dug in a corner.

*Someone has been keeping a sharp eye here.*

Albert Garrick did not like to be seen unless it was on the stage. He would have preferred to take some time to dismantle the landing pad, but, with eyes on the house, he decided to return when the heat was off. Garrick skipped upstairs, checking the pockets of his greatcoat for weapons. He was delighted to find that the three FBI handguns had made it through the wormhole with him, one with laser sights attached.

These weapons alone will make my fortune, he thought. I shall engage a gunsmith to tool up ruder versions, then it's off to the patent office. This time next year, I shall be taking tea with the Vanderbilts in New York City.

Garrick toted up his bullets and vowed to stab contracts to death whenever possible in the future to conserve these precious shells.

"Thirty bangs, and that's my lot," he muttered.

The house on Half Moon Street was in reasonable nick, but it was obvious from the knee-high rising damp on the walls that this place had been a dead lurk for quite some time. Garrick slipped out the servants' entrance at the rear and vaulted from the coal bin to the yard wall. From there he leaped nimbly to the alley, enjoying the shock of the impact thrumming through his young bones. All of his old twinges and weaknesses had been subsumed by the wormhole.

Garrick ducked into a gateway and held himself stock-still, to see if anyone was on his coattails. When he was satisfied that he was not being followed, he drew himself erect and strolled around the corner, setting his beak toward Piccadilly.

In a hundred years' time, he thought, I would not be able to escape so easily. There will be DNA and fingerprinting and UV-wanding, not to mention cameras on every corner and in outer space. But now, in my time, once I am clear, I am gone, and none can say different who did not witness it with their own eyes.

The sun was shining here, as it would be in a century's time, though it had a harder job busting through the smog. Garrick spotted a boy wearing the familiar red coat of the Shoe-black Brigade and hailed him.

"You! You there! What day is it?"

The boy shuffled across the street, not bothering to avoid the puddles of seeping sewage. As he came up, Garrick could see that his jacket was tattered and closer to dirty pink than red from a hundred rough launderings.

He scowled at Garrick. "Well, it ain't Christmas Day. And you ain't no Mr. Scrooge."

On a normal morning Garrick would have striped the cur's cheek with his glove, but today he was feeling charitable toward most of England.

"Yes, well spotted, you educated scamp. Now, fetch me a cab to Holborn. Hop to it and there's a shilling in it for you."

The boy stretched out a hand. "Shilling in advance, guv'nor."

Garrick laughed. "In advance? You'll be getting your payment when I see you on the backboard of my cab. As you so cleverly pointed out, I ain't no Ebenezer Scrooge."

As the boy hurried off, whistling the customary three-note

cabbie summons, Garrick realized that he had lost his wallet in the wormhole.

No journey can be embarked on for free, he thought. Not even one through time itself. Another thought occurred to him: I hope that boy can wait for payment; I don't like to commit murders this early in the day.

The morning was not progressing swimmingly for Riley and Chevron Savano. Just moments before Garrick's arrival in the basement, the time-traveling pair had been swathed in rough burlap, torsos mummified by bailing twine, and manhandled up a flight of stairs.

By the time Chevie shook off the wormhole bliss, she was on her back on polished floorboards with a knee wedged to her throat. She tried to call out to Riley but could do nothing more than croak through an obstructed windpipe.

Apparently her croak was enough to arouse the ire of her captors, as one rapped her on the crown.

"Shush yer gob, miss," he ordered. "We is tired and hungry men and not in the mood fer shenanigans."

Chevie responded by heel-kicking her captor in the knee.

*How do you like those shenanigans?* she tried to say, but all that emerged was a series of grunts.

Her stricken captor howled lustily, to the great amusement of his comrades.

"Aw, Jeeves, did the maiden injure your person?" said one, the chicken-wing man by the smell of him.

"Shall I carry you to a hospital, or is you too far gone?" said another, then spat noisily to punctuate his derision.

The injured party recovered himself, cracking Chevie once more on the head. "Do we need 'em both? Malarkey might be satisfied with one to spill the beans."

Inside his sack, Riley jerked at the mention of the name Malarkey.

*Otto Malarkey? The king of the Battering Rams?* How had they come into his sights?

As there was no knee on his throat, Riley spoke to the men. "Which one of you bludgers wants to tell Mr. Malarkey how you murdered his kin?"

This question was met with a moment's silence, until Jeeves spoke. "Oh, ho! That's a fine bluff. A man would have to admire a lie so brazen, would he not, Mr. Noble?"

Noble spoke. "Are you calling it, Jeeves? 'Cause I certainly ain't."

"It's no bluff," shouted Riley through the sacking. "Trussing us up was insult enough, but threatening our persons will land you in the river by moonlight."

Noble whistled. "Malarkey does favor the river by moonlight for his bye-bye business."

"There is a safe way to put the quiets on these two," said the third man.

Riley heard the pop of a cork from a bottle, and a sharp odor cut through the dull musk of burlap.

Ether! he thought. They're putting us under.

"Chevie!" he called. "Close yer gob."

Jeeves cackled. "That's wot I told her," he said.

Riley felt a dampness spread across his face as the liquid anesthetic seeped through the material. He held his breath until one of the men jabbed him below the rib cage, forcing a sharp intake of etherized air.

*I pray that Garrick is not already here or we'll never wake up*, was the last thought he had before his mind sank down like a stone dropped into the midnight Thames.

Riley did survive to wake up, but before he opened his eyes to whatever new dreadfulness awaited them, he spent a moment reexperiencing his visions from the wormhole.

*My family lived in Brighton, where Father was in the FBI. Mother was Irish and the most beautiful lady I have ever seen. My mate Ginger is in actuality my own half brother, Tom. Ma and Pa were slaughtered for money by Albert Garrick. But who shelled out for the job? And was my own pa from the future? How do these strands tie together? Where is Tom now?*

These were big bites of information to swallow in one gulp. Everything he had taken for gospel was a falsehood spooned into his ear by Garrick.

Riley opened his eyes and was relieved to find he could see.

A second cause for relief was the sight of Chevron Savano seated opposite him, tied to a sturdy chair, and they were alone. Her bonds, though not expertly fitted, were many and varied. Her captors had used whatever hodgepodge of tethers that lay handy, and therefore her torso was bound with twine, her ankles with manacles, and her forearms and wrists were done up with twists of waxed paper. There was a leather lanyard drawn tight around her neck, securing it to the chair's high back.

At least she still has the Timekey, he thought, seeing the instrument's outline through Chevie's shirt.

Riley was sure, without glancing down, that he was similarly trussed.

"Chevie," he whispered as loudly as he dared. "Agent Savano. Stir yourself."

Chevie opened her eyes, blinking away the ether's aftereffects.

"Riley! You're okay."

"I am well, Agent. The ether fog will lift momentarily, trust me—I have experience."

"Get out your pick," said Chevie. "Free yourself, then me."

Riley wiggled his ankle. "My pick is gone. Lost in the day's exertions, or found by the coves what lifted us."

Chevie breathed heavily through her nose, like an angry young bull. "Great. So now we gotta sit here, trussed up like Thanksgiving turkeys, and wait for this Malarkey character to show himself. Who is that guy, anyway?"

"Otto Malarkey is a person of considerable importance in the city. He is the mister-master of the Battering Rams, a criminal gang of bully boys who take a slice of everything from thimble rigging to opium dens. Nobody pulls a stroke in the Great Oven without first tipping their cap to Mr. Otto Malarkey."

"I understood about half of that," admitted Chevie. "So what you're saying is that we're in trouble again."

Riley looked around. They were imprisoned in a large

storeroom, possibly underground, judging by the chill. Sides of beef lurked in the shadows, suspended by chains from a ceiling beam, and wedges of light shone through gaps in the ill-fitted floorboards overhead. The hubbub of both commerce and merriment filtered down from above, punctuated by crashes and cries of dispute. Various liquids slopped through the boards, splashing on the mud floor. Riley saw wine, beer, and the slow drip of blood.

"We ain't swine food yet, Chevie. Now, tell me a tale."

Chevie started. "Tell you a tale? I gotta say it, Riley. I was not expecting that request."

Riley began to tense and relax his muscles. "I am Garrick's apprentice in murder and magic. One leaf of that book is escapology. But a get-out like this one is the veriest devil of a job. I don't know the knots and I ain't humping no tools. So tell me a tale while I wriggle my way free."

Chevie was stumped. "I don't have any stories, Riley. Books are not my thing. I like a good movie, though."

"Tell me something of yourself, then. Why the strange tattoo?"

Chevie glanced at her right sleeve, which covered the tattoo spanning her upper arm. "The chevron? Yeah, maybe that is a story."

"This may be your last chance to tell it."

"True enough." She rattled her manacles in frustration. "I cannot believe any of this is happening. How can I be trapped in the past?" The rattling produced nothing but noise, so Chevie settled down. "Okay, you want to hear about my tattoo?"

Riley's face was slick with sweat, and his body was rigid as a board. "Please."

Chevie closed her eyes, trying to imagine herself out of the past, and into her own past in the future. "My mom and dad grew up on the Shawnee reservation in Oklahoma. They call it trust land, these days. As soon as my dad could afford a motorbike, my mom hopped on the back and they took off across the country. Got married in Vegas and settled in California. I came along a while later, and Dad told me that things were just about perfect for a couple of years, until Mom was killed by a black bear over in La Verne." Chevie shook her head as if she still could not accept this fact. "Can you believe that? A Native American on a camping trip killed by a bear. Dad never got over it. Oh, we were happy enough, I guess. But he drank a lot. 'When love dies,' he told me, 'there are no survivors.'"

Chevie was silent for a moment, wishing for the millionth time that she could remember her mother's face.

"We had ten years together before his motorcycle blew up on the Pacific Coast Highway. Dad had a tattoo just like mine, a chevron symbol. It's what I was named for."

"You were named for a symbol? That is a strange custom."

Chevie scowled. "You asked for a tale, remember?"

Riley twisted his own arm backward at the elbow. "I apologize, Agent. Please continue."

"My dad had the same tattoo. Same shoulder. He told me that all the Savano men back to the Shawnee wars have borne this mark. William Savano fought the Long Knives with Tecumseh at Moraviantown. For every officer he killed in battle, William daubed a chevron on his arm in blood, as this was the sergeant's symbol. He was a fearsome warrior. So, in memory of William, the Savanos have worn the symbol. I am the last of the Savanos, so I bear the name and the symbol. The first girl to do so."

"That is indeed a fascinating tale," said Riley, shrugging off his bonds until only the solid manacles on his wrists remained. "And well told."

"Yeah, a pity I can't talk off your handcuffs."

Riley winked. "These are screw bracelets. The walking dummy what put 'em on botched the job. See these barrels? They should be at the bottom."

"Because?"

"Because if the barrels are on top, a prisoner can do this . . ."

Riley brought his hands together as close as he could, crossed thumbs, and used the opposable digits to unscrew the handcuffs.

"Hey, presto," said Riley, taking a deep bow.

A slow handclap echoed across the room, floating down from the top of a rickety stairway.

"Bravo, boy. Well done to you."

A giant meat cart of a man ambled down the stairs, each step creaking under his weight.

"Otto Malarkey," whispered Riley. "The big boss himself."

Malarkey jumped the last three steps, sending the hanging carcasses swinging on their chains. This man would be a character in any age. He wore leather breeches with pirate boots, no shirt covered his barrel chest, and his flowing black locks were barely contained by a shining silk top hat. Two revolvers hung in cowboy holsters on his hips, and in one massive meaty paw he swished a riding crop.

"You show some considerable talent, boy," he said, his booming voice bouncing off the ceiling. "Of course that glocky tree stump, Jeeves, screwed on yer bracelets rump-ways. I could use you in the Rams. With that clean mush and full set of teeth, you would make a fine burglar boy for the genteel jobs up at Mayfair and the likes, where my oafs attract peelers like horse biscuits attract flies."

Malarkey stepped forth, emerging from the shadows, and Chevie noticed a ram's head tattoo on his shoulder and a price list on his chest that read:

Punching—2 shillings
Both eyes blacked—4 shillings
Nose and jaw broke—10 shillings
Jacked out (knocked out with a blackjack)—15 shillings
Ear chewed off—same as previous
Leg or arm broke—19 shillings
Shot in leg—25 shillings
Stab—same as previous
Doing the Big Job—3 pounds and up

Malarkey noticed her gaze. "Some of the diverse services offered by the Rams. Of course my prices have elevated with my stature. I've been meaning to update the ink since they booted me from Little Saltee prison. I was king of that dung heap." He spread his muscled arms wide. "Now I am king of the greatest dung heap on earth."

Riley circled the giant warily. "What is your interest in us, Mr. Malarkey? Why were the Rams keeping eyes on that particular basement?"

Malarkey kicked Riley's vacated chair, sending it skittering across the floor.

"Cheeky cur, posing questions to me in my own gentlemen's club. The Rams took a contract to murder anyone who showed up in that lurk. For two years now we've been pocketing quite a stipend for doing nothing but keeping an eye, and that's all the information you'll be needing on the subject."

"Of course, sorry, guv'nor. My mistake."

"Hark at him," said Malarkey. "All manners and how-do-you-do. I suppose that'll be the rearing I gave you. You being my kin and everything." His chuckle was gruff with cigar smoke and whisky. "That's a smart mouth you have on you, boy, and it kept the both of you alive. You are a deal smarter than the numbskulls who brought you in, saying you appeared in a puff of genie magic. I could have room for you in the Rams. The girl, however, seems less valuable."

Otto squatted before Chevie, taking a lock of her hair between two fingers and sniffing it. "Mind you, you do have the glossiest hair, miss. How do you make it shine so?"

"Well, Mr. Malarkey," said Chevie sweetly. "What I do is I slap the hell out of Battering Rams, then wash my silken locks in their tears of shame."

Taken at face value, these comments would seem unprofessional at best and psychotically foolhardy at worst, but as Cord Vallicose at Quantico had informed his young students in the Negotiating Tactics class, *In certain confrontational situations, for example when dealing with a narcissist or psychopath, an aggressive tack can sometimes prove useful, as it will pique your captor's interest and prompt him to keep you alive a little longer.* Chevie had never forgotten this quote and used it to justify her regular outbursts. Riley, of course, had not been to this lecture and could not understand why Chevie repeatedly antagonized their captors.

"She's a simpleton," he blurted. "There was an accident with a high wall . . . and some laudanum. Her marbles rolled clean out her earholes."

Malarkey was nonplussed. He stood and paced awhile, uncertain how to react.

"Well, I never," he said rather quaintly. "I ain't accustomed to vinegar from gents. Now I meet my first Injun lady, and she's spouting all this color at me. What's a gang leader to do?"

Malarkey slapped the riding crop against his massive thigh. "Here's the scoop, folks. My predecessor took a job in good faith to keep eyes on that house in Half Moon Street and slit the neck of anyone who arrived in it. So I find myself in a dilemma. Mine is not to wonder why the man who contracted us would want you two snuffed, but Otto Malarkey don't like to kill without reason, especially a cove like you, boy, who could be of service. But the brotherhood accepted coin for a job of work, and the Rams be nothing if not reliable."

Riley had a thought. "But you couldn't kill another Ram."

"Quick thinking again, boy. But you ain't a Ram. A cove's gotta be born into the brotherhood, or fight his way in. And, with respect, you might be able to climb a drainpipe, but you couldn't bend one."

"I might surprise you," said Riley, and to prove his point, leaped high in the air and smashed the empty chair with a blow from his forearm.

"Not too shabby," admitted Malarkey, flicking a splinter from his trouser leg. "But I got a dozen better. I need something with a little theater about it. The men are bored watching dullards pound on each other."

Riley held out his wrists. "Put manacles on me, and I'll still whip whoever you nominate."

"I don't know. We've been paid already."

"Don't you want to know *why* this man needs us dead? Knowledge is power, ain't that so? And a king can't have enough of either."

Malarkey slapped his thigh with the riding crop. "You is a dazzling one, but perhaps too smart with your verbals. I have found in this particular kingdom that it is generally prudent to keep the gob shut, do your business, and ask no questions. I *would* like to know why such a celebrated man would want to see you in the dirt, but in this game knowing too much can see you dead quicker than knowing too little."

An idea popped into Chevie's head. "What if I fight, big man? How would that be?"

Malarkey's crop froze in mid-swing. "*You*, fight? We couldn't abide that here. We only started admitting ladies into the Hidey-Hole recently."

Riley was thinking three steps ahead. "Mr. Malarkey, this lady has special Injun skills. I seen her punch out a Cossack *and* his horse. She don't look it, but she's a dervish, sir. A foresighted man could make some serious coin betting on Chevie."

Malarkey rubbed the price list on his chest. "The odds would be long, so the gamble would be small. But one fight for one place. That still leaves you out in the cold, boy."

"Not a problem," said Chevie. "You pick your two best bruisers, and I'll fight both of them."

Malarkey guffawed in surprise. "Both of 'em? Fight 'em both, you say?" He winked at Riley. "Just how high was this wall she took a tumble from?"

# 8 » THE RED GLOVE

ALBERT GARRICK HAD MIXED FEELINGS ON THE subject of the Orient Theatre. On the one hand he was too much in love with his memories of the performer's life to ever let it go, and on the other it caused him great pain even to gaze on the mechanics of his once-famous illusions.

He trod the boards now, tightening a rope here, adjusting a mirror there. Each contraption brought a rueful smile to his thin features.

*Ah, the Chinese water bowls. How the crowd cheered in Blackpool. Lombardi, they cried. Lombardi, Lombardi.*

It occurred to Garrick that with his improved physicality, no illusion would be off-limits to him.

*I am more supple now and could wind myself into one of the Chinese water bowls if need be. The Great Lombardi could be the most famous illusionist on earth.*

It was a tempting notion, to travel the courts of Europe, dazzling tsars and kings. To have jewels strewn on the tail of his velvet cape.

*So many possibilities.*

Garrick retired to his larder, preparing a simple meal of cheese and meats, which he consumed standing, with a crust of slightly hardened bread and a flagon of watered beer.

*Of course I would need an assistant. This time I will choose wisely, and not show so much kindness. It was my own soft hand that spoiled Riley.*

Garrick returned to the Orient's stage, pulling his velvet cape from its peg and wrapping it around his shoulders. Then, as a sentimental comfort, and because he felt somewhat alone, the magician placed the original Lombardi's silk top hat on his head.

Assistants are troublesome creatures, he admitted, often developing their own personalities. Their own wants and preferences.

Sabine had also caused him considerable pain. Had her treachery not forced him to quit performing altogether?

*But she had been so beautiful. So perfect.*

Garrick felt a tiredness come over him that he could not ignore, so he settled into an armchair that was positioned on a low circular dais center stage and decided to allow himself a few hours' sleep before he began the hunt for Riley and Chevron Savano.

And, as they often did, his dreams turned to Sabine. His first, beautiful, perfect assistant. Perfect until . . .

In the beginning it had seemed to young Albert Garrick that his life had entered a new phase, edging away from the horrors of his youth. He was gaining mastery over Lombardi's works and growing into the Italian's boots very nicely. Not a single engagement was canceled, and Sabine seemed more than satisfied to renew her contract.

Garrick was besotted, and he showered the girl with tokens of his esteem, which she accepted with squeals and hugs, calling him *her Albert* and kissing his cheek. Garrick was content for the first time, and even his nightmares of blood and cholera grew infrequent and seemed somehow less potent when they did occur.

Unfortunately for young Garrick, Sabine's heart was colder than the baubles she loved so much, and her intention had always been to ditch her employer at the first sign of a better prospect.

In the summer of 1880, a young Albert Garrick—the Great Lombardi now—was second on the bill below the well-known Anglo-Irish dramatist and actor Dion Boucicault at the Adelphi, when Garrick noticed Sabine's flirtatious manner as she fraternized with young Sandy Morhamilton, one of the lighting boys. This vexed and puzzled Garrick, as generally Sabine had no patience for the crew. But a little investigation revealed that young Morhamilton was no hand-to-mouth pauper; he was, in fact, the heir to a large coffee-trading company and was spending a year at the Adelphi to exorcise the theater from his system.

*And if I have uncovered Sandy's true identity, so too has Sabine,* Garrick reasoned. He began to keep watch on the pair, discovering a talent for lurking that would serve him well in later years. Day by day his heart was broken as the woman he had worshipped for years gave her attention to a dolt, a high-born halfwit.

Garrick's love curdled into a hate that turned inward, souring his very soul. The entire affair blossomed tragically on the third Sunday of June, during the matinee. As he was preparing to insert the steel blades into their slots for the Divide the Lady trick, he noticed that Sabine's gaze was directed to the gantry above the stage. To his amazement, the trollop actually blew a kiss skyward. Garrick leaned close to issue a stern admonition and, almost incredibly, he saw his rival reflected in his beloved's eyes.

An irrepressible fury consumed the young Garrick and he slammed the center blade into the slot without reversing the handle, which meant that Sabine had no chance of avoiding the sharp steel when it eventually fell.

Garrick's fury was replaced by cold satisfaction and, with a shake of his bloodied glove toward the young Morhamilton, he fled through the stage door and into the night, never to return to the Adelphi, though superstitious theater folk swear that the Red Glove still haunts the stalls, searching for the man who cuckolded him.

Albert Garrick was never prosecuted for his crime because,

ironically, he was found guilty of a lesser one. Two days later the destitute magician attacked a sandy-haired youth outside the Covent Garden Theatre and beat him half to death. His sentence gave him the choice of a fair stretch in Newgate or a spot in the Queen's army, on a train leaving for Afghanistan that very evening. Garrick chose the latter, and by nightfall he was squeezed into a troop carriage on his way to Dover, without anyone ever realizing that Albert Garrick's hat fitted snugly on the Great Lombardi's head. He arrived among the Afghans just in time for the great battle of Kandahar and covered himself in bloody glory. Garrick was offered a commission and could have made a career for himself in the army, but he reckoned there was more coin to be made if he struck out as an independent.

"Sabine," Garrick muttered to himself, half in slumber. "Riley."

Garrick was not alone in the Orient. In fact, a band of dyed-in-the-wool knaves had been lodged there for the past couple of days, waiting for Garrick to return from his mission in Bedford Square. These were no ordinary kidnappers, but a trio of superior punishers handpicked for the grisly mission. Their boss reckoned them the bloodiest in his stable and trusted them with this contract, which was bringing in a considerable pocket of chink for the brotherhood.

"One body only?" Mr. Percival had asked, the most experienced of the three, a man who often boasted of having performed at least one killing on a different continent for every decade of his life.

"Yes, but an exceptional body," his boss had assured him, "and worthy of your combined talents. Take no half measures with this cove, lads, or you will find yourself looking down Old Nick's throat. When he returns from his own bloody work, just wait for him to bed down, then do the business. You wait as long as it takes. Got it?"

The men nodded with feigned sincerity and pocketed their advance guineas; but once the big man was gone, they congratulated each other for landing such a soft job.

"We are the luckiest of beggars," Percival had confided in his confederates. "This Garrick mug will have his entrails on the boards by dusk, and we will be scoffing mutton stew for supper."

So now Percival and his two mates roused themselves from behind Row F of the Orient stalls and walked crabwise to the aisles. One took the left, the second went right, and Percival himself advanced straight down the center. Apart from the delay, events could hardly have turned out peachier for the intruders. This cove Garrick, far from being a specter of death, as advertised, had actually plonked himself center stage for a wee nod. The brave trio intended to flank their mark, then close in with diverse blades.

Percival hefted a short-handled chopping ax that he'd purchased in a supply store in California and later used to punish a teenage boy for pointing a finger at him. The second man, known simply as Turk, wielded a curved scimitar that had been in someone's family for generations until Turk nicked it.

And the third man, a Scot with unusually short legs, had a baling hook slotted between his fingers that had seen more eyeballs dangling off its tip than hay bales. The Scot, Pound, also carried a pistol, but bullets were costly and a wide shot could startle their mark into action, so best to do the job quietly with blades.

These men had worked together before and had developed a system of nods, whistles, and signals that precluded any chatter on the job. Chatty assassins did not last long in London. Percival was the captain, so the others looked to him for their lead. With two jabs of his ax, he directed them to the wings. Garrick would undoubtedly fly to one side or another should he somehow detect Percival's approach. This was unlikely in any case, as Percival made about as much noise as a leaf floating across Hyde Park. Turk and Pound resigned themselves to the fact that the kill itself would be Percival's, as it generally was.

Percival mounted the stage bridge and crept across the orchestra pit, enjoying the weight of the ax in his hand, relishing the *thunk* it would make chopping a wedge out of the mark's skull.

*Four more steps, then it's mutton stew for me and the lads. Three more steps.*

Percival sprang onto the stage proper, and he knew that at this distance there was not a man or animal on earth who could escape the deadly arc of his swing.

I could fell a bear from this distance, he thought.

He raised the ax high and brought the blade down with terrific force. It struck nothing but chair, slicing through the padding and biting deep into the wooden backrest.

Percival's brain could not understand how certainty had become uncertain.

"Magic," said a voice. "All is not as it seems."

Percival yanked the ax free and whirled toward the source of these mysterious words. There in the corner stood the mark himself, Garrick, wrapped in his conjurer's cape.

"Do you approve of my cloak? It's a little theatrical, but this is a performance, after all."

He don't know about the others, thought Percival. Else he would not be blathering on.

Percival whistled two notes, high and low. The signal for Turk to advance from the folds of velvet curtain that concealed him.

Turk made even less noise than Percival, as he wore silken slippers, which he called his murder shoes. He came up on Garrick from the rear and reached out for a shoulder, to steady the magician for the scimitar's blade, but his questing fingers skinned themselves on glass instead of flesh and bone.

A mirror, thought Turk. I have been misled.

Terror sank into his gut like a lead anchor—he had the wit to know that he was done for.

The mirror image of Garrick reached out through the mirror and plucked Turk's own sword from his hand.

"You will not have need of this," said Garrick's image, and he plunged it directly into Turk's heart.

Turk died believing a phantasm had killed him. His final wish was that he could return as a spirit to this place in order to decipher the events leading up to his death, but unfortunately that's not the way the afterlife works, especially for black-hearted killers.

Percival would have attacked then, but he was uncertain of his enemy's position. He heard an ominous creaking behind him and turned to see a large set piece being lowered from the flies. The piece was circular and constructed of canvas stretched over a wooden frame. On the front were circles painted within circles.

"Stone me," breathed Percival. "A target."

"Stone you?" came a voice from the blackness of the stalls. "I fear you are missing the point, but not for long."

Percival backed up until his shoulder blades bumped the target and his head sat squarely in the bull's-eye. Before he could twig the implications, a veritable hail of blades hissed from the darkness.

I am done, thought Percival, and closed his eyes.

But done he was not; instead the various knives, forks, swords, and bayonets pinned him tightly to the target, drawing no more than a pint of blood from minor wounds.

Was this by accident or design? Percival knew not, but he took advantage of his still-pumping lungs to call to his final confederate.

"Damn the blades, Pound. Plug this cove."

Pound rushed from his place of concealment and waved the barrel of his pistol around, searching for the mark.

"Where are you, Garrick? Show yourself!"

By some device, Garrick appeared where he had not been a second before, his face pale in the stage lights, dark hair rippling over his shoulders.

"I am insulted by this attack on my home. Insulted, I say."

"Quit yer jittering and stand still," ordered Pound.

"That you may shoot me dead? An odd request. However, as you wish. Pull your blasted trigger, but take care—if you miss, I shall not."

The cards were apparently all in Pound's hands, but with his boss pegged to a target, he was nervous.

"Shoot him, man!" Percival urged. "A monkey could make the shot."

Garrick spread his arms wide. "Make your shot, Scotsman. Unto dust."

Pound blinked the sweat from his eyes, wondering how this job had turned into such a dog's dinner.

"On yer knees, Garrick."

"Oh, no, I kneel for no man."

Percival strained against the knives that secured him. "Shoot him, Pound! Pull the trigger."

"You are weak," said Garrick mockingly. "A coward!"

Pound fired his pistol and a flute of blue smoke billowed from the barrel. The noise was deafening, and for a moment Garrick's upper torso was wreathed in a flickering cloud.

When the smoke cleared, Garrick was revealed, hale and hardy, with no changes to his appearance but for the blood on his teeth and the bullet between them.

"Oh, my God," breathed Pound. "He caught the bullet. This is no mortal man."

"Shoot again, you fool!" cried Percival. "You hold a revolver in yer hand."

Garrick spoke between his teeth. "One chance only. Now, you must stand still for my bullet."

Pound was so confused that his feet were like anchors and tears streamed down his ruddy cheeks. "But you are without a pistol."

Garrick rubbed his fingers before his mouth as though warming them, then spat out the bullet with such force that it penetrated Pound's forehead and dropped him where he stood.

Percival realized then how deep in the mire he stood.

"Please, mister. We have cash in our pokes. Take it and let me go. I will be on the next boat to America."

Garrick's eyes held no hint of mercy. "I need the name of the man who pulls your strings."

Percival ground his teeth. "I cannot. I swore an oath."

"Aha, an oath," said Garrick, meandering toward the massive target. "That in itself is a telltale sign."

"I'll say no more," said Percival stubbornly. "Do your worst, you devil."

"That, sir, is quite an invitation," said Garrick, removing one by one the knives sticking Percival to the target. "You may have surmised that I was once an illusionist of some fame. Some called me the Great Lombardi, but notoriety bestowed upon me another name."

Garrick paused and Percival could not take it. "What name? In God's name, stop toying with me."

Garrick whipped a covering sheet from a coffin-shaped box stage left. "I was known as the Red Glove."

Percival's eyes rolled back and he fainted where he stood, held aloft only by a cleaver and a stiletto.

"You've heard the legend, I see," said Garrick, plucking out the remaining blades.

Percival woke in the box, strapped down tight, bare feet poking from the end.

Garrick leaned over him, dressed now in full evening wear, with silken hat and dinner gloves—one white, one red.

"This is my most famous illusion," he said. "A somewhat irksome truth, as it is the only illusion that ever went fatally awry."

"Awry?" said Percival, his head fuzzy. "Does that mean *wrong*, sir?"

"Oh, it does. And do you know what *fatally* means?"

Percival searched his vocabulary, which consisted of little more than two hundred words, most of them food related. "Dead, sir—is it that someone was killed?"

"You are more educated than you look, Mr. . . . ?"

"Percival, guv'nor."

"Percival. A good strong Welsh name."

"Welsh, yes. Perhaps you have Welsh kin and will spare me?"

Garrick ignored the question, drawing from behind his back with quite a flourish a large, wooden-handled, square blade.

"This is the key to the illusion, Percival: the blade. The audience assumes it is a fakement, but I assure you it is of the finest steel and will cut through flesh and bone with barely a stutter."

And, with great panache and dexterity, Garrick tossed the blade into the air, caught it, then rammed the tempered steel square into the leg slot, appearing to sever Percival's feet from his legs.

"Mercy!" screamed Percival. "Kill me and be done. This is torture, sir. Pure torture."

Garrick clicked his fingers and from somewhere overhead came the sound of an orchestra.

"You must indulge me, Monsieur Percival. I so rarely have need of the old togs."

Percival's face seemed to swell with fear. "I ain't no blower. The judges could never make old Percival blab, and neither will you."

"Why so hysterical, Percival?" asked Garrick innocently. "I have done you no harm. Look."

Percival saw that there was a large gilt-edged mirror suspended above the proscenium arch. He commanded his toes to wiggle and was mightily relieved to see them do it in the looking glass.

"But the light is so bad in here, Mr. Percival. I should afford you a closer spy."

And with that Garrick separated the lower box from the main body, and Percival screamed as his feet rolled away from him, toes wiggling furiously.

"My little piggies," he howled. "Oh, come back, piggies."

"Who sent you?" demanded Garrick, brandishing a second blade.

"No. Never."

"I admire your stoicism, Mr. Percival, really I do, but this is a battle of wills, so you leave me little choice . . ." Garrick steadied himself against the saw-box, then drove the second blade into its slot.

Percival gibbered, tears flowing from eyes to ears, and he unconsciously began to sing the ditty of freemasonry loyalty that he had warbled in many a public house with his tattooed brethren.

> *We stabs 'em,*
> *We fights 'em,*
> *Cripples 'em,*
> *Bites 'em.*

Garrick was not surprised. "Ah, Mr. Malarkey, would you insert yourself in my affairs? Thank you, faithful Sir Percival. You have done all I asked of you. So I will inflict no further harm upon your person."

Percival was beyond rational thinking now, and continued to sing.

> *No rules for our mayhem.*
> *You pay us, we slay 'em.*
> *If you're in a corner,*
> *With welshers or scams.*

Garrick sang along for the last two lines, inserting a clever harmony.

> *Pay us a visit,*
> *The Battering Rams.*

Garrick applauded, his red glove flashing in the lights. "You have a fine tenor, Percival. Not professional standard, but pleasing. Won't you delight me with an encore?"

Percival obliged, his voice becoming more tremulous with each note, dissolving entirely into a terrified, burbling scream as Garrick took hold of the head box and sent it twirling across the stage.

Percival's last sight was his own receding torso and the wiggling tips of his fingers, straining to be loose from their bonds.

Garrick could have told him that it was all done with mirrors and prosthetics, but a good magician never reveals his secrets.

He danced a quickstep jauntily across the orchestra pit bridge.

"'Pay us a visit,'" he sang, deciding to sing high for the last phrase, "'The Battering Raaaaaaams.'"

And he thought, I intend to do just that.

The magician stamped on a powder bomb hidden beneath a patch of carpet in the center aisle and disappeared in a magnesium flash and a ball of smoke.

# 9 » GOLGOTH GOLGOTH

*I*T HAD OCCURRED TO SPECIAL AGENT CHEVRON SAVANO that she might be the victim of some massive sting operation. There were files from World War II that told stories of prisoners in war hospitals who had been convinced by English-speaking enemies that the war was over and allowed themselves to be debriefed, but they were high-ranking prisoners and the operations were hugely expensive. She was barely more than an FBI wannabe with a tin badge. No one was going to go to such fantastic lengths for the piddly secrets in her brain.

Any lingering doubts that she might not actually be in nineteenth-century London disappeared the moment Chevie emerged from the dungeon into Otto Malarkey's den of thieves, cutthroats, and wastrels.

Riley grabbed her elbow.

"Agent . . . Chevie, let me be the mouthpiece in the Rams' Hidey-Hole. I know these people."

"Relax, kid, I can talk for myself."

Riley's expression was pained. "I know. Your impetuous nature seems to land you in hot water no matter what the era."

"It's psychology, Riley," said Chevie defensively, though she knew it was only half true. "You wouldn't understand it."

The Battering Rams' Hidey-Hole did not seem much like a hole, nor did it seem like they were hiding from anyone. The storeroom's rickety stairs opened into the entire ground floor of a wide house with no dividing walls to hold up the ceiling, which sagged alarmingly and would have collapsed entirely but for the brick chimney breast. The grand room was crammed with so many lifelong thieves that such a concentration of criminality would have been difficult to achieve elsewhere outside of a prison compound.

Animals roamed freely through the hall, including chickens, hounds, and actual rams, tangling their impressive horns to the encouragement of the two-legged Rams.

There were several makeshift stages constructed from barrels and planks where burlesque ladies sang drinking songs or street conjurers ran thimble games. At least four parrots hid in the crystal chandeliers, swearing in as many languages.

"Wow," said Chevie, feeling the room revolve kaleidoscopically around her. "This is unreal."

"Say nothing," Riley hissed. "I may still be able to slip us out of here."

He dodged between a monkey and its handler to catch Malarkey. "Mr. Malarkey, Your Majesty. I have some conjuring skills. Doves, rabbits, that kind of thing. Think of a card, any card."

Malarkey strode into the center of the room. "No. We agreed on a bout, lad. Save yer politicking. Wasn't it you who suggested I bet on the battling lady?"

This was a good point.

"Yes," admitted Riley. "But that was . . ."

Malarkey stepped over an unconscious sailor clutching a roasted leg of pork. "That was when you was belowdecks in the killin' basement, with blood on the floor and waste seeping through the walls, and you thought you would spout off whatever it took to see the light of day, but now you see said light of day and are thinking to yerself, Maybe I can stall poor old simple Malarkey and finagle a way out of here for me and the pretty lass."

Riley had a shot at arguing. "No. I have genuine top-notch skills. Watch." He snatched a vicious dagger from the belt of a nearby sailor and jammed it between the ribs of a man who, for some reason, wore a striped swimming costume. The blade stuck but did no apparent harm.

"See?"

"Not a bad effort," said Malarkey. "But I have my mind set on a fight." A thought struck him and he stopped abruptly, turning to Chevie. "Do you know the Marquess of Queensbury Rules?"

Chevie was stretching out her shoulders. "Nope. Can't say that I do."

Malarkey tapped her on the head with his riding crop. "Capital. Neither do we. No holds barred is all the legal we have here."

With a single bound, Malarkey mounted a central platform where there was a squat wooden and velvet throne, resplendent with a mightily horned, shaggy ram's fleece. He aimed a kick at a monkey who sat in the king's spot, then twirled on his heel, falling neatly into the throne. Malarkey smiled for a moment with paternal indulgence at the various forms of criminal mayhem unfurling all around, then snagged a brass speaking trumpet from its leather holster on the arm of his throne.

"Listen, Rams," he called, his voice projected yet tinny. "Who among you fine sporting gents fancies a wager with your king?"

The word spread like the plague through the assembled rabble, and soon they were clamoring for sport at the feet of their king.

"Very well, Rams," said Malarkey, rising to his feet. "I have a belter for you this evening, to delay you indoors awhile when you should be outside performing your customary honest labors."

A raucous laugh rose to the very roof at the partnering of the words *honest* and *labors*.

"I, your chosen monarch, in sight of the sacred fleece, offer you a wager. And I am telling you coves right from the off that you won't be taking a ha'penny of my hard-earned. So, who's got the bottle?"

Many hands went up, and some even tossed coins to the foot of the dais.

"Not so fast, my eager bucks. Let me fill you in on the details, lest there be accusations of cheatin' flying around later-wise." Malarkey leaned over, plucking Riley and Chevie from the crowd. "So, my people, what we have here are two possible recruits. A fine little grifter with fast 'ands, and his Injun princess. I've instructed 'em only one fights, and that one fights for two."

"I'll take him," said the knifed swimmer.

Malarkey waved him away. "No, you ain't heard the best bit. The one that's stepping up is the young lady."

This announcement was met with pandemonium.

"We can't have a lady on the canvas," objected the challenger, backing into the throng.

Malarkey stamped a foot. "You have beheld my champion, Rams. Now, show me yours!"

There was no immediate response to this challenge. It was not a matter of cowardice; it was the left-footed awkwardness of tussling with a female in public.

But not all were awkward: one man soon skipped to the front of the line.

"I will crack her skull for her."

The contender was a bald six-footer with bandy legs from carrying his beer gut.

"Can I use me bludgeon? I never fights without it for reasons of balance."

Malarkey was shocked. "Use yer bludgeon? Of course

you can use yer bludgeon, Mr. Skelp. I would never deprive a brother of his beloved weapon of choice."

Skelp drew from behind his back a blackthorn club the size of Chevie's leg. As if its dimensions were not formidable enough, Skelp had hammered on armored plates that had doubtless once been shining steel but were now dull with congealed liquid and matter.

"Charming," said Chevie. "You guys are a classy bunch."

Malarkey laughed. "Skelp is one of our more sophisticated brothers. Betimes he reads stories to the illiterates.

"The odds are ten to one on Skelpy. Cash only, no markers. Give yer coin to my accountant."

A small man in a waistcoat was suddenly besieged by aggressive men with money and dealt with them all efficiently, using a complicated system of facial tics and swearing.

Once the betting was done, a space was cleared in front of the dais. Riley guessed that this was the traditional bare-knuckle arena, and he hoped that the dark splashes on the floorboards were simply wine or beer.

Chevie did not seem anxious, though there could be nothing familiar to her about the proceedings.

Riley realized that the attention of every man in the room was on Chevie, and that this was a perfect time to look for a way out for them both. He couldn't abandon her now. *We are partners, till the end of this affair.*

The Battering Rams jostled for a ringside view as the opponents readied themselves for the competition. Chevie carefully stretched her muscles and tendons, while Skelp stripped to his waist and spoke soft words to his darling bludgeon.

"I will call the match," said Malarkey through his speaking trumpet. "Last man . . . or woman . . . standing shall be proclaimed victor. Both parties prepared for the bout?"

Skelp spat a gob of chewed tobacco, mostly on his own boot. Chevie simply nodded and balled her fists.

"Then begin!" called Malarkey.

The Rams were expecting the little lass to be brim-full of vinegar and take a run at Skelp, possibly causing him to fall down laughing. They were prepared to berate their comrade good-naturedly as he was eventually forced to tap the girlie on her noggin in order to claim his winnings.

They were utterly unprepared for what actually happened, and several burst out laughing, presuming that it was some manner of jape orchestrated by King Otto for a bit of a giggle.

Before the echo of Malarkey's words faded, Chevie rushed in low, used a basic judo disarming maneuver to twist the club out of Skelp's grasp, then unleashed an out-of-the-ballpark uppercut with the man's own beloved bludgeon that knocked out three of his teeth and sent him flying into a gaggle of his comrades. The whole lot went down like ninepins.

"Next," said Chevie, which was a bit melodramatic, but no more so than the entire situation.

A silence followed Chevie's victory, the like of which hadn't been heard in this arcade in twenty years, not since Gunther No Nose Kelly earned his nickname during a rat-eating contest.

"Wait for it," said Malarkey out of the side of his mouth.

When the assembled Rams realized that their invested

chink was in serious danger of disappearing beyond their grubby grasp forever, the short-lived silence was shattered by a collective moan that rose like an ululating wave and crashed in a sea of objections.

"Hold on there!"

"Unfair! Unfair!"

"Will you beat a man with his own club?"

"She ain't no female. She's a witch."

Malarkey silenced the clamor with a bellow through his trumpet, then addressed the stunned congregation.

"You fellers seem a mite surprised by my little whirling dervish here. I warned you, but no—you fine gentlemen knows better than yer beloved regent."

Malarkey rubbed Chevie's head as though she were a favored puppy and even instructed Riley to relax in his throne.

"Here," he said, tossing a purse of gold to Riley. "A share for the Injun princess, even though that were not part of the deal; but I am a fair and benevolent monarch."

Malarkey faced his subjects.

"Listen, my gallows-bound busters, there is another twist to this tale. You have witnessed what my champion can do, so maybe yer regretting monies wagered. So I offer you one chance to retract yer wager without penalty. But if you leave yer ill-gotten gains in the kitty, then among the benefits that will accrue to you are shorter odds, a free toddy, and the admiration of your peers. And who steps up to spill the blood is your affair. You coves have leave to select the burliest muck-snipe from among your ranks to set against my little girlie. Choose whomsoever you fancy, so long as he bears the mark."

Riley found his discomfort swelling with every passing second. This was a fine penny-show for the Rams, but Chevie and himself were sitting ducks. If Garrick had managed to dump his carcass into the tunnel-of-time, it wouldn't be long before some tidbits concerning a battling squaw dropped into his ear hole.

*And then the Thames water rats will be raking two extra floaters out of the dawn currents.*

Riley perched on the throne's cushion.

"Chevie," he whispered, "do the business quick as you like, then we can make ourselves scarce. My skin is crawling with the feeling that Garrick is coming."

"Roger that. We need to be on our way," said Chevie. Every one of Riley's *Garrick is coming* hunches had been bang on the money so far.

Malarkey overheard the exchange. He plucked Riley from the throne, depositing him at his feet like a royal puppy, or jester. "Don't worry about Albert Garrick. My best team of murdering scum have been lying in wait for him at his digs, their time bought by the very same fancy gent who ordered your deaths. As to you two foundlings being *on your way*, I think you have misremembered our arrangement."

Chevie punched her fist into her palm and several large men jumped backward. "What arrangement?" she asked.

Riley's chin dropped to his breastbone, and he answered the question for Malarkey. "We are fighting our way into the Rams, the alternative being a sudden case of violent death— yours and mine. Once we are in, then we are Malarkey's for life."

Malarkey pointed at Riley. "A shilling to the boy for keenness. You fight for the very breath in your lungs, little lady. And if you wrestle your death from my grasp, then I still hold your life. Remember that well."

He swiveled on the balls of his feet like a trained swordsman until his riding crop pointed at Riley. "Take this one and mark him. He is ours now."

Hands descended on Riley from the crowd, so many that it seemed as though he were being swallowed by a sea anemone. Riley fought, dropping several of his captors with well-placed blows, but whenever one fell another sprang to take his place. The Rams lifted him high and carried him through the throng to a far corner of the room, where a decrepit old man sat surrounded by books, boxes of needles, and little ink bottles of dense, jeweled colors. The man's fingers were small like a child's but gnarled and inked in the wrinkles, each knuckle a rainbow. Riley found himself plonked in a wooden chair and held in place by viselike fingers on each shoulder.

"A young recruit, is it?" said the man.

"That is the case, Farley," said Riley's restrainer.

Farley set his store of needles tinkling as he poked through them. "Not really a Ram," he muttered. "More a lamb than a Ram. Still, mine is not to wonder why . . ." He selected a thin needle to make the mark.

"Mister, ain't you going to a-sketch it on first?" Riley asked nervously.

Farley's cough rolled in his throat. "Sketch, is it? Boy, I been doing the ram for years, could do it in me sleep, I could.

Now, quit yer vibrations, or it's a goat adornment you'll be sporting in place of a ram."

"That needle is clean, ain't it? I don't want to lose an arm."

"Worry not, the tool is sterilized better than any steel in St. Bart's. No one ever saw a bubble of pus from Anton Farley's needles. I will do her small and quick, and the time will pass. And presently I will select a second, alcohol-swabbed needle to pick out the ram on your friend."

At the mention of his friend, Riley craned his neck, trying to look back toward the boxing circle without moving his shoulder. From his seat he couldn't see so much as the top of Chevie's head, just a throng of Rams who had set up a chant.

"Golgoth, Golgoth," intoned the criminal coterie, and again, "Golgoth, Golgoth."

"Ah, me," said Farley sadly. "Just the one needle, then."

Chevie was not yet accustomed to the sheer pungency of Victorian London. Even the air seemed to have a sepia tinge to it, and mystery flakes landed on her head and shoulders, mottling her skin.

That can't be good, she thought. I don't even want to think about where those flakes come from.

The Rams had formed a loose human cordon around her and seemed to have developed a certain prudence in approaching the Injun maid, probably due to the large club dangling from her dainty fist and the blood dripping from its *howjadoo* end.

And now the men were chanting the word *Golgoth*, which

Chevie suspected would turn out to be some particularly vicious incarnation of Battering Ram.

*Battering Rams. If these guys got any more macho, they could have their own show on cable TV fixing motorcycles and pumping iron.*

The ocean of men parted and a malevolent hulk strutted into the circle like he was the world's best at something violent.

So this is Golgoth, thought Chevie. It's probably going to take two wallops to knock out this guy.

Golgoth reached up a delicate forefinger and thumb, pinching his crown and removing his hair, which apparently was some kind of hairpiece.

"Hold Marvin for me, would you, Pooley?" said Golgoth, dropping the hairpiece into the hand of his much smaller friend, who did what his far larger friend requested of him, which was probably the basis upon which their relationship was built.

Two things about Golgoth and his friend surprised Chevie.

One: the creepy hairpiece had a name.

And two: no one besides her seemed to find the word *Pooley* hilarious. It sounded a little bit rude, but she wasn't sure why.

"Okay, Golgoth," she said, cracking her knuckles. "I will try to hurt you humanely."

"I ain't no Golgoth," said the giant. "I is his little bruvver."

Which was the last thing she heard before something the size of a cement block hit her square in the chest with the speed of a freight train.

• • •

Chevie may have been strong and quick, but she was also small and light. The blow from her mystery attacker knocked the FBI agent over and sent her skidding across the floorboards, picking up dozens of splinters in the process.

The pain was so huge that Chevie wondered if her lungs had been crushed, and she was relieved when her breathing started up again.

"Oooh," she groaned, a blood-string swinging between her lip and the ruined shards of her Timekey on the floor.

*I am stranded here.*

"No fair."

"Golgoth! Golgoth!" chanted the Rams, stamping their boots to set the floorboards a-jumping.

Chevie raised herself to all fours, wondering if her skull was fractured, thinking, Where is this Golgoth guy? Can Victorians do invisible?

She struggled to her feet, shaking her head to extinguish the stars in her vision, casting around for her attacker. There was no one in the fighting arena but Otto Malarkey.

"Where is he?" Chevie asked blearily. "Point me toward Golgoth."

Malarkey touched two fingers to his lips, a gesture of guilt. "I am afraid, princess, that I am Golgoth. My old circus strongman name."

Oh, crud, thought Chevie. "But I'm fighting *for* you!"

Malarkey removed the fingers from his lips, wagging them

at the assembled Rams. "I said they could pick any Ram, and the clever bleeders picked me. After all, who better? Now I must choose between purse and pride."

Let me guess, thought Chevie. Pride wins.

"And in that tussle, pride wins every time. I must sacrifice my wager to save my position."

Chevie adopted a boxer's stance, dipping her chin low behind raised fists.

*Not that it matters much. With those hands, Malarkey could punch straight through my guard. I will have to rely on my speed.*

The crowd's attitude shifted from raucous encouragement to quiet, feral anticipation. There was much at stake here. Both combatants were being tested, but while Chevron was fighting for her life, Malarkey fought to prove himself loyal to his men, and he knew that there would be more than one Ram praying for him to fall and leave a vacancy for the top position.

The contestants circled each other with wary respect. Chevie's ear was ringing with what she couldn't help feeling was the *Star Trek* theme tune, which was extremely distracting. Malarkey rolled his shoulders and danced light-footed back and forth in a complicated jiglike routine that was almost as off-putting as the ringing.

After a minute or so of sizing each other up, both fighters attacked at the same moment, to a tumultuous roar from the Rams. Malarkey's swiftness was limited by his sheer bulk, and only his eyeballs could move with sufficient quickness to capture Chevie darting under his ham-fist to punch him twice in the solar plexus. Which had about as much effect as throwing a snowball at Mount Everest.

Punches not working, Chevie realized, straightening her fingers and jabbing them into Malarkey's kidney. It does not matter if a man is as big as a house and made from red brick: if he gets a solid poke in the kidneys, it is going to hurt.

Malarkey roared and reflexively jerked his torso, which bumped Chevie into the human cordon around the fighting arena.

Rough hands tousled her hair and one cheeky so-and-so even patted her bottom.

"See that? What she done with her fingers there?" said one Ram, behind her.

"Fingers? I coulda sworn she used her thumb," replied his comrade.

"Nah, dopey. Four fingers, held stiff, like so." And the Ram demonstrated the move on Chevie, sending her lower back into spasm and giving Malarkey enough time to get a grip on her neck.

Game over, thought Chevie, as her feet left the ground.

She chopped at Malarkey's forearm and pinched the nerves in the crook of his elbow, just as Cord Vallicose had assured her would break the grip of the *biggest son of a gun on this green earth.* Apparently he hadn't taken Victorian crime bosses into account.

Malarkey laughed in her face, but Chevie thought she detected a spark of relief in his eyes.

"You had help, Otto. Remember that when you're gloating on your throne."

Malarkey squeezed her windpipe, choking off the accusation along with her air. Chevie hung on to his arm, taking the strain off her neck, trying to avoid spinal damage, but already the lack of oxygen was blurring her vision and draining the strength from her limbs.

"Riley," she croaked, though she knew the boy was under guard outside the throng. He could neither see her nor help her if he did catch a glimpse.

Malarkey drew back his free hand. "This pains me greatly, little maid. Yes, I prove my physical supremacy once again, but it will cost me a pretty pound to honor all the chink bet against you, not to mention the fact that I lose me own wager. I bet on you, girl, and you let me down."

Malarkey clenched his fist, his knuckles creaking.

"I won't kill you," he promised. "And you should wake up with most of yer teeth and marbles."

Chevie tried to draw away, but she was held fast. The ringing in her ears changed from *Star Trek* to something more strident. A simple bell. Was her subconscious trying to tell her something?

Malarkey cocked an ear, and Chevie thought for a second that he could hear what was inside her head; then the Ram king called, "Shush! Shut yer babbling gobs. Can you not see I am listening?"

Silence fell almost instantly, except for Mr. Skelp, who was just waking up.

"Wot's occurring, mates? I remember having me porridge this morning and then . . . nuffink."

Malarkey took three steps into the crowd and silenced Skelp with a boot to the chin.

"I said quiet, you dolts!"

There was dead silence, except for the curious ringing.

Malarkey's eyes widened as his mind connected the noise with an object. "The Telephonicus! 'Tis the Telephonicus Farspeak!"

A chorused *Awww* rose through the Hidey-Hole's ballroom, and all the heads swiveled, lemminglike, toward Malarkey's throne. On a walnut parlor table stood a device, carved from ivory, in two parts: a base and cylinder, connected by twisting cables. The device jangled with each ring.

Malarkey summarily hurled Chevie into the arms of the throng.

"Hold her. Not too tight now, boys. No one hurts the maiden but me."

He ran to the Telephonicus Farspeak and delicately answered the call, little finger raised like a duchess taking tea.

"Helloooo," he said, his accent a little more refined than usual. "This is Mr. Otto Malarkey speaking from the Hidey-Hole. Who is it on the hother end?"

Malarkey listened a moment, then pressed the earpiece to his chest and hissed to the Rams.

"It's Charismo. I can hear him so clear, like he's a fairy in my ear hole."

No one was particularly surprised to hear that it was

Charismo's voice emanating from the earpiece, as it was Mr. Charismo who had installed the Farspeak in the Hidey-Hole. Even so, at the mention of his name, several of the villains blessed themselves, and a couple of the Catholics genuflected. A few more Rams formed triangles with their thumbs and fore-fingers, an ancient gesture to ward off evil.

"Come now, brothers. Mr. Charismo is a friend to the Rams," said Malarkey, but his words sounded forced and hollow.

Malarkey listened some more, his face falling. When Charismo had finished speaking, Malarkey nodded as if that could be transmitted over the phone line, then replaced the ivory earpiece in its holder on the base.

"Well, Rams," he said. "There's good and bad in it. Mr. Charismo has heard *somehow* of the Injun and the boy. He instructs that we deliver them direct to his residence. There is not to be a mark on either, he says."

"And the good news?" asked a Ram in the front row of the throng.

"The good? The good is that the bout cannot technically be concluded, so all bets are off." Malarkey smiled broadly. "Which *is* good news. For your king, which is me."

A few of the Rams grumbled, but not too loudly, and Malarkey knew that his luck would not be questioned. All in all, it was the best possible result for the Ram king: his reputa-tion was intact, his purse no lighter, and Mr. Charismo had been in a much better mood than expected, considering. A good day's graft all around.

• • •

Farley finished the simple Ram motif on Riley's shoulder and swabbed it with medicinal alcohol.

"Don't pick at the scab," he advised, "or you'll end up with scarring, which makes my design look bad."

Riley could not work out what had happened. "Is my friend safe? Is the fighting done?"

Farley placed a clean rag across the tattoo. "The fight has been suspended. A client has expressed an interest in meeting you, as I thought he might."

Riley frowned. There were politics at work here.

"So, you sent word to this gent? It was you that saved us, Mr. Farley?"

Farley tied the knot tightly. "Quiet now, boy. I took a few bob for sending a message, that's all."

Riley touched the bandage gingerly. "Who is this client? What would he want with us?"

Farley carefully and methodically capped his inks and replaced them in a wooden case.

"This *client* is a most singular individual," he said. "A genius in many fields, he is, and a generous benefactor to those who keep him informed. As to what he wants with you, well, that's a question he will answer in person."

"Any words of wisdom for me, Mr. Farley? Regarding this mysterious client and how to keep him sweet?"

Farley smiled and his teeth were remarkably white inside wizened lips. "You are a smart one, boy. That is possibly the best question to have asked, when there was only time for one." Farley thought while he wiped his needle. "I would advise you to keep yourself interesting. Be amusing in your conversation. Mr. Charismo is unlikely to send you back here for as long as he finds your company scintillating."

Riley stood on the stool and caught sight of Chevie, who was terrorizing the Rams trying to restrain her.

*Scintillating*, he thought. *That shouldn't prove too difficult.*

Then the name mentioned by Farley penetrated his brain.

*Mr. Charismo? Surely not Tibor Charismo, the most famous man in all of England. What was his involvement in this whole affair?*

Whatever Mr. Charismo's intentions toward their persons, they were sure to be less lethal than those of either Albert Garrick or Otto Malarkey.

*Perhaps we will have a moment's respite. Perhaps even a bite to eat.*

Riley waved at Chevie and smiled encouragingly.

*Our situation is about to improve*, he wanted to tell her. *Be of good cheer.*

But Chevie was not in good cheer and would not be for some time; for lying in the palm of one hand were the remains of the Timekey, which had been smashed utterly by Otto Malarkey's surprise blow.

THE ORIENT THEATRE, HOLBORN, LONDON, 1898

Before quitting the Orient in search of the Rams, Garrick checked that his cashbox was still hidden in a steel safe below the conductor's podium in the orchestra pit. It would be a galling shame to return after dumping the bodies of Percival and his cronies in the Thames to realize they had raided the stash before his arrival.

Garrick loaded all three bodies onto a cart in the yard and made a quick trip across to the low-lying marshes on the Isle of Dogs to lighten his load.

More food for the fish, he thought as the macabre packages slid below the murky waters.

And now, with the day's donkey work completed, he could attend to more important business. Specifically, to find out who had hired the Rams to do him in. There was one man who would surely be able to answer that question, and Garrick knew precisely where that man would be.

*The Hidey-Hole. Is that not how the Battering Rams refer to their infamous club?*

As if it were hidden. As if every bobby in London were not perfectly aware of its exact address. As if constables did not extend their routes by miles simply to avoid going anywhere near the Rams' headquarters.

*Yes, the un-hidden Hidey-Hole. The next port of call for the Red Glove.*

The sun was already long past the spire when Garrick purchased a mug of coffee from his regular man on the tip of Oxford Street, but his palate had been educated by twenty-first-century coffee, and he judged this mug as bilge water not fit for the Irish. He flung it to the cobbles and vowed to take his custom elsewhere in the future.

The coffee soured his mood briefly, but the memory of his

artful disposal of the three Rams who had violated his beloved theater cheered him somewhat.

I behaved righteously, he realized. My enemies came to murder me and I defeated them.

Self-defense was unusual for Garrick, and he allowed a grim and righteous anger to build in his breast.

An eye for an eye, sayeth the scriptures, thought the magician, deciding to ignore the New Testament for now, as *Turn the other cheek* did not suit his argument.

In daylight hours the Haymarket was little more than a rowdy thoroughfare, with an uncommonly high number of gin houses; but the rising of the moon had a more alarming effect on the tiny borough than it would have had on one cursed with lycanthropy.

First came the bonfires, plonked directly onto the pavement, and no sooner lit than surrounded by half a dozen ruffians, pulling on pints of gin and passing around pungent cigars. Then, drawn perhaps by the bonfires' smoke signals, came the dandies and the players, and a veritable brigade of ne'er-do-wells, all destined to embroil themselves in heavy drinking, illegal betting, and cardsharping before the night was out.

Garrick generally considered himself too fine a gentleman to frequent the Haymarket after dusk, but needs must; and if he was to have the contract on his head lifted, he would have to visit the king in his broken-down palace.

By the time he arrived at Rogues' Walk, the corner was

already six deep in night owls, with a glut of brawn outside the Hidey-Hole's double doors as patrons lined up for a ringside view of the Battering Rams' infamous fighting ring, which on any given night could feature exotic warriors, dogs, roosters, and even, on one notorious occasion, a dwarf and an Australian miniature bear.

This is not the time to speak with Otto Malarkey, Garrick realized. *Even a man of my talents could not hope to penetrate such an army. But my moment will come.*

Garrick was distracted from his task by the sight of a sometime stooge of his sauntering toward the bonfires, then begging nips of gin from the lowlifes warming their hands.

*Lacey Boggs. My West End songbird.*

Lacey Boggs's con was to sing for tipsy gents after the theater while her accomplice dipped into their pockets. The dodge had not been pulling in the revenue it once did after Lacey passed a summer at Her Majesty's pleasure and came out of the clink minus her teeth and plus a set of wooden dentures.

Garrick took Lacey by the elbow and propelled her beneath a gas streetlight, so that her head bonged against the pole.

"Here, what's all this rough stuff?" she objected. "I'll 'ave your hand for a spittoon, mate."

The bluster was replaced by terror when Lacey realized exactly whose hand she had just threatened.

"Oh, not you, Mr. Garrick. I never meant you. Be rough all you like, I know there's no harm in you."

Garrick tightened his grip on Lacey's elbow. "There's harm in me, Lacey Boggs. Gallons of harm and hurt, a-waiting to be spilled onto some poor unfortunate."

Lacey smiled, and Garrick saw that she had taken to dying her wooden choppers with lime. "Not me, Mr. Garrick. Ain't I always done as asked to the letter? Who was it that located that French count for you? The one what was brutally murdered . . ." Lacey's eyes went wide and she covered her mouth with her hand. "I never meant that *you* had nothing to do with that. A fine gent like yourself . . . Coincidence, surely."

Garrick had no patience for this bleating woman. "Calm yourself, Lacey. The harm in me is not for you. I have a job, that's all. Do you remember my boy, Riley?"

Lacey's face muscles relaxed. "Aww. I remembers him. Cute little beggar with the wonky eyeballs. Suffers with the nervosity a bit, I'd say."

"That's him. I need you to find him. Employ whomever you need. Have old Ernest send a pigeon to the theater if I cannot be found."

Lacey sniffed, as though she could smell a sovereign. "London is a big place, Mr. Garrick. Three million souls big. Could you give a girl a clue?"

"I shall be generous. Two clues I have for you. Firstly, Riley may fly to the Old Nichol, for he is well aware of the abhorrence I hold in my heart for that disease pit."

"And the second?"

"It is possible that he travels with an Injun maiden. A pretty lass, but dangerous."

Lacey Boggs clacked her wooden teeth in rumination. "An Injun in Old Nichol. That fox will hunt herself, so she will."

Garrick took a half sovereign from his coin supply. "There are another ten shillings to go with this if you are successful. If not, I will be reclaiming this one from your dead hand. Do you understand me, wench?"

Lacey Boggs shivered as though suddenly cold, but one hand flicked from below her shawl to claim the coin. "I understands. Find the boy and send word."

Garrick took her chin in his bony fingers. "And no gin until the job is done."

"No gin. Not even a tot."

"Very well, Lacey," said Garrick, releasing his grip on the woman. "Off to Old Nichol with you. I have business here."

Lacey rubbed the fingermarks on her chin. "Is you placing a wager, Mr. Garrick? If so, think twice, sir. Otto Malarkey always fixes the odds so he can't lose."

Garrick patted his coat and trouser legs, checking the blades concealed in secret pockets all about his person.

"Even the great King Otto can't fix these odds. He has started a fight that he cannot win. So if I was you, I would quit this place in case the blood flows onto the street."

Lacey Boggs hitched up her petticoats as though the blood already pooled about her feet. "I am making myself scarce, sir. I am an employed woman with a job to do."

Garrick watched her go, and he knew that the news of a bounty for Riley would sweep through the city faster than cholera through a rookery.

*If I know my boy, he will follow the pattern of his previous escape attempts. Riley will find himself a bolt-hole, with a view to making a run for it when his trail has cooled. In this case, he will run for the future, and there are only two doors leading that way. One is in the basement of Half Moon Street, but I could be there waiting for him; or I could have simply dismantled the apparatus, so he will give it a few days, then make for Bedford Square. And that's where I shall be, just as soon as I have myself a little chat with Otto Malarkey.*

Inside the Hidey-Hole the revelries continued until the wee hours, when Otto Malarkey called a halt by abruptly losing his temper, as he did, regular as clockwork, just before sunrise, urging anyone who did not wish to bear a stripe of his riding crop to find themselves a hammock out of his sight.

"Except you, Mr. Farley," he called to the elderly tattoo artist. "I would have you update my price list as I doze." It was a testament to the man's tolerance for pain that he intended to sleep while Farley labored over his chest tattoo.

The enormous room cleared slowly as the weary shuffled toward their resting places. Malarkey hung his hat on the throne and placed the ram's fleece on his head. He snagged a bottle of brandy from the grip of an unconscious sailor on the floor and staggered to Farley's corner.

"How now, my faithful artist," he said, dropping into the tattoo lounger, which creaked alarmingly under his prodigious bulk. "I need you to update my price list. Add a half sov to every service. After all, I am king now."

Farley was tired and his fingers were cramped, yet he knew

better than to complain. He provided a valuable service to the Rams, but Malarkey's moods were unpredictable and a man would do well not to visit his dark side.

"A half sov it is," he said, tapping the ink bottles into a pleasing straight line. "Some will be straightforward enough; the *same as previous* ones won't need touching. But may I 'umbly suggest leaving the denomination as shillings? Then all's I need to do is diddle with the numbers a bit. Save a little on the ink and needles."

What went unsaid was that Farley's method would cut down the needle time.

Malarkey uncorked the bottle with his teeth and took a long draft. "As you wish, Farley. It is of little matter to me, hardy as I am. Your needle is like a pinprick compared to the many rapier punctures I suffered on the prison island of Little Saltee."

*That's because it* is *a pinprick*, Farley wanted to say, but he thought better of it.

"Enough blabber, and on with it," said Malarkey. "I needs me sleep. Rest is vital for a shining head of hair. Rest and the touch of the fleece. Which I happens to know is vital for keeping my mane glossy."

Malarkey was vain about his hair. It was his weakness, and too many people knew it, in Farley's opinion.

"Rest and the fleece, boss. You see to your hair and let me work on this chest. When you wake it will be done."

Malarkey belched almost contentedly, arranged the fleece so it covered his eyes, and allowed his muscles to relax, then jumped as Farley's needle made its first puncture. It had been a long time since he'd taken ink, and it was a mite more painful than he remembered.

"Apologies, boss. The sting will ease soon enough."

Malarkey relaxed once more. Jumping and a-twisting was not a wise idea when taking the ink.

*A cove's T could end up a J.*

Farley had spoken true, and soon the needle pricks faded to a dull buzz. Malarkey felt his entire chest assume the numbness that often went with extreme drunkenness. Within minutes he felt at peace with the world.

The surrounding hubbub faded, to be replaced by loud snoring and the occasional squeal of night terror from the upper levels.

*I love this time of day,* thought Malarkey.

He was on the point of slipping away when he felt the tattooist's needle slide in uncommonly deep, like an icicle perilously close to his heart. The Ram king's eyes flew open, and one hand raised itself to knuckle Farley on the crown for his carelessness; but when he tore the fleece from his head, Malarkey saw that it was not the decrepit Farley bent over him but the assassin Albert Garrick, in full evening wear, including a heavy velvet cape that rippled in the low light like the fur of a satisfied panther.

"Have you lost your senses?" Malarkey shouted.

"Keep your voice down, Malarkey," said Garrick, twisting the needle a fraction. "Or you may startle me into popping your heart like a rancid bag of pus."

From his position, Malarkey could not see the tattooist. "Where is Farley? Have you murdered the old geezer?" he asked quietly.

"Not murdered," replied Garrick. "I etherized him is all, and rolled him under the stairs. I am not an animal."

"What you are is a dead man, Garrick," hissed the king of the Rams.

Garrick smiled and his teeth were like corn husks. "I would be a dead man already if you had had your way. Isn't that the truth of it, Your Majesty?"

Malarkey paled slightly as it occurred to him that if Garrick was here, then his murder boys were more than likely getting their eyeballs examined by mud crabs in the Thames.

"It was a contract from a valued customer. Business is all."

"I appreciate that," said Garrick, who had surmised as much. "But I need to know the name of this customer whose value outweighs the risks of crossing swords with yours truly."

"That's a name you ain't extracting from me," said Malarkey, who had borne terrible tortures before now.

Garrick sighed, as if it were a tragedy how people drove him to commit acts that were against his nature. "Let me tell you a story before you makes up your mind proper. It is the story of Samson and Delilah. Samson was a great Israelite warrior who laid low all before him, a little like your good self, Otto. But then the treacherous Delilah chopped off his precious hair and drained his power. It's a brief story, but I think you get the point." With every phrase, Garrick slipped the cold needle in a whisper further toward Malarkey's heart.

Malarkey's face was drenched with sweat, but he held firm. "Shave my head then, you devil. You will get no name from me."

Garrick expected this resistance from a man of Malarkey's reputation, but he had another card up his sleeve.

"Personally I think that whole head-shaving business is a euphemism for stealing the man's power, but I know how fond you are of your gorgeous head of hair, so my threat to you is that if you do not tell me who put the black spot on my head, then I will . . ."

"You will shave my head. This is old news, Garrick."

Garrick made a noise that could be described as a titter. "No. I will burn your scalp with my little bottle of acid, so that no hair will ever grow on your crown again. And then, in one month, when the men have bellyache from laughing, I will return in the dead of night and kill you."

Malarkey's lip twitched. "That is a powerful threat. A man would have to be soft to ignore a threat like that."

"It makes you think, does it not?"

Malarkey squinted past the brim of Garrick's top hat, searching for the magician's eyes. "Perhaps, I am thinking, Garrick did not bring his acid, and this whole affair is bluff."

"Well, then," responded Garrick, a sickly glow emanating from his teeth, "at the very least you shall die in this chair, and I shall tattoo something tasteless on your barrel chest."

Malarkey was bent but not broken, and Garrick realized from his new knowledge of psychology and interrogation techniques gleaned from Felix Smart's studies that a proud man must be given an *out*: a way to supply the information needed that left him with some dignity.

"I respect you, Otto. So I have a proposition for you. I will buy out your contract, simple as that. Fifty sovereigns in your poke, right this second, which I'll wager is more than you ever had from the instigator. Fifty sovs and you suspend all operations undertaken on the word of this man who hired you. A nice purse for the name of he who pointed the Rams my way. And I'll sweeten the pot. I seek a day's amnesty only. If I have not taken care of the problem by sundown, then you are free to hunt me once more."

This was indeed a tempting offer. "We can murder you tomorrow?"

The teeth glinted again. "You can try, but three of your top bludgers have already tried, and I am sorry to say that Mr. Percival and Co. will not be attending this evening's soirée."

Malarkey thought as much. "Here is my counterproposal to you, Garrick. I am planning to close my eyes and sleep. Betimes I say things in my sleep that I would never say when in my waking mind. When I rouse myself, I expect to find you gone and a purse of coin stuffed into my paw. What do you think of that plan?"

Garrick withdrew the needle from Malarkey's chest. "Close your eyes and find out."

# 10 » MR. CHARISMO

CHEVIE FIRST THOUGHT THAT RILEY WAS ANXIOUS in the carriage, but she quickly realized that the boy was excited.

"Hey, kid. Are you okay?"

Riley was bobbing up and down in the brougham's seat, bumping shoulders with Jeeves and Noble, who had been tasked with escorting them.

"Yes, Chevie, I am dandy. Don't you know where we are going?"

Nowhere, thought Chevie glumly. We are staying right here in Victorian London. I could end up being my own great-grandmother.

She looked out of the carriage's window.

*Check your surroundings, Special Agent.*

They were somewhere in Piccadilly, perhaps driving toward Mayfair, judging by the spruced-up surroundings. The shoals of urchins had stopped clustering around the carriage's rear wheels soon after they had left the Haymarket, and the number of beggars on the street had decreased as the number of bobbies walking the beat increased.

Riley answered his own question. "We are being sent to Mr. Charismo's house. *The* Mr. Charismo. Surely you must have heard of him?"

Chevie elbowed Noble, who sat on her left, for a little more room. "No. I have not heard of this Charismo guy."

"You have not heard of Mr. Tibor Charismo?" said Jeeves, laughing. "Where've you been bunking? In a wigwam?"

"In a wigwam," repeated Noble, slapping his knee. "You do occasionally throw up a good comment, Jeeves."

Chevie scowled. "So who is this Charismo person? Somebody famous?"

All three were struck momentarily dumb by Chevie's ignorance. Riley was the first to recover. "Somebody famous? Mr. Charismo is like Arthur Conan Doyle, H. G. Wells, and Robert-Houdin all compacted into one individual. He is our most illustrious novelist, composer, and, of course, spiritualist."

"Sounds like I should have seen this guy on the History Channel."

"Queen Vic herself consults Mr. Charismo," said Noble, touching the brim of his shabby bowler at the mention of Her Majesty.

"And Gladstone, too, before he popped his clogs," added Jeeves.

"You are familiar with the James Bond series?" asked Riley.

Chevie jerked in her seat. "Er . . . yeah, actually."

"The novels featuring Commander James Bond of Her Majesty's navy. He is second only to Holmes himself for exposing villains, though his methods are a little more direct."

"The name is Bond. James Bond," chorused Noble and Jeeves, shooting finger pistols into the air.

"And of course Charismo's symphonies are world famous," continued Riley. "*Another Brick in Yonder Wall* is my favorite, featuring the crazed lute player Pinkus Floyd."

Chevie frowned. "*Yonder Wall?*"

"Yes. And who does not adore the stage play *The Batman of Gotham City?*"

Jeeves seemed genuinely scared. "That Joker character gave me the right willies!"

*James Bond. Pink Floyd. Batman?*

Chevie was pretty sure these things should not exist for decades. Whoever this Charismo character was, he seemed to know an awful lot about the future.

*So how come the future doesn't know about him?*

The carriage transported them to higher ground, and the street noise subsided almost completely but for the far-off rattle and clang of an omnibus and the *click-clack* of genteel horses pulling plush carriages. If this was not the richest area of London town, then it was certainly no more than a stone's throw away. Chevie would have been willing to bet that she and Riley were the only people on this street wearing manacles. The carriage creaked to a halt outside a six-story town house that would cost untold millions in the twenty-first century.

"'Ere we are," called the driver's booming voice from above. "Grosvenor Square. North side, all ashore wot's going ashore."

Before the passengers could disembark, a small, rotund man came barreling down the steps and across the footpath, clapping his hands delightedly. He was impeccably dressed in a gold-brocade waistcoat and navy trousers. But what really caught Chevie's attention was the purple jeweled turban perched on his head.

"Visitors," he sang. "Visitors today for Tibor."

The man leaped nimbly onto the carriage step and flung the lacquered wooden door wide.

"Children, welcome," he said, poking his head into the doorway. His broad smile changed to pantomime horror when he saw the manacles. "But no! This is unspeakable! Remove these chains from the delicate limbs of my guests. *Tout de suite!*"

Jeeves was somewhere between starstruck and dutiful. "I dunno, Mr. Charismo. King Otto told me not to take off the bracelets till we get inside the house. I adores yer work, by the by. *Behold the Rooftop Fiddler* is the wife's absolute favorite."

Tibor Charismo's eyes flared, and Chevie thought she spotted eyeliner. "Inside the house? You will never set foot in my dwelling. The carpets are from Arabia, for heaven's sake."

It pained Jeeves to argue with his wife's hero, but he knew that Otto was a stickler for his orders being followed. "Be that as it be, but orders is orders, sure as the early bird and so forth."

Chevie noticed that Charismo was sporting a molded theater mask that covered the left side of his face from hairline to cheekbone. It was cleverly painted to blend in and would only be noticed close up. Chevie wondered if this was a kind of show-business affectation, like the turban, or did it hide something?

Charismo's curled mustache actually quivered with rage. "I do not understand you, sir. Tell Charismo your name."

Jeeves pressed himself against the carriage wall. "There's no call to be looking for a man's name when he's only doing his job."

"Don't tell him, Ben," advised Noble. "He'll have the evil eye on you."

Jeeves actually shrieked. "You glocky toad."

"Aha!" said Charismo. "Benjamin!"

Noble rolled his eyes. "Calm yourself, there must be dozens of Bens in London. He don't know Jeeves, does he?"

Chevie groaned. Stupid criminals were stupid criminals in any century.

Charismo placed the thumb of his right hand on a large ruby in his turban, then pointed the index finger at Jeeves, who at this point was cowering in the corner.

"Benjamin Jeeves," he intoned, and by some trick of the light his eyes seemed to glow. "Beeenjamin Jeeeeeeeves."

And that was all it took. "Look, Mr. Charismo, see," said Jeeves, fumbling a key from the band of his tatty hat and getting to work on Chevie's handcuffs. "I am removing the bracelets. No need to look into my future."

Charismo broke contact with his ruby. "Very well, uncouth lout. Now free the boy."

"No need," said Riley, tossing the cuffs to Noble. "I took 'em off back on Piccadilly, while these two were spying on a group of Oriental ladies."

"I ain't never seen one before," mumbled Noble guiltily.

Charismo stepped down onto the footpath. "I shall take delivery of the *prisoners*, and responsibility, too. Please inform Mr. Malarkey that I am delighted with his service and to await my call on the Farspeak."

Even the mention of the miraculous Farspeak had the henchmen touching their brims, as though the machine was royalty.

"We will do that, Mr. Charismo, and thank you."

Suddenly Tibor Charismo stiffened and pressed both forefingers to his temples. "I am getting something from a year hence. I see crowds cheering and I hear hooves galloping. *Manifesto*, the word *Manifesto*. Does that have any significance to you gentlemen?"

Noble and Jeeves clutched at each other in a flurry of excitement. Charismo's tips were famous. He was never wrong. A man could make his fortune on a tip from Mr. Charismo.

"Manifesto," said Jeeves in hushed tones. "I bet on that beauty last year at Aintree. She won by twenty lengths. I ate beef for a week."

"She's going to win it again," said Noble. "Not a word of this to anyone. No need for the odds to shorten."

"No. No need whatsoever. Me and you only, Noble."

Charismo clapped his hands briskly. "Gentlemen, our business is done, and I would feed my guests."

Jeeves more or less booted Chevie from the carriage, followed by Riley.

Charismo raised his face to the gigantic coach driver, who kept a cudgel on the seat beside him in case of hijack. The driver gave the impression of someone who had seen every horror London had to offer and had probably been responsible for inflicting a good portion of them. His head was completely shaved, with a star-shaped scar above his right ear.

"Barnum, take these two gents wherever they want to go and then come directly back here."

"Yessir, master," said the driver, and he whistled to the horses to move along.

"I know," said Charismo, as the carriage rumbled down the avenue. "*Master.* It's so melodramatic, but I get a shiver every time I hear it. Humble beginnings, you see."

Chevie rubbed the cuff marks on her wrists and wondered when her world would make sense again.

What should I do here? she thought. What does the FBI handbook say about dealing with spiritualists in the past?

The pavement seemed hard and gritty beneath her feet, and she could smell flowers from the window boxes in the evening air.

We have been beaten, drugged, dragged, and beaten some more, she thought. We need rest.

"Perhaps you are considering flight," said Charismo, linking arms with them both. "After all, who is this mysterious benefactor who has pulled you from the frying pan? Perhaps only to toss you into the fire, eh? If that is your decision, then leave now. Charismo will be devastated, as I have prepared for your coming. A hot bath, fresh linen, soft pillows, roasted fowl, and beer for the boy, but, as you wish. I saw you both in my vision, and I felt that somehow you were special. I would simply like to talk with you, and perhaps document something of your story for my next novel. I was working on a comedy of errors for the stage entitled *The Panther That Was Pink*, but that can wait; I have a feeling that your story is far more interesting. So, you may stay with me for as long as you wish, and in return for a few hours of your time each day, I shall treat you like royalty and perhaps introduce you to some. What say you?"

What say we? thought Chevie. I have no idea who this guy is or what is going on here. The Panther That Was Pink? Riley and I need a few minutes to talk.

She turned to consult her young friend, but he was already halfway up the steps to the spectacular town house.

"It looks like we are staying," she said to Charismo.

The tiny gentleman squeezed her arm. "Capital. You have no idea how happy that makes me. We will get you cleaned up and find you some ladies' clothing, instead of that boyish rig-out that you were obviously forced to wear by your abductors."

Chevie spied two young women stepping from a nearby carriage wearing enormous bonnets and a million layers of skirts.

Ladies' clothing? she thought. Not in this lifetime.

• • •

Chevie was woken by a vertical shaft of sunlight slicing through a gap in the curtain. She ignored it for as long as possible, but whichever way she turned her head it seemed to follow, lighting the inside of her eyelid. Eventually she summoned the energy to drag a pillow over her head, and she would have drifted off to sleep once more had it had not been for the sheep.

*Sheep? Aren't sheep supposed to help a person go to sleep?*

Her subconscious threw up the idea that she should try to count the sheep.

No, Chevie thought. I am not counting sheep.

But the mind is its own master, and hers was soon trying to figure out how many sheep were in the flock, based on the tones of their bleatings.

*It is amazing how each sheep has its own little personality, if you really listen.*

And this thought finally forced Chevie to open her eyes. A thought like that could be enough to get a person kicked out of the Bureau if you happened to voice it aloud to the agency shrink.

"Sheep!" she moaned. "Why are there sheep in Bedford Square at this time in the morning?"

Then she sat up and saw that the bed was a showy brass affair heaped with flounces, ribbons, and crocheted cushions, and she remembered that she was not in Bedford Square anymore.

She sighed. "Not a dream, then. What a pity."

Chevie pulled aside the gauze drapes, climbed out of bed, and padded across a deep carpet to a purple velvet curtain with golden ropes and tassels.

Chevie stood in the tall sash window and looked down on a perfect Victorian mews, thronged with staff and traders, their industry hidden from the view of important people.

She remembered something Charismo had told them at dinner the previous night.

*The Duke of Westminster, one of my society clients, lives nearby in Grosvenor Street, and I have a Farspeak line running directly to his office. All I have to do is pick up this receiver and one of the most powerful men in Great Britain listens attentively to whatever I have to say.*

Whoever this Charismo guy was, he had all sorts of clout. Funny that the same guy would have one line to the Duke of Westminster and another to Otto Malarkey.

Something caught Chevie's eye. An elderly gent was walking down the back lane, tugging four sheep on a string behind him.

*Four,* thought Chevie. *I knew it.*

Charismo had ordered a maid to remove Chevie's clothing for burning, promising a selection in the room that would be suitable for a young lady about town. Chevie checked the wooden wardrobe and found that in the ladies' half there was room for two dresses with their voluminous bustles, while the men's side held a selection of suits and hunting wear. Chevie chose a pair of jodhpurs, probably tailored for a teenage boy, tucked them into knee-high riding boots, and topped the lot off with a crisp white shirt.

We need to get out of here, she thought. I don't trust this guy: he is being too nice to us. And he knows far too much about the future to be from the past. I do not buy this spiritualist story for a minute.

She placed her ear to the door and could hear sounds of conversation from downstairs.

*No doubt Riley the fan-boy is asking any question he can think of.*

The conversation drifted up to her with the aroma of coffee and fresh bread. Chevie realized that she was starving, in spite of the feast Tibor Charismo had served up the previous night.

*Chicken, guinea fowl, turkey, pheasant. How many birds can a person eat in one sitting?*

She twisted the painted knob and found the door locked.

*Odd. Why would our supposed benefactor lock me in?*

As far as Chevie was concerned, this was simply another tick on the evidence sheet against Charismo.

*This guy has some kind of link to the future. He is connected to this case, and with any luck he can show us the way home.*

But before she confronted him with her suspicions, Chevie decided that it would be wise to snoop around and gather some evidence.

I'm a federal agent, she thought. Snooping is what we do best.

The window was also locked, which slowed Chevie down. She discovered a cushion that had been embroidered with Charismo's own face and thought of ramming her elbow through Charismo's nose to crack the pane beyond.

But the glass breaking was not a clever idea. The noise would still be heard in the mews, and there were people on the flagstones in the yard. As soon as she smashed the window there would be a hundred eyes on her.

There must be another way out besides the window. Chevie spent a minute knocking on the walls, searching for the secret passage that all Victorian houses had in the movies, but there was no hollow echo, just the flat rap of solid brick. Then she noticed a silk screen, again embroidered with Charismo's face. In petty annoyance she put the toe of her riding boot through the screen, only to feel a draft. It was a fireplace with a dried-flower arrangement in the grate.

*The chimney. Garrick came down the chimney in the Garden Hotel. I never thought I would steal one of his tricks.*

Chevie knelt and poked her head into the flue. It led to a redbrick chimney. Chevie saw the bricks were red, even through a scaly skin of soot, because a splash of light fell across them from above.

Light, thought Chevie. That means there's another fireplace one floor up.

She wriggled her shoulders into the flue—while there was enough space for a wriggle, there certainly was no room for a shrug.

I had better not shrug, then, thought Agent Savano, and twisted herself completely into the fireplace.

While Chevie was scraping her nose along the redbrick of a chimney, Riley was being interviewed in the writing room by society darling Tibor Charismo. Riley was an adoring fan of Charismo's work, and Tibor seemed extremely satisfied to take this as the starting point of their relationship.

They sat at an extraordinary mahogany writing desk fashioned in the shape of a stylized gryphon, with a lion's body and the head of an eagle, covered in gold leaf, protruding from one side. The lion's flat back was upholstered in pale orange leather, with cubbyholes for bottles, pens, and blotter.

And even though Riley had visited the twenty-first century, he believed this desk to be the most fantastic single object he had ever seen.

"You are admiring my desk, I see," said Charismo. On this morning he wore an old-fashioned powdered wig over his dark curls, his mask was painted in garish orange and red to give him a slightly demonic appearance, and his dressing gown was quilted silk with a lush fur collar.

"Yes, sir," said Riley. "It's the most beautiful thing I have ever seen."

Charismo drummed his fingers on the wood. "A gift from the tsar of Russia. I baked a poultice for a boil on his nose, if you can credit that. The offending blemish was reduced in circumference by more than sixty percent. Alexander was most grateful."

Riley's jaw dropped. "You are a doctor, too?"

"I have no formal qualifications," said Charismo, in a way that suggested *formal qualifications* were a waste of a gentleman's time. "I am connected with the spirit world, which is composed of the sum of human experience, past, present, and future. The spirits communicate with me in my dreams. They whisper to me of words and music, but also of future events. Wars, catastrophes. Plague and famine. It is a terrible burden." Charismo rested his weary, tortured brow on his knuckles. "No one can ever comprehend the cross I bear."

Riley dared to pat his hero's elbow. "Sherlock Holmes said, 'Genius is an infinite capacity for taking pains.' And surely, sir, you are the greatest genius who ever lived."

Charismo smiled a touch sadly. "Dear boy. Yes, perhaps I am. And how pleasant it is to have the fact acknowledged. You truly are a perceptive young fellow."

Charismo dabbed a lace kerchief near his right eye. "Perceptive and mannerly. You have no doubt noticed my various masks and yet made no comment." Tibor Charismo tapped the smooth plaster of the mask molded to the left side of his face. "This particular model is a Japanese Noh mask representing the devil." He giggled. "I wear it for séances; a little melodramatic, I know, but it gives the ladies such a naughty thrill." He paused, his mouth drooping in long-suffering sadness. "I know what they say, those so-called gentlemen of the press. Charismo hides his warts. Or Tibor Charismo cultivates mystery because he is a sham. But the truth is, I wear these masks to hide a terrible disfigurement. A birthmark that was the subject of so much childhood ridicule that I cannot bear to expose it now. Even at night I wear a silken veil." Tibor banged his fist on the desk. "Why must Tibor endure this curse?" he shouted to the heavens, and then, "Oh, look. Tea!"

Barnum, the enormous driver, was also a butler. He now

entered, squashed into a uniform and pushing a trolley heaped with cakes and hot drinks.

"I know how you young scamps enjoy your treats," said Tibor, filling a plate for Riley.

"Oh, no, sir," objected Riley, his stomach already full to bursting after a glutton's breakfast. "I'm not used to such rich food."

"Nonsense," proclaimed Charismo. "You must sample *les macarons*. My chef is French, and they are his speciality. Though I have been credited with inventing the different flavors. A tip from the spirits."

"Perhaps just one," said Riley, selecting a small cake.

Charismo filled his own china plate and ate for several minutes with concentration and enjoyment, growling low in his throat with each mouthful. Eventually he sat back and belched into his handkerchief with such force that the material fluttered.

"Now, what was our topic? Ah, yes, the trials of Tibor, but enough of that. You will think me a terrible boor. We are here to talk about you. The spirits assure me that you have had a fascinating life. Let us start with those unusual eyes." Charismo placed a finger to his temple. "The spirits inform me that this condition is known as anisocoria, and it is usually the result of trauma, but it can also be inherited." Tibor leaned forward, suddenly paying very close attention. "Can you remember, my dear boy?" he asked, flecks of sugar on his lips. "Can you remember your parents? Did they have anisocoria?"

Riley sipped his tea. "I do not know for certain, sir. Sometimes I have dreams, or visions. I was young when my parents died . . . were murdered, actually. By a man named Garrick. Now he's on my trail."

Charismo stuffed his kerchief in his mouth. "*Quelle horreur!* Murdered, you say. But this is terrible, awful." He patted Riley's knee. "You are safe here, my boy."

Riley placed his cup on its saucer, tracing the pattern of dancing girls on the china with his index finger. "I can't stay long, sir. You have been wonderful to grant us shelter, but Garrick will find me, and then you would be in danger. My conscience could not bear that responsibility."

Charismo harrumphed. "With your leave, Riley, I shall worry about this Garrick individual."

Riley scratched the scab on his shoulder, though the tattooist Farley had warned him against this. "Everyone says that, sir. Then Garrick kills them."

"Shall we make a gentlemen's agreement?" asked Charismo. "We will have our little talk and I shall take my silly notes, and then I will set all the resources at my disposal, which are considerable and include Otto Malarkey and his stooges, a-looking for your Garrick. How does that sound?"

Riley forced a smile.

"Capital," he said, resolving that he and Chevie must be away before nightfall.

Chevie's first thought upon emerging through the fireplace into the chamber directly above her bedroom was that perhaps she should not have worn a white shirt.

I am not having much luck with clothes these days, she

thought, and then, These days? What does that even mean anymore?

The climb had been difficult, but far from impossible for someone whose first month in training had included a half-mile crawl along a disused latrine drain, with barbed wire overhead and a permanently disgruntled FBI instructor above the wire. Her only worry in the chimney had been that she would lose her purchase on the mortar between the bricks and slide down to the cellar.

Chevie climbed over the grate's brass railing, then stood upright, grateful to have space on every side—she had been about two minutes away from developing claustrophobia.

She looked around. This room was three times the size of hers and infinitely more luxurious. The bed was the size of a trampoline and seemed to be built on a nautical theme, with posts designed to look like masts and drapes rigged like sails. Blue-and-white-striped cushions were heaped in a mountain in the center, and what looked like a veil was tied to a brass hook on the headboard. Chevie counted over a dozen gas jets on the walls, as well as four electric lamps. One of Charismo's Farspeak devices stood on a marble-topped bedside table and another on the rolltop writing desk. Gold-framed pictures lined the walls, and all depicted Charismo. Some were seated portraits, but others documented his extraordinary career. Here he was onstage with Robert Louis Stevenson in Covent Garden, and there was Tibor presenting a leather-bound book to Queen Victoria herself. By the window was a framed cover of *Harper's Magazine*, split by a Union Jack ribbon into two halves, the left depicting Charismo speaking into his Farspeak device, the right showing an amazed mother with her petticoated daughters listening raptly to the receiver.

Chevie looked around for anything that might justify her nagging suspicions about Tibor Charismo. She knew in her gut that something was wrong. Her instincts had served her well when she'd been undercover in Los Angeles.

*I knew those guys were clean, and I just know that Tibor Charismo is dirty. I need to find the connection. There were only two men from the future hiding back here. One was Riley's father, an FBI agent, and the other was the man he was guarding.*

Charismo's collection of half-masks was displayed on a board on the wall, each dangling from a dedicated brass hook.

This guy sure likes his masks, Chevie thought, tapping a mask that looked like solid gold but was actually painted plaster.

*Nothing is as it seems.*

Almost unconsciously, she began humming the intro of a song that her father had played over and over again on his beat-up turntable: Eric Clapton, "Behind the Mask."

*Now this is real music, squirt,* her dad said every single time he dropped the needle on the record.

*"Behind the mask." I wonder, what is behind the mask?*

There was a crack in the display board running right down the center. No, not a crack—a gap, because the board was actually a set of doors.

*Where is the handle?*

There was no handle, so Chevie put a finger against each

door and pressed. The doors gave slightly and then swung open to reveal a recessed cupboard and bulletin board. There were line drawings pinned to the board and an assortment of objects placed on the shelf.

Calm down, she cautioned herself. And don't miss a thing.

"Oh, my God," she said aloud, surprised that her suspicions had proved to be spot on. "I've got you now, *Tibor*."

What a fancy name he's given himself, Chevie thought. Much fancier than Terry.

Suddenly she heard the rapid footfalls of a big person jogging up a nearby set of stairs.

*I need proof for Riley.*

Chevie snatched two small objects: a glittering ring from its velvet cushion, and a Timekey to get her home again.

I don't know why Tibor Charismo would have a Timekey, Chevie thought. But I am glad he does. Or did.

She was back in the chimney before the masks stopped rocking on their hooks.

Inside the chimney, Chevie plotted her next move.

*I need to get Riley alone and show him what I found. I hate to destroy his hero, but Charismo is not quite as gifted as he pretends to be.*

She inched down the shaft toward the light below.

*The light. My room.*

No one entered the chamber above. The footsteps she'd heard had been a false alarm. Still, it would be foolhardy to go back up. She should count herself lucky that she'd escaped detection this time.

Chevie imagined her Quantico instructor screaming abuse in her ear, and this motivated her to descend a little faster. In three minutes flat her boots were sticking out of the fireplace in her bedroom.

She twisted onto her stomach and pushed herself into the room, once again feeling that immense sense of relief at being free from confinement.

*I made it*, she thought.

A voice above her said, "Well, well, well. What do we have here, a-droppin' down the chimney? One of Father Christmas's elves, perhaps?"

If that voice belongs to Barnum, the humongous coach driver, then I am in trouble, thought Chevie.

It did, and she was.


Albert Garrick always felt a little jittery passing through Mayfair. In spite of his dandy getup and his long hair, a style affected by many a lordling, he had the nagging idea that his humble origins somehow shone through his eyes for all to see.

*In spite of everything I know, everything I have seen, I cannot make myself comfortable on these streets.*

He tried to bolster his own confidence with an inner pep talk: *Buck yourself up, Alby. You are no longer a starving urchin combing the cobbles for the scraps from a rich man's table. Time to scrape that shame off your soul like dog filth from the toe of your boot.*

A flower girl actually curtsied as she approached. "A carnation for your buttonhole, m'lord."

This simple greeting raised Garrick's spirits more than his own strictures ever could, and he smiled with more sincerity than he had in some time. He reached behind the girl's ear and found a shiny sovereign.

"This is for you, my dear. Buy something that is as pretty as yourself."

The maid stammered a thank-you, then stood a-staring at the currency in her hand as though it would melt.

Garrick continued down the north side of Grosvenor Square toward the residence of Tibor Charismo, the man who had hired Otto Malarkey to kill him.

There was a well-tended private park opposite Charismo's famous dwelling, reserved for residents only and accessible by a heavy, locked gate. Armed with his magician's tools, Garrick was no more troubled by the gate than a dog would be by a KEEP OFF THE GRASS sign. In seconds he was reclining on a clean, varnished bench, admiring the Himalayan rhododendrons, and keeping a close eye over their bobbing heads on the fabulous Charismo residence.

*So, now Tibor Charismo wishes me dead, as he once did Riley's family.*

For it had been Tibor Charismo who had contracted Albert Garrick over a decade ago to dispose of Riley's entire family in their Brighton residence. And now, all this time later, he had obviously discovered Garrick's deception and decided to settle the affair with some finality.

*Could that be the entirety of it? Charismo would pit himself against me over the life of a boy?*

Garrick thought that if the situation allowed, he would put this question to Charismo before he killed him.

There was some movement in a window. Garrick's rejuvenated eyes had no difficulty recognizing the figure, even from this great distance.

*Charismo.*

Garrick sat up as though the bench had been electrified.

*So, my nemesis is at home today. That makes my job easier.*

He was suddenly glad that he had tipped the young flower girl so heavily.

*You see, Albert. It is like Felix Smart's mother always said: If you do nice things, then nice things will happen to you.*

Inside the house on Grosvenor Square, Tibor Charismo was treating himself to yet another *macaron* while the barbiturates he had mixed into Riley's tea took hold of the lad's brain. The sweet delights of the belly had always been Riley's weakness.

Once the boy's eyes had glazed and his arms hung limply by his sides, Charismo began his questioning in earnest, revealing the true motives for his kindness.

"Now, Riley, let me explain what is happening. I have given you a blend of barbiturates that I cooked up myself. A truth serum. You could try to fight it, but you would simply damage your brain, so it would be far better for your mental health if you answered all my questions truthfully. Do you understand?"

"Yesh," said Riley, around a fat tongue. He felt drunk and compressed by the weight of air above him.

Charismo clapped his hands. "Excellent. Now, first question: Did you come through the wormhole, or were you just squatting in the house on Half Moon Street?"

It did not seem strange to Riley then that Charismo should know about the wormhole. Perhaps the spirits had told him?

"Wormhole," he slurred. "From future."

Charismo frowned. "I imagine you somehow were pulled into the time tunnel on Bedford Square, then returned through Half Moon Street, correct?"

"Yesh. Pulled and returned. Future smells lovely."

"And Miss Savano—what is that sweet girl's part in this affair?"

Riley closed his eyes and smiled. "She is FBI. Special agent pretty."

Charismo stood, wringing his hanky like a turkey's neck. "FBI? F . . . B . . . blooming . . . I."

"Like my old dad. FBI. I saw his shield."

"Like your old dad?" said Charismo slowly, allowing the words to sink in, confirming his suspicions. "Of course. I heard Garrick had a boy. But I didn't know you were *that* boy." He steered his mind back to Chevie.

"Has she come for me?"

"For you, sir? Oh, no. We simply flee from Garrick. He wants the Timekey. It's the last one for this wormhole. Or it *was* the last one, till Otto Malarkey pulverized it."

"The last one," breathed Charismo, relaxing considerably.

"Well, then, I am safe. Garrick should be deceased already, and even if he isn't, he will have no inkling that I have another key."

"That's wrong, sir."

Charismo flapped his kerchief, irritated. "What's wrong, boy?"

"Garrick is not deceased. Everyone makes that mistake."

"Not Tibor Charismo," said Tibor Charismo. "I have taken care of Albert Garrick. He crossed me once, but never again."

Tibor popped the final *macaron* into his mouth and hummed while he chewed. "That's the chorus of a new song I am crafting entitled 'We All Live in a Yellow Submarine,' which I won't be able to release until submarines become commonplace."

The door burst open and the manservant Barnum entered, dragging Chevie behind him. She was bound fast with coils of rope, but still struggling.

"What ho!" said Charismo. "This is unexpected."

"I found 'er in the chimney," said Barnum, tossing Chevie to the floor at Charismo's feet.

"Unexpected?" said Chevie, cheek burned by the carpet. "Didn't the spirits warn you?"

Charismo poked Chevie's shoulder with the tip of his pointed slipper so that she lay on her back. "That is not how it works"—he placed a finger to his temple—"Agent Savano of the Federal Bureau of Investigation."

Chevie sneered. "Hey, why don't you ask those spirits if they can tell you anything about Terry Carter, a crooked banker from New York City?"

Charismo shrieked at the mention of Carter's name, then kicked Chevie in the stomach, driving the air from her lungs.

"Put her on the chair," he ordered Barnum, sitting down to rub his toe. "Then leave us."

Barnum's hands were quick to the job, but his brow was puzzled. "Leave you, master? But this gal has strange maneuvering in her, and you are not yourself entirely, throwing kickings and such."

"She is tied, is she not?" said Charismo irritably. "Do as you are told, but wait outside the door. There will be some lifting before long."

Barnum threw Chevie a threatening look and left the room, muttering about how a man never knew where he was, and a little manners would not go astray.

"Apologies," said Charismo. "Sometimes Barnum forgets his place."

Chevie jerked herself upright in the chair. "Nice desk. Who gave you that? The spirits of cheap and vulgar?"

"I shall not be manipulated to anger," said Charismo. "The great Charismo rises above base emotions."

"How about Terry Carter? What does he do?"

Charismo toyed with a letter opener in the shape of a dagger. Or perhaps it was a dagger in the shape of a dagger. "Terry Carter is dead. He died almost thirty years ago, when I arrived here."

Chevie noticed that Riley was not reacting to any of this and seemed to be humming a Beatles song.

"What did you do to the boy?"

"Oh, him. I gave him a few drops of sodium thiopental and a little deadly nightshade," said Charismo conversationally. "I favor it as a mix. You speak the truth and then die. Don't worry about the lad. Riley will drop off to sleep and never wake up, which is about the best way to go in Victorian London. You're going to adore it."

Chevie struggled against her bonds, but they had been tied by a man who tied things up as part of his job description.

"The great Tibor Charismo. You're nothing but a common murderer."

Charismo seemed genuinely offended. "No. Absolutely not. I am the greatest human being since Leonardo da Vinci, whom I suspect may also have been a WARP veteran. I write, I compose, I *see*. In the twentieth century I was nothing, a Mob banker. Here, I am the darling of high society. Why on God's green earth would I ever go back?"

"I see how it could happen," said Chevie. "You knew the Mob would track little Terry down eventually. No matter how many of them you put away with your testimony, there would always be more wiseguys. But in Victorian London, you could really be somebody."

"Exactly," said Charismo. "And do you know how? I have a photographic memory. Everything I ever read, saw, or even heard, I remember forever. Simple as that."

"Genius," said Chevie, half meaning it.

Charismo rose to his feet. "Queen Victoria herself listens to my advice. As soon as the Feds told me I was moving to

Victorian London, I read everything I could about any subject I thought might be useful. I know things about world politics, sporting events, simple inventions, fashion trends. It's a gold mine."

Chevie took a few breaths to calm herself. "Okay, Terry, listen to me. Just let us go. Give the kid an antidote. Don't become a murderer on top of everything else."

"Become a murderer?" said Charismo, laughing. "This is Victorian London. Even with my gifts, you have to carve your way to the top, or hire a big strong Barnum to do it for you. When I found Barnum, he was bleeding to death in Newgate prison; now he is loyal to me unto the grave."

"Really?"

"No. I hired him in the pub, but I plan to use the Newgate story in my memoirs."

"You don't have to kill the boy, Charismo. I'm the law here. He's just a kid."

Charismo smiled, perching on the edge of the desk. "Oh, he's the one I need to kill most of all. You still haven't put it together fully, Agent, have you?"

"Oh, I think I understand most of it," said Chevie. "It's a pretty basic tale of human greed. Little Terry Carter decides he likes it in the Victorian era and so hires Albert Garrick to cut any ties to the future, specifically Agent Riley and his family."

Charismo showed no remorse. "That was not my fault. I was meant to be his priority, but, no, Agent Riley decides to fall in love. So I had little alternative but to order Garrick to kill Bill Riley and his precious family. No loose ends."

Chevie looked at him. "But you needed Bill Riley's Timekey?"

"Yes, indeed," said Charismo. "Garrick delivered it to me without ever suspecting what it was. How could he? All programmed and ready to suck Bill back to the twentieth century—the twenty-first now, I suppose. I have it secured safely, just in case I need to escape this time zone. There will always be medical procedures—chemotherapy, for example—that I may need to avail myself of. That is the only reason I have not disassembled the portals. Of course, I only recently found out where the portals were."

"Well, poor little Mob banker Terry wouldn't be told the locations. Information like that would be strictly need-to-know."

"Precisely. On the night I arrived, they hustled me out of there with a sack over my head. Can you believe it? In my condition?"

When he said the word *condition*, Charismo touched his mask lightly, and Chevie wondered again what precisely was under there.

"So, even with Agent Riley out of the way, you still needed to find Charles Smart and whatever portals there might be; otherwise you could never be sure that they wouldn't come after you."

"The alternative was keeping a low profile," explained Charismo. "And what was the point in doing that?"

"Yeah," said Chevie. "Why be a nobody in two centuries?"

"You're doing awfully well so far," said Charismo coldly,

adjusting his devil's mask. "Would you like to continue? Or should I kill you now?"

"It takes a while to build up your funds, but as soon as you can afford it you cultivate a relationship with Otto Malarkey, because only the Battering Rams have the network you need to find Charles Smart and the portals."

"All I had was a sketch of Smart, which I drew from memory, and a description of a basement with a bed mounted on a metal plate. Not much to go on."

Chevie took over the narrative. "It took years, but eventually the Rams found that Smart was actually living in this century in Bedford Square. And they followed him to Half Moon Street."

"I kept him under *surveillance*, as you Feds might say, until I was satisfied that Smart was the only one using the portals. No one was looking for him or coming for me."

"And you wanted to keep it that way. You wanted sole control of the wormhole, so Charles Smart had to go. And that's when you contacted Garrick again, to finish the job he began a decade ago."

"Yes. After all, my freedom to evolve was at stake."

Charismo leaned forward and parted Chevie's hair with his letter opener. "I had forgotten how much effort it is speaking with my fellow Americans. So confrontational."

"You made one mistake, Terry," said Chevie.

"Oh, I don't think so. After all, you are prostrate before me, as is the entire city."

"Garrick. You should never have hired him. He can't be controlled."

Charismo covered his smug smile with a kerchief. "Believe me, Garrick has been *controlled* into an early grave. Otto Malarkey has seen to that. He was the last direct connection between me and the future."

"Until we came along."

"Otto was supposed to kill anyone who arrived at either portal, but it is in his nature to try to squeeze a few extra shillings from every situation. Luckily I have a man in the Rams who is loyal to my gold, and he informed me there was activity in the Half Moon house. Can you imagine my surprise when one of the fugitives from Half Moon Street bore a striking resemblance to William Riley? It must be a coincidence, I told myself, and I almost believed it, until the boy himself revealed to me that his father was an FBI agent. So young Riley here is the only wild card in this game, and he is, as you can see, not really playing anymore."

Charismo clapped his hands, which seemed to be something of a trademark. "And so, the game is over, and Charismo has triumphed."

Riley moaned and spasmed in his chair.

"Come on, Carter!" said Chevie. "Cure the boy! Let him go. What harm can he do to you?"

"None whatsoever. Little Riley is harmless. And soon that will be a permanent condition."

Chevie's pulse pounded in her forehead. "That boy idolized you, and you've killed him."

Charismo fluttered his kerchief. "Well, you know what they say? A person should never meet his heroes. And I haven't killed him yet, he's simply dreaming. The poison is still in his stomach. He won't die for hours."

Riley *was* half-dreaming, and he would have loved to lose himself entirely to slumber, but something was glinting in his eye. The boy squinted, attempting to focus, but he could see nothing, except the small shining object on Chevie's finger. It was blurred and surrounded by a golden nimbus, until Charismo moved in front of the window and blocked the sunlight, bringing the golden object into relief.

It was a horseshoe ring.

*A horseshoe ring. There was a man with a horseshoe ring. Mr. Carter.*

In his dream state Riley was closer to his visions; he remembered that his father had protected the man wearing this ring, and this was enough to wake him slightly, just in time to hear Charismo say, "I was meant to be his priority, but, no, Agent Riley decides to fall in love. So I had little alternative but to order Garrick to kill Agent Riley and his precious family. No loose ends."

Bill Riley, thought Riley groggily. My dad.

Riley could not fathom the circumstances, but he had heard a confession, and the ring made him believe it was the truth.

With superhuman effort, he breathed himself back to the surface of consciousness. It took several moments, but finally he had the energy to act. Riley dragged himself from the chair and flailed at Charismo, striking out clumsily.

"Oh, please," tutted Charismo. "This is embarrassing. I am embarrassed for both of you, really."

He placed a hand on Riley's forehead and tipped him over backward. Riley fell awkwardly, knocking over a marble-topped table and sending the Farspeak skittering to the end of its wire.

"Now look what you have done!" said Charismo, mildly irritated.

"You animal!" shouted Chevie, lurching from the chair; but she was well trussed and succeeded only in toppling herself onto the floor, cracking her head on a gryphon wing on the way down.

Charismo rolled his eyes. "Oh, now look, there is blood on Tibor's special desk. I shall be exceedingly glad when you are dead, Miss Savano. I had hoped to interrogate you as I did the boy, perhaps learn how the world has turned since my day, but now I think I shall forgo that pleasure and proceed directly to the endgame."

Chevie spat blood on the rug. "What about your queen? How would she feel about all these murders?"

"Old Vic?" said Charismo. "I do not care a fig for Her rheumatic Majesty, beyond the fact that her patronage secures my status. At any rate, she will die confused at the dawn of the new century, and her daughter the following year, which will ring the closing bell on the house of Hanover."

"And what of your precious Duke of Westminster?"

Charismo laughed bitterly. "That old coot will be gone before Christmas. Would that he should survive another twenty years, as it is extremely convenient to have the ear of the richest man in Britain. But no, the outdoor life will sow the seeds of bronchitis, and that shall do the duffer in."

Charismo knelt and tousled Chevie's hair. "Do you know, I would have preferred to have kept you alive. We could have spoken of the future. I have so many plans. One, for example, is that I could change the course of wars. Imagine how different World War One would be if the Germans were warned not to torpedo the *Lusitania*. America would never enter the war, and by 1918 England would be a German colony, with Tibor Charismo very nicely placed in its court. That is just one of my many ideas."

"You're mad," said Chevie, trying hard to keep Charismo's attention on her. She suspected that Riley had pulled a fast one, in spite of his drugged state. And even if his actions were accidental, they could work in Chevie's favor, as long as Terry Carter didn't turn around.

"Mad, delusional, comatose. Who cares? I am happy, and I intend to remain happy for as long as possible."

Charismo dinged a service bell on his desk and Barnum entered, still a little sulky from his recent dismissal.

"Oh, you wants me back in the room, does you, master?"

"Don't be petulant, Barnum. Your boxer's countenance does not suit the expression."

"Very good, master. What's the drill with these two? I was

thinking a quick stab over the kitchen sink, for to catch the blood, then into a sack and roly-poly down the embankment."

Charismo tick-tocked his letter opener, considering this. "No, Barnum. I want these two to disappear entirely. Not so much as a hair left."

"Then there are two avenues we can advance along. One, there's my old army pal and his pig farm by Newport. Pigs will eat from crown to toe, brain and bone—makes no differ to a pig, as we know from those two gypsies last year, master."

"I think not," said Charismo. "The last time you tramped pig dung all over my carpets. What is our second choice?"

"Burning," said Barnum simply. "I chop 'em in the kitchen and feed 'em slow into the furnace. Takes a few days and is grisly labor, but once the job is done, all the king's horses couldn't put these two bad eggs together again."

Charismo giggled. "Nicely put, Mr. Barnum. You do make me smile. The furnace it is, but do your stabbing business in the kitchen."

"Very good, master," said Barnum, and he slung Chevie over one shoulder. "Can you manage for an hour while I make a start on the butchering?"

"You go ahead," said Charismo magnanimously. "I shall be perfectly fine. . . . Oh, perhaps you might bring some more cakes when you have finished cutting. Tibor is peckish."

"More cakes. Of course, master."

Charismo winked at Chevie. "*Master*. I get shivers, every time."

To Tibor's utter surprise, Chevie had enough spirit for one

last comment. She looked the WARP witness directly in the eye and said, "You talk too much."

A statement not just of opinion but of fact, as it would turn out.

Barnum swung Riley by the belt in an arc toward his other shoulder. However, as soon as the manservant's hand was free, the poisoned boy somehow found the strength to roll off and land on Charismo's chest.

"Murderer!" he slurred. "You killed my family."

"Eeek!" said Charismo. "Get him off me, Barnum. He could have lice."

Had Riley been more alert, he might have been able to land a painful or even fatal blow, but in his drugged state it was all he could do to squirm a little and pat Charismo's chest like an infant.

"C'mere, boy," said Barnum, and he reclaimed his prisoner with strong fingers, tossing him back onto his free shoulder.

"Take care, Barnum," said a shaken Charismo, checking his mask. "Even a dying dog can be dangerous."

"Sorry, master," said Barnum, inserting the toe of his boot into a crack in the door and nudging it open. "I should have taken more care that you were not overpowered by the incapacitated child that you had just poisoned to death."

Charismo glared after his manservant as he left, wondering if perhaps he should begin docking his wages for insolence.

Barnum bundled the condemned pair into the dumbwaiter in the adjoining room and winched them down toward the kitchen.

As the elevator dropped into its shaft, Chevie heard Charismo's voice drift through: "You are such a slacker, Barnum. The dumbwaiter, honestly."

The small compartment creaked slowly toward the basement, and Riley moaned and tried to stretch, which was impossible in the confined space. The air was heated, the walls stank of meat, and the box seemed incapable of sustaining their weight. Though she could not see it, Chevie felt the shaft yawn below them, waiting for the box to pop its cord and drop down and down.

"Hey, Riley," Chevie said, nudging the boy's leg with her elbow. "Are you okay?"

Riley was not alert enough to reply.

*I wonder, has the poison begun to do its work? No. Charismo said he had hours left. There is still time.*

The dumbwaiter came to an abrupt halt, and the trapped pair could do nothing but breathe recycled air and wait until Barnum pulled them out. Chevie was first.

He tossed her on the wooden worktop like a side of beef, then tied on an apron and ran his fingers across a row of kitchen knives.

It's funny, thought Chevie. I am not afraid. That is because I still believe we will get out of this alive, in spite of all the evidence.

Barnum selected the largest knife, with a stained bone handle and serrated blade.

"Ah, Julia," he said to the knife. "You knew I would choose you."

He talks to his knives, thought Chevie. I bet Garrick would love this guy.

Barnum froze suddenly, like a deer that has heard a sound not meant for the forest.

*What does he hear?*

Then Chevie heard it too: a trundle of carriages, but also the clatter of marching feet.

"What now?" said Barnum, then cocked his head, waiting for the commotion to rumble past. But it did not. Instead, the cavalcade came to an abrupt stop outside Charismo's residence.

"Next door," muttered Barnum to himself. "Surely the militia have business next door?"

But it was not next door, as was made abundantly clear by a barked command from outside: "Halt! Charismo residence, blue door! Ready the cannon."

"Cannon?" said Barnum, in a voice that was surely two octaves above his usual register.

The manservant dropped his beloved blade, drew a revolver from inside his coat, and raced across the kitchen and through the service doors.

The doors had not yet finished flapping when a thundering explosion rattled the very foundations, channeling compressed air through the house's stairwells and passageways. The blast threw Barnum and his gun back through the service doors. The six-shooter pinwheeled across the kitchen, shattering a wall tile with its butt, then skittered into a sink.

Barnum himself was not in good shape. His waistcoat

had been shredded, and a hundred small wounds on his chest allowed his life's blood to leak onto the wooden floor.

Barnum had seen enough of death to know that his number was up. He turned his gaze laboriously to where Chevie lay on the worktop.

He attempted to speak, but before he could get it out, a final rattle signaled his departure for the next world.

Chevie rolled herself from the worktop, landing with a thump on her shoulder, which did not break.

*Lucky break, or lucky non-break.*

Barnum's battered face was two inches from hers on the cold floor, and his blank stare motivated her to keep moving in spite of the pain in her shoulder.

*Find the knife,* she urged herself. *Find Julia.*

It was not far away, jutting from between the floorboards, like Excalibur from the stone. Embedded where Barnum had dropped it.

Another stroke of luck, Chevie thought.

She wriggled like a snake toward the knife.

*Come on, Julia. I hope you're sharp.*

She was. Once Chevie got a palm on either side of the knife, it took seconds to saw through the rope securing her wrists and, with her hands free, the rest of her bonds could be sliced off easily.

Overhead was regimented chaos. Chevie could hear the battle roar of a dozen troops as they stampeded through the house, searching for Charismo. Their tread knocked dust from the fractured ceiling, and one gas jet on the wall seemed to catch fire spontaneously, shooting a blue flame across the kitchen.

We need to get out of here, thought Chevie.

She heard footsteps split off from the others and descend the steps to the kitchen.

Chevie grabbed Barnum's gun from the sink and squashed herself inside the dumbwaiter next to Riley, back into the oppressive heat and stale food stink, closing the hatch behind her.

Through a crack she saw a soldier's black boots and pants push through the door. He strode briskly around the room, turning quickly as he looked behind the table and chairs. He paused over Barnum's corpse, checking that the giant had indeed passed on.

Riley moaned in his half-conscious state, and Chevie stuffed her knee in his mouth, stifling whatever noise he might make next.

Luckily for the concealed pair, the soldier was still a little battle-deaf from the cannon's roar, and he missed the muffled sound.

"Big," he said loudly, nudging Barnum's corpse with his toe. "Big, big." Then he snapped to and exited the room.

Chevie waited till the sound of the soldier's footsteps had faded, then she yanked the leather strap, opening the hatch, and backed herself out into the kitchen.

Riley was moaning when she tugged him out of the tiny space, but also smiling.

"Agent Pretty," he said. "A kiss from pretty Annie Birch."

Boys are the same down through the years, thought Chevie, then punched Riley in the stomach.

"Sorry, kid," she said as Riley doubled over, retching. "One more should do it."

She punched him again and stood clear as the boy vomited a stream of half-digested *macarons* and, she hoped, deadly nightshade onto the floorboards.

"Okay," she said, to herself mostly. "He should make it now. I hope."

Chevie swabbed Riley's face as best she could with a damp cloth from the sink, then she helped the boy stagger to the kitchen door, which led conveniently to the back of the house.

We need to get out of here, thought Chevie again, grabbing a heavy overcoat from a hook by the door. But I wish I could stay long enough to see the look on Charismo's face. I bet the spirits didn't warn him about this.

The look on Charismo's face was a blend of disbelief and petulant terror, an unusual cocktail of emotions for a set of features to display. The result was that Tibor appeared to be sucking on an invisible bottle when Colonel Jeffers of the Knightsbridge Barracks strode into his office, flanked by two privates and a doctor.

Once they were certain that Charismo was unarmed and alone, the soldiers relaxed a fraction, though the barrels of the privates' Lee-Enfield repeater rifles were rock steady and aimed squarely at Charismo's torso.

Charismo fluttered his kerchief, as though that could deflect bullets from their course.

"Am I in danger, Colonel?" he inquired querulously. "Has the duke sent you to protect me? Is there a credible threat?"

"There is a threat, sir," replied Jeffers. "Indeed there is, and I have the misfortune to be staring directly at it."

Charismo's hanky fluttered like a hummingbird's wing. "Right at it? I am the threat? Tibor Charismo threatens? And whom does he threaten, Captain? Answer me that."

Jeffers did not answer, but he followed a cable on the floor until his eyes lighted on the Farspeak, which lay where Riley had tipped it.

"Somebody wishes to speak to you, sir," he said, picking up the device and holding it out to Charismo.

Charismo understood then, and his curled mustache quivered. "I do not wish to converse at present," he said, almost childishly.

"I advise you to take it," said Jeffers firmly, and Charismo correctly inferred that to refuse again would have dire consequences. He accepted the Farspeak with trembling hands and pressed the transmitter close to his mouth.

"Hello? Your Grace?"

On the other end was the rattling breathing of a pipe smoker, then: "I am dreadfully disappointed, Tibor. Dreadfully."

Charismo tried to talk his way out of it. "Your Grace, I can only imagine what you must have thought. Sometimes when I am in the grip of the spirits, my words are not as I would choose."

"Silence!" thundered the Duke of Westminster. "I am to die! The queen is to die. The rheumatic queen, for whom you do not care a fig! The end of the house of Hanover."

"Perhaps I overstepped the mark," admitted Charismo.

"Overstepped the mark? You plan to aid the Germans in a war against Britannia! Germany is our friend. This is high treason, nothing less."

"It was idle chatter. A passing notion."

"Imagine the scandal. Imagine the heartache this would inflict on Her Majesty, at her age. Her own spiritualist conspiring against her. *My* blasted spiritualist. We trusted you, Tibor. Damn you, sir."

Charismo thought fast. "A trial would cause considerable scandal."

The duke chuckled, the laugh of a harsh man. "There will be no trial, sir. I have declared you insane and, while you languish inside Bethlem Lunatic Asylum, I shall systematically erase you from history. Your works will be unofficially banned, your books burned, your songs will never again be heard on the music-hall stage. We shall see which of us survives to see the new century." A loud click from the earpiece signaled that the conversation was over.

"No!" Charismo protested to Jeffers. "No, I will not stand for it. I am Tibor Charismo."

Jeffers drew himself to attention. "You are a traitor, sir, possibly foreign to boot. The madhouse is too good for you."

"This is all a mistake, Colonel. If you search downstairs

in the kitchen, you will find my manservant. He is the real criminal here."

"We found your manservant. He, at least, died with honor."

Reality finally dropped on Charismo like an anvil from the sky. "Barnum dead? I am lost."

Jeffers stepped close. "There is an option, sir, but I would be amazed if you availed yourself of it. You may accept my challenge and we can end this affair right now." The colonel took off his left glove and struck Charismo across the cheek, causing his mask to fly off.

Jeffers stepped back in momentary horror, but his stiff upper lip quickly reasserted itself.

"My God, man. You are an animal."

The left side of Tibor's face was covered with green and brown reptilian scales, which seemed to change color as he moved.

"It was the wormhole!" he howled. "Quantum mutation. The professor swore it would not happen to me."

Jeffers clicked his fingers. "Take him. I will not fight an animal."

Tibor continued his rant, even as the privates dragged him from the room to the ambulance outside.

"Make sure he is locked away from the other inmates," said Jeffers, stamping on the Farspeak until the casing gave up its entrails of wires and fuses. "And send up some squaddies. I want everything taken from this house and burned."

Charismo's cries echoed through the ruins of his devastated hallway and set the ambulance horses a-whinnying in distress.

Albert Garrick watched events unfold, leaning forward on the park bench in rapt attention. One minute all was quiet on Grosvenor Square, and the next a squad of Her Majesty's finest had double-timed it to the front door with an honest-to-God cannon in tow, followed by a black carriage.

"Well, blimey," he said, forgetting his carefully cultivated accent for a moment. "This is a right royal turnup."

Whatever maneuver was about to be employed would certainly not go off half-cocked. There were enough troops here to fight the Afghans.

The soldiers expertly swiveled their cannon and blew the door in, sending a flock of starlings soaring into the sky.

*A battle in London town. How extraordinary!*

It occurred to Garrick that the presence of all these soldiers would hamper his efforts to cancel Charismo's contract with the Rams.

*And all because I neglected to kill Riley in his bed all those years ago. Could that be the whole reason? Would Charismo pit himself against a man of my caliber over the life of a child?*

Suddenly Garrick remembered the first time he had spied a Timekey.

*Riley's father had one on his person. I took it from his corpse and delivered it to Charismo. He asked for the device specifically.*

This was indeed a revelation and for a moment Garrick held his breath, accessing both his own and Felix Smart's memories to assemble the pieces of this quantum jigsaw.

*Riley's father was FBI. Why would England's most famous man want an FBI agent murdered?*

It occurred to Garrick then that Mr. Tibor Charismo had seen the future and was benefitting from his knowledge.

*But not anymore. Charismo has gone too far with someone, and now the military are involved, which would suggest a government connection, perhaps even the monarchy.*

This pleased Garrick greatly, as he had always thought the man a trifle smug and had never liked his music. *Another Brick in Yonder Wall.* Honestly.

The spirit of Felix Smart suddenly made the connection, and Garrick physically reeled with the realization.

He knew that song, or rather Agent Smart knew it, because it originated in the future. Tibor Charismo had not only been to the future, he belonged there.

Garrick closed his eyes, focusing on his train of thought. He pictured Charismo's face, then allowed his memory to make it younger and draw on a ratty beard.

Tibor Charismo was Terry Carter, the missing witness. Agent Smart had the file in his desk. William Riley had been his handler.

This put a completely different complexion on the matter. Charismo could not be allowed to talk to anyone. If he had a Timekey, then he could demonstrate its workings, and Garrick could become a fugitive once more.

I must act now, he thought. Carpe diem. The circumstances are far from ideal, but the risk is acceptable.

Garrick's on-the-hoof plan involved subduing the carriage driver and then hopefully absconding with Charismo in the back.

*He might even believe I am rescuing him.*

Garrick smiled grimly. This misapprehension would not last for long.

The blossoming scheme dried up and withered when two soldiers emerged from the house with Charismo suspended between them, his short legs bicycling the air.

*There is no time. No time.*

Garrick knew that, even with his speed, he could not vault the railings and overpower the driver in time.

But all was not lost. Garrick was nothing if not adaptable. He stepped behind the trunk of a large hawthorn bush and pulled his laser-sighted pistol. It was a shame to waste a bullet on the likes of Charismo, but at least it would be only one.

Garrick sighted quickly along the barrel and placed a red dot over Charismo's heart.

*I will never know the full truth of why you wished me dead*, he thought. *It is a pity we could not chat, you and I, but better a niggling mystery than a dangerous loose end.*

Garrick's finger was about to squeeze the trigger when he noticed that the carriage was actually a secure ambulance, with the Bethlem Lunatic Asylum logo inked on the side.

They are taking him to Bedlam, Garrick realized.

He watched bemused as Charismo was stripped down and roughly bundled into an asylum work shirt. His clothes were tossed onto a growing pile of his possessions on the basement stairwell, which was doused with lamp oil and set alight.

Charismo's Timekey is busted now, if he kept it, Garrick realized with some satisfaction. *Tibor can talk of wormholes to his heart's content, and all it will earn him is a beating from the screws.*

Garrick pocketed his gun and strolled casually toward the far side of the park.

*I will come to find you, Tibor,* he thought. *Before very long I will know all of your secrets. After all, you don't need them anymore.*

In seconds, Garrick's mind was once again focused on his main mission to find Chevie and Riley, with absolutely no idea that he had come within a hair's breadth of snagging them for the second time.

*By this time, my spies will be scouring the city,* he thought, *all craving the reward for information on the boy with the odd eyes and his Injun companion.*

Although slightly aggrieved at being denied the opportunity to question Charismo, Garrick judged it to be a fair morning's work, all in all.

*One more enemy safely out of the way,* he thought, whistling the opening bars of *Another Brick in Yonder Wall.*

*Only two remain.*

## 11 » THE OLD NICHOL

THE OLD NICHOL ROOKERY, BETHNAL GREEN,
LONDON, 1898

CHEVIE TRIED TO FLAG DOWN A CAB, BUT SHE was filthy from her trips up and down Charismo's chimney and no driver would halt until she stood half in the road, waving Malarkey's gold purse. As the hansom clattered away, Chevie slumped on the seat beside Riley and wondered where in the universe they could go in order to earn a minute's respite. Her ribs ached from the various scrapes that Victorian London had inflicted on her person, and she realized that somewhere in the midst of this misadventure she had developed a constant ringing in her left ear.

Riley was recovering, but in no shape to journey far. They

needed to find a place to hide until she could figure out their next move.

It would be irresponsible to allow Garrick to run amok in London with all the knowledge in his head, which he would definitely not be using to put an end to war and starvation. Simply put: Garrick had to be stopped. But how? She had no idea. This was Riley's world, and they would have to put their heads together on a problem as big as Garrick. And to do that they would have to lie low somewhere until they were fit enough to fight back.

Chevie slapped Riley's cheek gently.

"Come on, Riley. Wake up, partner. There must be somewhere this lunatic won't follow us. Where is Garrick afraid to go?"

She was forced to repeat the question several times before it penetrated Riley's addled skull, but as soon as he understood the question, he knew the answer: the Old Nichol. His face paled and his hands shook at the very idea.

"There is a place," he said, then coughed long and harsh. "Somewhere Garrick has sworn he would never go. He would rather smash his artist's hands with a mallet, said he, than return to the rookeries of Old Nichol."

Chevie sat straight in the hansom's seat, brushing the soot from her shirt. "Off we go, then. The Old Nichol it is."

Riley was not so eager, for to see the devil afraid of a place is a powerful incentive never to pay that place a visit. He gazed at the road ahead, remembering how Garrick had described the Old Nichol.

"Garrick told me that the air in Old Nichol is charged with sulfur, enough so that the rats and small dogs will turn snow white and asphyxiate."

Chevie sat back beside her traveling partner. "Rats turning white is never good," she admitted.

"At the rear of each tenement or rookery there is a pile of raw sewage, which is fed by the entire building. The only creatures who thrive in Old Nichol are those that feed on offal—you know, animal entrails."

Chevie felt her stomach sour. Offal-thriving did not sound like much of a way to get by.

Riley remembered something else. "Old Nichol is slow death for all. Garrick told me of a strongman who fell on hard times and took a bunk there. In six months he had wasted away to nothing and died of blood poisoning from bedsores. They buried him in a flour sack."

"Oh, come on," objected Chevie. "We're not getting married and raising kids there. You just need a few hours' sleep to get the poison out of your system, then we can figure out a way to defeat Garrick."

"It takes only a moment to suck down whooping cough."

This was a sobering statement and almost turned Chevie from her purpose, but she held on to her reasoning. Garrick would not set foot in this Old Nichol hellhole, so they must, if only for a single night.

She rapped on the cab's roof.

"Hey, buddy. Take us to the Old Nichol."

The cabbie slid back an aperture and stuck his head in the

hole. "Beggin' your pardon, miss. This heat have me addled. I could've sworn you said *Old Nichol*."

"You got it, pal."

The cabbie's luxuriant eyebrows arched like small fish. "Old Nichol? West End to the Old Nichol? Is the tourist having me on, young sir?"

"No," replied Riley gloomily. "She ain't."

The cabbie spat into the street. "Well, beggin' yer pardon, but I ain't taking you into the stink. The bleeders would have the shoes off me mare. I'll drop the pair of ye at Bethnal Green, and you can risk yer own skins from there."

Poverty and crime are never very distant in London. Even in the modern metropolis, cast an eye down any alley and there is an unfortunate making himself as comfortable as the pavement allows. But in the nineteenth century, the Old Nichol rookery had been saturated so thoroughly by destitution and neglect that not even a postcard-sized area was exempt. Each building was a tenement, each citizen was crooked with disease, and every occupation dealt with the immediate preservation of life. Even the climate seemed worse there, creating a chill, damp principality inside the boundaries of London proper.

As Chevie Savano and Riley walked along Boundary Street, all hope of a bright future seeped down into their boots and onto the uneven cobbles. There wasn't a shantytown in the modern world that could compare with the Old Nichol for sheer grim despair.

Walls of greasy bricks rose from the cracked paving

stones, story plonked upon story. Windows, apparently placed at random, were rarely glazed, and were curtained by busted crates or flapping rags. Street stalls were piled with decayed objects that would have been on the rubbish heap in any other market. The fruit was gray and pulped, the bread tinged with green, and rock hard.

Even the people in this place seemed the offspring of a different, meaner god. Gone was the irrepressible cockney spirit, and in its place the hacking cough or the threatening leer. The inhabitants moved with a peculiar shuffling gait, shoulders hunched and elbows tight to their sides, protecting themselves as much as possible.

Chevie could not keep the shock from her voice. "This is . . . It's like hell on earth."

Riley hung on to her elbow. "We need to get ourselves inside. Put some solid planks between us and Old Nichol before nightfall. I must get my head down."

A slovenly woman stood, elbows on a half-door, staring vacantly into the street.

Riley approached her, ignoring the filthy urchins nudging his knees like cleaner fish.

"Any spare digs, ma'am? We are requiring a lurk for the night."

The woman eyed them suspiciously from underneath a fuzz of curls.

"Chink?"

Riley nodded tightly, hiding his nausea. "At the ready. We have firearms, too, but only shot enough for the bluebottles."

*Firearms* was a bit of an exaggeration. They had Barnum's revolver and six shots only.

The woman barked with laughter, and there was sour gin on her breath. "Bluebottles? I ain't seen the law in here since ninety-two, when they tried to take in the traitor Giles. What a morning that was. There was enough blue blood in the gutters to wash out the cholera."

"Have you got a room or not?" Riley insisted.

"I gots the loft spare. Cove gave up the ghost on Wednesday. Someone took him to the heap, I think."

"How much?"

A crafty light sparked in the stinking woman's eye. "I would take a florin."

"I'll wager you would, if I would be sap enough to fork one over. I have a shiny sixpence here, which you can take or not. If it's not, then we'll be moving along down the street for ourselves."

The woman rubbed a finger along a sparsely populated bottom gum. "I shall be taking that shiny sixpence, young gent."

Riley handed it across. "And warn any likely lads about the firearms," he said. "I hate to waste shots on fellow killers, but if anyone tries to crack our drum, I will make an exception. Also, my companion here is a black-magic witch, and she will set fire ants a-crawling in yer brain."

The woman flicked the coin with her yellowed thumbnail and listened to it sing.

"Fire ants," says she, unimpressed. "I've had those bleeders inside me head for years."

• • •

Riley and Chevie picked their way down a hallway where the floor could have been removed from a salt-warped shipwreck: the boards jostled with each other for space and rose or fell like the ends of a seesaw, depending on the point of pressure. The passage was lined with young criminals—a collection of snakesmen, smashers, palmers, hoisters, and prowlers the likes of which would rarely be seen this side of Newgate's watchtower. These boys smoked what they could find, which seemed to be mostly rolled-up strips of wallpaper that burned out after a drag or two and covered the lungs with paste, which made running from the coppers more troublesome than it should have been for a group of young feller-me-lads.

Every one of those boys gave Riley the evil eye on his way past, but they did not know what to make of Chevie, with her shining hair and white teeth.

"You are like an angel to these poor coves," Riley whispered to her on the stairs. "Seeing as they do not know you like I do."

One of the urchins had the bottle to clear his throat, calling from the upper landing, "Here, miss. Is you the Injun princess what humbled them Rams?"

Riley stepped forth, trying to appear more energetic and aggressive than he felt. "Aye, this is the very specimen. She ain't got none of the Queen's English, so I does her talking. She's high-strung, too, so you gotta approach her careful and always frontwise."

"My name is Bob Winkle," said the boy, who could have been any color under the dirt that encrusted his skin, and who had about as much fat on his bones as a tinker's ferret. He was no taller than a ten-year-old, but his voice and face were older. "You need anyfing? Booze, bread, or contraband? Bob runs a clean service. Robs to order, too, whatever you like."

Riley reckoned that young Winkle's service was about as clean as his face.

"If we have need, we will rap on the floor. But if you come up, no arm waving, or the Injun princess is like to rip yer throat clean out."

The boys covered their throats and cleared a path, waving Chevie through like royalty.

They mounted the stairs toward their rented loft, steeling their hearts against the glazed eyes of the residents they encountered on the climb. Young girls brawled, dragging clumps out of each other's matted hair. Grandfathers sat wedged in corners, sucking on empty pipes and swearing into space, and everywhere the clamor of despair rose through the house, funneled skyward by the stairwell like a cry to heaven.

Three flights up, they arrived at a door at the end of an uncommonly rickety set of steps. Riley twisted the wooden knob and was not surprised to find their room unlocked. A heavy brick stood against the wall inside, to be used as a stopper if the occupants required some privacy; but what would be the point when the walls of the loft were pocked with sledge-hammer holes?

Chevie hurried in and hefted the brick.

"Come on," she urged Riley. "Let's get this secured."

Riley obliged with some reluctance. "I never dreamed these poor people could sink so low."

The brick scraped across the floor as Chevie wedged it against the door. "You've never been here?"

"Never. I fled to Saint Giles once and thought that a proper slum, but I've seen nothing like this before. I understand now why Garrick vowed never to return."

Chevie tore brown paper from one corner of the small window to let some air into the rank chamber, though it was hardly worth the effort.

Riley wrapped his arms around himself, sinking to the rotting wooden floor. "We are between the workhouse and the grave here," he said quietly. "Londoners fear Old Nichol because it awaits us, each and every one." He shuddered. "I should not have brought you here, Chevie, and you a lady."

Chevie draped her arm around his shoulder, moving close for warmth. "No. We had to come." Chevie remembered the question she had been meaning to ask Riley for the past few hours. "Tell me something, Riley. Did you knock over the Farspeak on purpose?"

Riley stopped himself from shivering long enough to answer. "Yes. Charismo handed us the rope to hang him."

"Yes," agreed Chevie. "That guy talked too much."

"He had my poor mum killed," said Riley, sniffing. "And my dad—he was one of your lot."

"I know," said Chevie. "Special Agent William Riley. I read his file. He was quite a boxer. Before he disappeared, he was known for having fast hands."

"I have fast hands. Garrick said he never seen hands faster."

"We will need your hands, and your wits, if we are to defeat Garrick."

Riley huddled close for warmth and so that his nose would register Chevie's healthy odors rather than his rank surroundings.

"But what do we have to work with? Everything's gone. Even the Timekey."

"Smart's key is gone," admitted Chevie. "But I have another one."

She reached down the leg of her riding boot and tugged out a Timekey by the lanyard.

"Charismo's," guessed Riley. "You took it when you lifted his ring?"

"I did take it, but it's not Charismo's."

Riley's eyes widened. "My dad's. Bill Riley's key."

"That's right," said Chevie, passing the key to Riley. "Your dad is still watching over you."

This notion seemed to give Riley comfort and determination.

"We must use our time in this dreadful place to plot. We cannot take Garrick in a straight brawl."

Chevie grunted, staring straight ahead. "Maybe not, but there's more than one way to skin a cat."

"Shhh," warned Riley. "Else people will believe that there's a cat in here; then we will have dinner guests."

Chevie groaned. "Cats? People here eat cats?"

Riley nodded. "If you let them, they would eat your boots."

"We have so got to get out of here."

"We will," said Riley. "You saved me in your world. Now I will save you in mine."

This was not simply idle babble. Riley clasped his own father's Timekey to his chest and judged it a good omen. Now they had hope. Now they had something to build a plan around.

*You taught me well, Albert Garrick,* thought Riley, seeing the assassin's face in his mind's eye. *Now we must see if your own lessons can be turned against you.*

In spite of the wretchedness of their surroundings and the constant assault on their senses, Chevie and Riley somehow managed to drop into a fitful sleep for a few hours.

They woke simultaneously, feeling both starved and disgusted by the idea of eating food that had been prepared in this place. Especially meat, as Chevie had noticed a suspicious absence of rats. The sulfur-infused air had set their heads throbbing and stripped their throats of moisture.

"We need to buy some water," said Chevie.

"Not here," advised Riley. "A delicate gut like yours could not stomach Old Nichol water. It would be out again soon enough, one road or the other."

Chevie did not ask for details, and she knew that being ill was not something she could risk right now.

"Okay. No water, spoilsport. You go back to sleep and let me think."

Riley wriggled closer. "I am also thinking. Garrick has given me gifts that he may not expect me to use."

"If you have an idea, please share."

"I have the seed of an idea," said Riley. "It needs . . . watering."

Chevie may have chuckled or possibly shivered.

They sat without speaking for a while.

"Can I ask a question?" said Riley, minutes after Chevie was certain he'd fallen asleep.

"Ask away," said Chevie.

"In advance I beg you not to be insulted, for I do respect you."

"Oh, I love these questions. Go on."

Riley considered his phrasing. "Chevie, I heard how those agents from the future spoke to you. Why do you want to stay in the FBI when they don't seem to want you? And how does someone of your years, and a female to boot, nab herself a position with the bluebottles?"

"That's more than one question. That's more or less my life story you're asking for."

Riley moved closer in case there was a candle's worth of heat to be had. "You saw my life in the tunnel, Chevron. I think you could speak of yours. We are close now, are we not?"

"We are close," agreed Chevie. She had never been closer to anyone. She was bonded to this boy by trauma. "Okay, I'll tell you about me."

Riley did not speak, but elbowed her softly in the midriff, which Chevie decided to interpret as *Go ahead*.

"You know I'm an orphan, like you. After my folks were gone, I was put in the foster system, but I was never adopted—too old and too loud, they said. Apparently that made me just perfect for another family, a much bigger one: the Federal Bureau of Investigation. The FBI was putting a program together in conjunction with Homeland Security to stop terrorist cells from getting a grip on the minds of high-school kids. And what better way to guard our schools than with undercover juvenile agents? Sounds crazy, right? Hollywood crazy. But they got funding from a CIA slush fund, if you can believe that, and they picked half a dozen orphans from California for a pilot scheme. We were trained in a place called Quantico and then inserted in a school." Chevie paused to check that Riley was still awake, half hoping that he would not be. "Any questions so far, kid?"

Riley stirred. "Just one. What is *Hollywood crazy*?"

A good question. "You like those adventure books, Riley. Well, *Hollywood crazy* is something so wild that it wouldn't seem out of place in an H. G. Wells story."

"I see. Carry on."

Chevie shifted a little on the boards, trying for at least a modicum of comfort. "My target was an Iranian family with four kids in the school. I was supposed to cozy up to the kids, get into their circle, and call the office if they had any terrorist plans. A simple observe-and-report mission. No weapons for teenagers, you understand. So I did what I was told, acted friendly, got close. And I realized that these kids weren't interested in terrorizing anyone—they just wanted to make it through high school, like the rest of us. If anything, *they* were the ones being terrorized. We had a group of real sweethearts in our school who couldn't tell the difference between Saudi, Iraqi, and Iranian, and couldn't care less. One night a Jeep full of these guys corners my Iranians outside a theater. It got real ugly real fast. One of them pulls a weapon, starts putting shots into the asphalt."

"I can guess what happened," said Riley. "You did not take kindly to this behavior."

Chevie scowled. "No, I did not. I twisted that gun out of his hand, but not before he managed to put a ricochet into his own leg."

"It appears to me as though you were something of a heroine."

"Yeah, you would think that, except I got a little carried away and fired a warning shot overhead."

"That does not sound so serious."

"No, except now the kid claims that I shot him. And I have gunshot residue on my hand, and some joker with a camera phone captures everything on film, but from a crappy angle that shows me doing all my martial arts but not the kid shooting himself."

"Ah. Gunshot residue sounds like evidence that Sherlock Holmes would look for."

"Exactly, or should I say, elementary. So now it's all over the news how there's a kid with a gun and a badge in a high school. It gets all the way to the senate. The Bureau realizes its teen-agent scheme is at best unconstitutional and at worst illegal, so quickly and quietly retires all the other kids."

"But Agent Chevron Savano has found her family and does not wish to retire."

"That's right. I don't want to go, and they can't force me out just yet because there is a committee looking into the whole thing and I'm not supposed to exist. So they ship me off to London, and I think you know the rest."

Riley did not comment outright, and once again Chevie believed he had fallen asleep until he said, "If we are to deal with Garrick, you will need to hold your temper."

Chevie felt a weight of responsibility settle on her mind like a vise. This was a big moment for both of them. Riley had never voiced the opinion that it was even possible to be saved from the devil Garrick.

"But," continued Riley, "this is a plan we should make together. After all, we fight for both our lives. We are brothers in this."

"Agreed," said Chevie. "So tell me about this seed we have to water."

Riley spoke and Chevie realized that this kid was even smarter than she had guessed.

When he had come to a full stop, Chevie commented, "A little harebrained, Riley, and I don't see how we can do it alone."

Riley rapped on the floor with the heel of his boot, sending echoes tumbling through the building. "I know a boy who runs a clean operation and will work for coin."

• • •

When the scheme had been hammered as straight as it could ever be, Riley sent Bob Winkle and his crew to fetch their provisions, and he joined Chevie in the corner of the room where the wall sweated a sickly sweet heat that warmed their fingers when they wormed them between the bricks.

"Winter would be worse," said Riley. "We would not last a night."

"No HDTV either," said Chevie, and began to laugh. After a puzzled moment, Riley joined in, not knowing what HDTV was, but happy to have any excuse for mirth.

When the poisonous air forced them to stop taking such gulps, their laughter petered out and the hubbub from beyond their window once again filled the room.

Chevie held Riley's hands inside the makeshift vent.

"You know that we're on borrowed time?" said Riley. "Even though Garrick won't come in here, he can pay those that will."

"We move as soon as Bob gets back," said Chevie. "Don't worry. It's a good plan. It will work."

"It must," said Riley, squeezing her fingers tightly. "There will be no second chances with Garrick."

There was a knock on the door.

"I gots a message fer the Injun princess," said a reedy voice.

Chevie opened the door and there stood a consumptive boy with blood on his gums and the rattle of phlegm in his windpipe.

Chevie dragged the boy inside, then pinned him to the wall

for a quick frisk. Garrick would not be above booby-trapping a child. He would probably consider it funny.

"Don't rip me froat out, miss. I only done it for the sweety."

The boy had nowhere to conceal anything, and there was nothing concealed. In his hand he held a square of brown packing paper and on it was carefully drawn a window.

The message was clear: *Go to the window.*

Sure, thought Chevie. Like I'm going to the window.

But she did, ducking underneath the sill, cocking one eye at the ripped corner of paper, peering out at the sun rising through the pearly fog, scanning the rooftops.

She could see nothing odd. Nothing, that is, odder than a view of the nineteenth century.

Bowed roofs and chimney stacks. A distant spire.

*No, not a distant spire. A man on the rooftops, a red light flashing in his fist.*

The strange red light sliced through the fog, a hundred years ahead of its time, painting a dot on the paper plugging the tenement window.

"Down," called Chevie, diving at both boys, dragging them to the floor, and not a moment too soon. Six shots punctured the paper and knocked fist-sized chunks from the brick wall. Dust clouds swirled in the tubes of light admitted by the bullet holes.

Chevie held the boys down until she felt that the attack had passed.

"He's found us," gasped Riley.

The boards creaked under their weight as though collapse

was imminent. The stench of boiled tripe was stronger with their noses to the wood, and through a gap in the floor Chevie could see a dozen figures rousing from their sleep in the cramped murk below.

"If you are well enough to leave," she said to Riley, "I have had quite enough of the Old Nichol."

"You try keeping up with me," said Riley, and commenced crawling for the doorway.

# 12 » UNTO DUST

THE OLD NICHOL ROOKERY, BETHNAL GREEN,
LONDON, 1898

ALBERT GARRICK HAD SPENT MOST OF THE
previous night in discreet observation of the house
on Bedford Square until one of his stooges sent
him word of the Injun princess's whereabouts. There had also
been a Battering Ram keeping an eye on the place, but the man
received news from a runner at twelve bells and cleared out of
his lurk.

*Doubtless Otto has heard of Tibor Charismo's fate.*

So now Garrick was on the border of the Old Nichol with
his marvelous weapons.

*A few warning shots,* he had reckoned, *to smoke out my
quarry.*

EOIN COLFER

Garrick spotted the twitch at the loft window, then utilized the beautiful and deadly laser to lay a few potshots into the room. The effectiveness of the sights made him quite emotional.

*It is a perfect creation in its blend of form and function.*

It was a simple matter for Garrick to take two paces eastward on the rooftop and thus have a clear view of the tenement's front door.

Riley knows I could never enter that building, he realized. The boy had a cruel streak in him. He could have made a worthy assistant, had he not betrayed me.

The rookery had only one exit, and it was through this doorway that Riley and Chevie must emerge, unless they planned to drown in the sewage pit at the rear of the house or batter their way through the one-story shack sublets that stood propped against it.

*And with my most excellent FBI weaponry, I will pick them off as they leave.*

He smiled. *The end is nigh, Chevron Savano.*

There was a flurry of activity at the door, precipitated by some yappy fighting mutts who tumbled into the street barking.

Here they come, thought Garrick, activating his laser sight. Two shots only; save bullets for the gunsmith.

But instead of two frightened fugitives, no less than a dozen youths erupted from the hovel door, bursting through the refuse littering the front passage, all sporting broad-brimmed hats, scattering like criminals on the run. It was impossible to tell if Riley and Chevie were among them.

310

Garrick grinned tightly from his perch. *A diversionary bunch. Clever.*

The assassin supposed that he could drop half a dozen, but that would be a shocking waste of ammunition, and the bobbies would be attracted by mass murder, even in the Old Nichol.

Garrick pocketed his weapon and ran for the stairwell.

*So now we race, my son. Only the swift shall survive. The future lies in Bedford Square for us all.*

Chevie ran straight across the road, avoiding potholes as she went. Directly facing the tenement's doorway was a forlorn alley barely the width of a man's shoulders, which Chevie and Riley darted down, avoiding the turgid stream that trickled down the middle. The black passage was lined with an honor guard of Bob Winkle's boys, all clapping and whooping with whatever enthusiasm their tarry lungs would permit.

Bob Winkle waited like an angel in the white fog at the alley's end, holding open a crooked wooden door.

"Get in, Yer Highness," called Winkle. "I fed the horse some peppers, and she is rearing for the off."

Chevie dived into the hansom cab's box while Riley clambered up to the driver's seat and Winkle landed beside him with remarkable agility for one so malnourished.

"You move sprightly-like," commented Riley.

"I threw down a few beers," admitted Winkle. "Just to perk myself up."

"This is your cab?" Chevie called to the boy from below.

"For the moment, it is your carriage, ma'am," said Winkle, winking through the roof hole.

Riley grabbed the long-handled whip from its holster and cracked it expertly between the horse's ears. Part of his magician/assassin training had been whip work, and Riley could snap a playing card out of a punter's fingers blindfolded. The horse reared once in fright, snapped strong teeth at its tormentor, then took off across the cobbles toward Bloomsbury and Bedford Square.

Garrick opted to run toward the house on Bedford Square. A hansom would be swifter, but there were none to be seen.

It vexed him, even as his lungs burned, that he, the great Albert Garrick, was forced to run down an urchin and a girl.

There was no question now of letting them live.

*They know my secrets, and I suspect that soon enough Agent Savano will turn her wiles to the task of plotting my downfall.*

Garrick knew that these two links to the future must be comprehensively severed lest they use the Timekey to reconnect with Chevron's time and bring justice down upon him.

The magician felt his hat fly off his head and he let it go, allowing his long hair to stream out behind him. The wind in his locks made him feel primal and unstoppable.

Riley drove the hansom as though the devil were on their tail, which was not far from the truth. The trip was a little more than two and a half miles, and Riley clipped almost every footpath on the journey, tossing Bob Winkle and Chevie like bull's-eyes in a jar, but they never complained or cried halt; they were all too willing to wear a few bruises if the prize was escaping Albert Garrick.

Riley, not content simply to graze footpaths, seemed determined to drive the cab to destruction. He thundered past a lord's carriage and was only saved from tipping upside down by the steadying steel of a lamppost, which buckled under the weight of the hansom's broadside.

Their progress along Gower Street was marked by two constables' whistles; a baker's tray tossed into the air, showering the boys trailing the cart with hot rolls; and a sea of roast potatoes rolling from an overturned grill.

Chevie tried to hold herself steady enough to look out for Garrick, but the city flashed past, and her senses were addled by the jostling.

"Nearly there," she said to herself, teeth clacking as she spoke. "I know this area."

And she did, as the general architecture and layout of the streets did not change substantially over the next century.

Riley stood on the board, hauling on the reins, and slowed the beleaguered nag to a trot. He leaned into the roof aperture.

"Out you get, Chevie," he ordered. "Bob, you dump this hansom in Covent Garden so as to draw the bluebottles away. Take it steady from here; no need to draw any sharp looks."

Bob took the reins, his face aglow with the sheer joy of flight. "Yessir, Mr. Riley. And if they nabs me, I'll not peach, Winkle's word on it."

Riley passed him the last of Malarkey's coin. "The princess thanks you, Bob."

Winkle stuffed the money inside his ragged waistcoat. "You know where I lurks, if you have need. Inform the princess that next time I'll be bartering for a kiss."

Chevie threw open the door. "You wash your face," she said, stepping onto the road, "and I might consider it."

Which caused the said mucky visage to churn in consternation, then grin widely as Bob Winkle snapped the reins and hurried off, vowing to wash his face at the next available opportunity.

The door of the Bayley Street house was solid wood with brass hinges and iron rivets and would obviously not succumb to a kicking.

Chevie was incredulous that a mere door might stop them, when they had come so far. She cast her eyes wildly around the square for some tool that would help them break in, but there was nothing in the street but nannies with strollers, enjoying the morning sun in the small park, or various street traders offering breakfast treats.

"How are we supposed to get in?" asked Chevie. "Our plan only works if we're inside the house."

"Calm yourself, Chevie," said Riley. "I have cracked this drum before, remember?"

The assassin's apprentice climbed on top of the ground-floor railings and sprang upward to grasp the sill of an upper window with his fingertips. Riley hoisted open the sash window and wriggled inside, just as he had during his previous, fateful visit. Last time the clasp had taken some forcing with a jemmy; this time it was already busted in two.

Half a minute passed, then Riley pulled open the door a slice.

"Duck inside," he said to Chevie. "I smell Garrick approaching."

Chevie obliged, saying, "I don't smell anything. I think I broke my sense of smell in the Old Nichol."

Riley closed the door, but he did not apply the chain. "I feel him near in the twist of me guts. It's something I've always been able to do."

Chevie placed the flat of one palm against her own stomach. "You know what, Riley? I think you may have something there. Let's get moving. My guts are twisting something awful."

Albert Garrick plucked another twenty-first-century phrase from the store in his mind: *the runner's high.*

I ain't a jot tired, he thought, as the adrenaline coursed through his system, maximizing his muscles' performance. That is because my adrenal gland is releasing epinephrine. Fascinating.

Garrick leaned into the wind, pumping his arms in the style of Carl Lewis, one of Felix Smart's favorite athletes.

The feeling didn't last, and darkness clouded his morning mood. Garrick couldn't rest until the Timekey was destroyed and the landing pad dismantled. He wouldn't be completely safe in this time until that happened.

*Riley shall know that I am his master, even unto dust.*

*When this is resolved, I will need to find myself a new apprentice. A less reluctant one.*

*I spared the rod. That will not happen again. I will select an indigent from the Old Nichol, feed him up, and teach him respect. And if he doesn't learn it, he shall go to the grave, as his predecessor is about to do.*

Garrick cut through the park, vaulting the iron railings onto Bayley Street, just in time to see the tail of Riley's coat disappearing into the shadowed hallway of Charles Smart's house.

Garrick's bloodlust rose in his throat like bile.

*I shall have them both,* he thought with raw savagery, *then away, before the alarm is raised.*

Garrick drew himself up to avoid conspicuous glances and strolled across the street, as easy as a man with nothing more on his mind than the purchase of morning coffee and sweet rolls. This casual manner was sloughed off once he put his shoulder to Charles Smart's door and found it unbolted.

*They are mine,* he thought, but then urged himself toward caution.

*Chevron Savano has considerable training. She is young and impetuous, but still capable of surprises.*

Garrick bolted the door behind him, then drew the laser-sighted pistol and walked rapidly toward the stairs. There was clattering ahead as someone went down to the basement. Garrick knew from the weight of the footfalls and the whistle of breath that it was Riley.

*It is possible that the boy is slightly asthmatic? Formative years spent in London's poisonous smog will have that effect,* he realized. And soon Riley's breathing problems will become more severe.

His own lungs were as clean as a whistle, thanks to the wormhole.

Garrick took hold of the banister with his free hand and swung himself into the stairwell, using a shoulder to check himself against the wall.

Riley was in view. *Ten steps below! A piddling, easy shot.*

"Riley!" he thundered, rather enjoying the melodrama. "Halt!"

The boy did not even turn, but his legs wobbled and something slipped from his hand.

*The Timekey! Riley has dropped it.*

Garrick could not quell an exclamation. "Aha!"


The Timekey slipped from Riley's fingers, and the boy knew that he must be seen to return for it, or else the plan counted for nothing. He spun around, only to find Garrick already crushing the key under his heel.

"You betrayed me, orphan," said Garrick. "And your punishment will be a slow death."

*You orphaned me*, thought Riley, fury building in his heart like steam in an engine, and he attacked, which was most certainly not part of the plan.

Riley balled his fists, as he had been taught, and punched Garrick in the nerve cluster above the knee. The assassin's leg had no choice but to collapse, causing Garrick to list sideways in the narrow stairwell. Riley got off one more punch to the gut before Garrick raised his guard.

"Some fighting spirit," he said, his voice reedy from the blow. "Too late for that, my boy. We are at the tail end of this story."

Riley fought on, searching for the chinks in Garrick's guard, finding them down low, around the hips and kidneys. And though Garrick's expression was untroubled, he was reluctantly impressed by Riley's skill, and surprised at how difficult it was to defend himself against the boy.

*I have never fought someone who employs my exact style,* he realized.

Finally Garrick grew tired of the game. He swept one arm around in a rapid arc, clouting Riley soundly on one ear, disorientating him utterly and sending him tumbling to the base of the stairs, into the basement corridor and out of sight.

*Riley will turn on his master no more,* thought Garrick.

All that stood between him and total peace of mind was one American teenager, who was probably unarmed. Still, he would take no chances.

Garrick spared a moment to finish crushing the Timekey beneath his boot, grinding the innards with great relish.

*I could leave now. Just ascend and go. I have destroyed the Timekey.*

This voice Garrick now recognized as the last wisps of Felix Smart's conscience, attempting to manipulate him. Garrick was delighted to realize that he could not be turned from his path.

*Riley knows my face. His voice must be silenced.*

Death was the only answer. *Unto dust,* as he always said.

And now he could proceed to the basement bedchamber without fear. The bed's metal frame was nothing more than that without a Timekey to activate it. In truth, Garrick knew he should have come here during the night and disassembled the bed, but he had been wary of ambush and had to ensure the price on his head was removed. No need for fretting now.

Garrick almost wished for twenty-first-century surveillance cameras so that he could record what was going to happen next. This was an episode he would like to view critically, to confirm that his presence was as striking as he supposed.

*There is always room for improvement in a performance.*

Garrick banished such thoughts and allowed a cold, efficient sense of purpose to encase his brain, like the cold steel of a dragoon's helmet.

*I must be the assassin now. Tomorrow my world changes—in fact the entire world may change—but for now, I am performing a job of work. And Albert Garrick always takes pride in his work.*

He strode down the corridor, eyes quickly adjusting to the gloom. There was scratching in the shadows that perhaps an amateur would have wasted ammunition on, but Garrick knew the claws of rats when he heard them and held his fire.

Riley moved slowly ahead of him, hampered by steamer trunks and mannequins, hunched over and casting fearful glances toward his mentor.

"She has deserted you, son," Garrick called after him. "You are alone."

"You murdered my parents!" Riley said. "I am no son of yours."

Garrick was about to deny it—after all, how could Riley know what had transpired all those years ago?—when the truth occurred to him: *The boy saw it in the wormhole.*

"It was a job of work," he admitted, shooting a wheeled mannequin for fun. "I did what I was hired to do. It was a matter of trust. And did I not save you? Against orders, I might point out."

"Murderer!" howled Riley, darting through the bedchamber door, into the gloom beyond.

Garrick prudently took up a position beside the doorway, unwilling to follow Riley directly, in case Agent Savano attempted an ambush.

*Remember, you have both had the same training. What is standard operating procedure when defending a room with a single entrance?*

Chevie would be waiting in a blind spot, aiming whatever weapon she possessed at the doorway.

*If she is there at all.*

Perhaps Agent Savano was not even in the building. Still, better to lose a few seconds than waste the opportunity to close this sordid chapter of the book.

Garrick summoned his memories of the room. He had passed quite some time here, waiting for Felix Smart to turn up.

*A rectangular space with a small alcove in the southern wall, with a dresser and writing desk. Rows of barrel-sized cylinders—crude batteries, I would guess, which Smart was building to power future visits to Victoria. Agent Savano will be in cover behind the desk. Upon my entrance she will have a clear shot at the optimum target zone.*

Garrick checked his pistol's load.

*Very well. Albert Garrick will indeed enter as expected.*

Chevie knelt behind the writing desk with Barnum's revolver pointed at the doorway. The instant Riley appeared, she was on her feet with the weapon cocked.

*Come on, Garrick*, she willed the assassin. *Show me that greasy smile.*

Garrick talked all the way, cock of the cockney walk.

"We have shared quite the adventure," he said. "But for me to realize my full potential, I need to be allowed to invest time in myself without constant interference . . ."

This speech surprised Chevie greatly, as she had shot Garrick three times between the first and third syllables of the word *adventure*. His cloak had twirled to the ground, and the magician keeled over stiffly, yet he *continued* to speak. And though she had been forewarned that there would be trickery, Chevie left herself exposed for a fraction of a second, which gave the real Garrick the chance to step calmly into the doorway and shoot Chevie square in the chest while still projecting his voice into the wheeled mannequin on the floor.

". . . constant interference from a juvenile agent who is completely out of her depth."

Garrick allowed the thought to flash through his mind that perhaps this FBI-style body shot was the most satisfying he had ever fired, in spite of Felix Smart's attempts to interfere with his conscience, or perhaps because of that.

*I am in control of myself once more.*

Chevie was knocked backward by the impact, lifted onto the tips of her toes, and almost somersaulted into a pile of blankets behind her.

Garrick, ever the professional, decided that he would savor the moment fully later, once he was safe in the Orient Theatre. Now was the moment to put the final nail in this coffin.

"Riley, boy," he said, his voice honeyed and sonorous, as seductive a tone as was ever heard on the West End stage. "Stop running, son. Let me end your pain."

Riley was facedown on the bed, his body heaving with sobs.

*At the end he was just a child. Perhaps better to die in innocence.*

Garrick pocketed his weapon, for it was important that this killing be more personal.

Two quick steps brought him to the bed.

*I shall choke off the air from his windpipe, watch his eyes glaze, but out of respect for our shared past, perhaps I shall speak kindly as he goes.*

Garrick reached for Riley's neck.

My fingers are so slender, yet strong, he thought. I could just as easily have been a pianist.

Riley was too beaten to attempt escape and simply lay on the bed, waiting for Garrick's fingers to close around his neck.

"No fight left in you, son?" whispered Garrick. "Perhaps it is time to sleep."

Garrick sprang catlike onto the mattress, but his fingertips did not land on Riley's soft neck, as expected. Instead they somehow clinked against cold glass, and the assassin's head followed, smashing into a pane of unseen mirror with a dull crunch, sending cracks racing across the glass.

"But . . ." he said, baffled, blood pouring into one eye. "But . . . I see."

Riley turned over and looked through the cracks in Garrick's direction, but not at him. "What do you see, mighty illusionist?"

Garrick's fingers tapped the looking glass, and he realized that he had been hoodwinked with his own magical apparatus; but the throbbing in his head grew louder than his thoughts. "Angled lights. A series of mirrors. Misdirection. But why?"

"To get you on the bed," said a voice behind him.

Garrick turned dully, and there, impossibly, stood Chevron Savano, hale and hardy, some form of throwing missile already flashing from her fingers, spinning in his direction.

Not so easy, thought Garrick, and he snatched the object from the air. *Even when dazed, I will not be struck down by the likes of you.*

The magician was irritated that he had been injured by one of his own mirrors. But what had the illusion accomplished, except to delay the inevitable? He was a little bloody, nothing more.

Garrick's hand tingled, and he saw orange sparks buzz around the fingers that held the missile. Sparks buzzing like quantum bees around honey. Puzzlement heaped upon puzzlement.

*Orange sparks? How?*

Garrick opened his fingers and saw a Timekey, and for a moment he thought it another illusion, until Felix Smart's experience assured him that it was real.

*The hazmat team I tackled earlier. Of course, they had Timekeys and body armor. This is one of their keys, as was the one I smashed on the stairs. Dropped deliberately as a ruse. Riley allowed me to see him enter the house. Chevron simply donned a bulletproof vest in the minute before my arrival.*

The Timekey's digital readout was divided into four quadrants, and the top two were flashing.

Garrick waited a nanosecond for the information to come to him.

*Top left activates the wormhole. Top right is the countdown, which already reads zero. The lower quadrants activate the reentry beacon. They are not active.*

"That's right," said Chevie. "You're going in, but you ain't coming out."

Garrick pawed at the Timekey controls with his fingers, but they had already become insubstantial; he was like a ghost trying to make contact with the real world. The Timekey slipped from his grasp and landed on the goose down, a vortex of light opening at its core.

"What?" said Chevie. "No last words? How about, *The world hasn't seen the last of Albert Garrick*? That's a good one."

Riley appeared at Chevie's side and his eyes were wet with tears. "You murdered my family. You stole me from my bed."

He shook Garrick's own cloak at him. "So that I could be your audience."

Garrick had bigger things on his mind than dealing with a boy's accusations. He felt himself slipping away.

I am nothing, he realized. There may have been comfort in this thought for many, but for Albert Garrick it held only terror.

*I shall be nothing for all eternity.*

The orange sparks spread like magical locusts along his limbs and torso, leaving a bare outline behind. Ghostly innards wobbled inside transparent flesh, and Garrick saw it all happen.

He opened his mouth to speak, but no sound emerged, so Riley said the words for him.

"Unto dust," said the boy, and he spat on the floor.

For an instant Garrick flashed silver, as though transformed into thermite powder, then he was sucked down into the Timekey, which stood on its point, spinning like a top.

A bolt of lightning shot from its tip, scorching the ceiling, then it too disappeared.

"Okay," said Chevie, grabbing Riley's shoulder and hustling him toward the steps, "I know where this is going."

Without an aperture at the twenty-first-century end of the wormhole, the time tunnel craved energy to sustain the matter conversion. The first things to go were the barrel batteries, which were grabbed with lightning fingers, squeezed dry, then tossed aside like dead husks. Then the lightning burrowed deep into the earth itself, siphoning geothermal energy until the soil cracked and split.

Chevie pushed Riley upstairs and toward the front door, hearing the earth itself open behind her with thunderous booms and sharp snaps. She could feel Bill Riley's Timekey buzz sympathetically against her chest.

"Run," she called, wholly unnecessarily. "The house is going to collapse."

Riley did not need any urging. He raced toward the door, thinking that this was the second time he had fled this house in fear of his life.

The house collapsed around them as they ran, sinking into the basement's maw, as the structure itself fed the wormhole with kinetic energy. Glass shattered and stone was crushed like sand. Chevie kicked Riley hard in the rump to shunt him past a falling chandelier.

Garrick had bolted the door behind him, but this didn't delay them, as most of the front wall had collapsed. The fleeing pair dived through a hole in the wall onto the pavement and scrambled quickly from the maelstrom of destruction behind them.

Streams of people flowed from the doors of adjacent houses, and screaming and howling rose up in the square as the wormhole gulped and swallowed the entire building, excising it from its neighbors with surgical precision. When at last the dust settled and the cacophony faded, the house had been removed, like a rotten tooth from a gum, leaving the others untouched save for a score of broken windows and a spiderweb of superficial cracks.

Riley and Chevie leaned on the park railing, as caked in

dust as any victims of Vesuvius, but intact and uninjured.

Riley spat a ball of brick dust to the ground. "Did you know that the entire house would be consumed?"

Chevie touched the tender spot on her chest where Garrick's bullet had struck the too big body armor. "I knew there was a chance, but it was worth taking."

There was chaos on Bedford Square as bobbies' whistle blasts filled the air and the bells of an approaching fire engine clanged across from the West End. Some people had fainted dead away, and young lads clambered over the rubble heap, calling for survivors.

"We should run," said Riley. "The police will question everyone in a posh gaff such as this."

Chevie tore off her bulletproof vest and took several breaths. "Yeah, okay, Riley. I make the strategy decisions, remember? Anyway, we should get out of here before the local police blame us for something."

Riley tucked the magician's cloak under his arm. "A good strategy. Lead on, Agent Savano."

The pair trudged to the corner of Bedford Square, against the flow of the crowd straining to see the collapsed foundations of what the *London News* would call the "House of Hell."

Riley and Chevie left a trail of dust behind them.

They did not speak for a while, both engrossed in thoughts of the future. Eventually they realized that they had linked arms as they walked.

"We are like a couple off to the opera," said Riley.

Chevie laughed and a puff of dust escaped her throat. "Yeah, a zombie couple." Her laugh petered out. "You could have died back there, fighting Garrick. That was not part of the plan."

"I thought of him, leaning over my dear ma," said Riley, "with his knife ready to do its business, and I couldn't help myself."

Hooves clattered alongside as a hansom cab slowed, the driver sniffing a fare, despite their appearance.

"We're content on foot," Riley called, without glancing upward. "Move on down the avenue."

"Perhaps I am content to ride beside my mates," said a familiar voice.

It was Bob Winkle, who had somehow kept a grip on the stolen carriage.

Winkle stood on the driver's seat, peering down toward the corner of Bedford Square. "You pair had a right knees-up in that gaff," he commented. "A cove might expect a life of high adventure partnering with such a duo. Like Holmes and Watson, ye are, but with extra munitions and explosions."

Chevie shook herself like a dog and something resembling a teenage female emerged from the dust.

"That's a nice face, princess," said Bob Winkle. "If you gave it the lick of a wet cloth, I might lower meself to kiss it."

They breakfasted like royalty on grub purchased with one of the sovereigns found sewn into the lining of Garrick's cloak. They ordered coffee with toast, oatmeal with brown sugar, fried eggs and sausage, curried chicken with potato, a platter of bacon, with extra grease for strength. All finished off with beer for the boys in spite of Chevie's health warnings.

They sat at a street table on Piccadilly after breakfast, watching the avenue fill up with the day's business.

Bob Winkle flicked a farthing at the first beggar to approach their table and set him guarding their little space so they could talk uninterrupted.

Riley sighed and rubbed his distended belly. "I am full as a prince on his birthday," he declared.

Chevie was less stuffed, having ignored ninety percent of what was offered to her.

I cannot stay here, she thought. My cholesterol count would kill me in a week.

"Okay, gents," she said, slapping the table with purpose, "we should draw up our plans before you guys get blind drunk."

Bob Winkle snorted. "Drunk on beer? I ain't been *beer drunk* since I were ten." He grabbed the rest of the black bread from the plate and shoved it into his pockets. "I better go and look to the mare. You two do your good-bye cuddling, and I'll be back to bring whoever's going to the Orient. I suppose there ain't much more than splinters left of that conjuring equipment me and the boys ferried over earlier."

Winkle dodged down the street, eyes and ears open for bluebottles.

"That guy will land you in trouble," warned Chevie.

"Well, he won't be spending his waking hours trying to murder anyone, or his sleeping hours dreaming of death."

"Maybe so. But I still think you should come back with me. A part of you belongs in the twenty-first century."

Riley sighed. "But a part of me is here. I have a half brother still living somewhere. Perhaps in Brighton? With Bob Winkle's help, maybe I can find him."

"You can afford Winkle's help?"

Riley shrugged. "For the time being. I know where Garrick kept his cash. I suppose the theater is mine too."

"So you will search for your brother?"

Riley pulled the magician's cloak tight around his shoulders. "I am a magician now. I shall put a troupe together and enjoy the theater life until I find Ginger Tom. Perhaps he knows my Christian name."

Chevie's eyes were downcast. "Yeah, I bet he does." She reached into her pocket and pulled out the final Timekey left behind by the hazmat team. "The team and their gear went down with the house, but I had Bob's boys collect their Timekeys while they were setting up the mirror trap, so, if you ever change your mind . . ."

Riley hooked the lanyard around his neck. "Thank you, Chevie. But this is my century, and I belong here."

Chevie wagged a finger. "Never say never, right?"

"Yes, you are correct. There may come a time when I need to escape."

"It's preprogrammed, set up already, so all you have to do is press the button. Make sure the four quadrants light up, or you'll end up stuck in the wormhole with you-know-who."

"I will be certain to check."

Chevie sipped her coffee, which had the consistency of mud and tasted like cough syrup. "I feel there should be more, you know. We've gone through hell, and now I'm just gonna walk away?"

"We will always be close, Chevie. I know the secret of your tattoo, remember?"

Chevie patted her own shoulder. "My tattoo? Yeah, well. I'm afraid I got sold a turkey on that one."

"Sold a turkey?" said Riley, frowning.

"A crock. A bowl of bull. A heap of lies."

"Your father lied to you? And you lied to me?"

"Afraid so, but I'm telling you the truth now, on account of all the bonding we're doing. Dad loved telling that story, but the whole Chevron thing came about because my father had a falling out with the owner of the local Texaco."

"Tex-a-co?"

"Yeah. A fueling station for automobiles. So, just to annoy this guy, and because of his beer problem, he gets a tattoo and then calls his firstborn Chevron, which is a competing gas station."

Riley pushed his tankard away with the tip of one finger. "So, no noble warrior?"

"No. And I based my whole life on that story, got the tattoo, told anyone who would listen, became an agent. Last year I meet the Texaco guy, who is broken up that my pop died, and he tells me the truth. I am named after a gas station."

"Wow," said Riley, who had heard the word used in the future and liked it.

"Wow? That's it, huh? No magical wisdom from the Great Riley?"

"We have both built our lives on lies," said Riley. "I was not abandoned to slum cannibals, and your ancestors were not great warriors; but the lies did their work, and we are who we are. I think you are the youngest agent in your police force for good reason. Perhaps in spite of the name Chevron."

Chevie smiled. "Yeah, okay, Riley. That's not bad. I'm gonna go with that."

They abandoned the cab and walked to the house on Half Moon Street. Bob Winkle was doing his utmost to decipher the limited facts he had been given.

"So, princess. You plan to enter this house and stay there for a hundred years?"

Chevie patted his shoulder. "Something like that, Winkle. I would say *See you around*, but it's probably not going to happen."

"So we should kiss now?"

"Of course," said Chevie, and she gave him a peck on the cheek that he would have to be content with.

"Next year I will be fifteen," said Bob Winkle, emboldened by the kiss. "We could be married. I could make fair chink off a battling Injun maid at the fairgrounds."

"Tempting as that offer is, I think I'll pass."

"Very well, princess. But now that I am part owner of a

theater, the ladies will be all over Robert Winkle. Six weeks I will wait for you, not a minute more."

"I understand," said Chevie, smiling. "It's the best you can do."

Riley walked her to the front step, while Bob perched on a neighboring set of stairs, watching for constables' helmets.

"Be careful, Chevron Savano," he said. "The future is a dangerous place. It is only a matter of time until the Martians arrive."

"Yeah, I'm gonna watch out for anything with tentacles."

"Hurry yourselves," called Bob Winkle. "This is a posh road. Two more minutes and our collars get pinched."

The boy was right. It would be a shame if this affair were to end in a prison cell.

Chevie hugged Riley tightly. "Thanks for everything," she said.

Riley hugged her back. "Thanks to you, too, Chevron Savano, warrior and fuel station. Perhaps one day I will put our story into words. It would rival the tales of H. G. Wells himself."

"Maybe you already did," said Chevie. "I'll Google it when I get home."

"Googling sounds like a painful procedure," said Riley.

Bob whistled loudly. "I see a helmet, Riley. Leave her be, now."

There was no more delaying it. Chevie kissed Riley's cheek and squeezed his hand, then closed the door behind her.

• • •

The basement room was dark and dank, just as Chevie remembered it from that brief moment before the sack went over their heads. She saw chicken bones in the corner with rats huddled over them like tramps around a bonfire. The rats did not seem concerned by her presence; rather they looked her over for the meat on her bones.

Being stared down by large rats was a good way to focus a person on getting to someplace with smaller rats, so Chevie pulled out Bill Riley's Timekey and walked briskly to the metal pad.

*No time like the present.*

She punched the Timekey's control pad and made very sure that all four quadrants lit up.

After a second's dry vibration, the key began sprouting orange sparks like a Roman candle.

Here we go, she thought. I hope Victoria's house doesn't fall down.

And then she thought, I hope Riley will be okay. That kid deserves a break.

She frowned. *Not that my own future will be a bed of roses. I am going to spend months answering questions. Thank God Waldo saw the whole thing. I hope he recorded it.*

Chevie held up the Timekey. All four quadrants were flashing.

*Good-bye, Riley. Be well.*

Chevie smiled and orange sparks flowed between her teeth.

Please, no monkey parts, she thought, and then was gone. Out of time.

• • •

Bob Winkle volunteered to steal a bicycle to ferry them both across to High Holborn, but Riley said no.

"I am your partner, you know," Winkle said. "How come you is issuing commands like some form of little Caesar?"

Riley decided to stake his claim right off. Winkle could swallow it or not as he pleased.

"I am the Great Savano, Master Winkle. I own the theater and the equipment, and I know where the gold is buried. If you want to work for me, then welcome, but do as yer bid. If not, then off back to the Old Nichol with your bones and smoke some wallpaper for yerself."

Bob whistled. "Harsh, Riley. Harsh and cold. But them are good traits in a master and will keep the others from getting out of line. Also, the Great Savano. That has a real ring to it."

"Thank you, Bob." Riley paused. "Others? I can't feed the entire rookery."

"I know, but I have three brothers that need looking after. We come as a set, you see. All or none."

"Who could split a fellow from his brothers?" said Riley. "That would be uncommon cruel. You should fetch them at once, and we will rendezvous at the Orient to draw up our plans. Can any of your brothers juggle?"

"Juggle?" said Bob, already crossing the road. "Why, Mr. Riley, they juggles *each other.*"

And he was off down an alley, making a direct line for the rookery, to break the news that the Winkles were saved from Old Nichol.

• • •

Riley walked on alone, casting furtive glances over his shoulder whenever a chill breeze cooled his forehead.

Garrick is gone, he told himself. Lost in the wormhole.

Lost in the wormhole? Could that be any more than a dream?

*Chevie was no dream.*

A beautiful maiden from an exotic land come to free him from the tyrant Garrick. It read like a dream and would make a capital novel.

*The only thing missing is a dinosaur come back to life.*

Riley walked on, realizing that it would be a long time before he could fully enjoy the sun on his face and ignore the chill.

*Every stone kicked in an alley, every creak of wood on the stairway—I will hear and see Garrick everywhere.*

But there would be a friend close by, and his brothers, and in time maybe his own brother.

*Ginger Tom*, he thought, *I am coming, and oh, boy, do I have a tale to tell you.*

Riley lifted the hem of his velvet cloak out of the city mud and gazed up at the triple span of the Holborn Viaduct, the city's most impressive feat of modern architecture.

Home once more, he thought. Home to a new life.

Riley stepped around a toppled fruit cart and in seconds was lost in the morning throng of everyday folk doing their daily job of staying alive in London town.

# EPILOGUE

THE BATTERING RAMS' RESIDENT TATTOO ARTIST, Farley, trailed behind Riley through Holborn, his face hidden by a silken hood of a kind favored by Arab mercenaries. Riley might not have recognized the tattooist even without the hood, had he caught sight of him. Farley did not seem nearly so decrepit as he had in the Hidey-Hole. His back was ramrod straight, and his sure-footed stride was that of a man in early middle age.

Pedestrians gave Farley a wide berth on the footpath for two reasons. For one, something red glittered from the shadows under his hood like the night eye of a wolf, and for another—if a second reason was needed to avoid a gent with a wolf's eye— this man was obviously a lunatic and destined for a bed in one of Her Majesty's asylums, for he was speaking into his closed fist as though there were a fairy living in there listening to every word.

So people stepped aside and cast quick, sidelong glances at Farley.

Talking to oneself is the first sign of madness, they thought. And there ain't no predicting when a madman will spring into sudden violence.

What the Victorian pedestrians could not have possibly known was that Farley was speaking into a microphone strapped to the back of his wrist rather than to a fairy. And the wolf's eye glowing from the shadowy recesses of his eye socket was, in fact, a monocular infrared scope with a visible-light-blocking filter. Simply put, to Farley, anyone who had been in a time tunnel and whose atoms had been coated in its particular radiation would sparkle gently, as though coated with gold dust. It was a very handy way to keep an eye on someone without getting too close.

"Rosie, patch me through to the colonel," he said into the microphone, his accent still English, as it had been in the Rams' Hidey-Hole. Farley had been in character so long that he rarely came out of it.

"You sure?" said a voice in his earpiece, male in spite of the name. "He's having a massage. You know what he's like."

Farley did indeed know what the colonel was like—no one knew it better, but he also knew that the colonel had asked to be kept up to date. In truth, Farley suspected that his superior was excited that something a little out of the ordinary was happening. This stage of the operation was all preparation, which was never very interesting, so this whole Agent Savano thing had put a little pep in everyone's step.

"I am sure, Rosenbaum. Just put me through. I'm out in the open here, talking into my hand like a halfwit."

"Connecting you now, Major."

Farley held for a moment, watching Riley open the door to a theater that had seen better days.

The boy knew where the other key was, noted Farley, stepping into the archway of a butcher's yard. Looks like he inherits the building.

His earpiece crackled as the colonel picked up the phone at his end.

"Hey, dude. How's it going on the street?"

Farley winced. He hated it when the colonel tried to be casual and chummy: that was not how the army worked. And, at any rate, it was an act. The colonel had no friends.

"It's fine, sir. On the streets. That situation we talked about is winding down. No need to deploy."

The colonel chuckled and it sounded like a well-oiled engine purring. "Come on, Farley. Why are you speaking in code? Who's going to be listening in? That clown Charismo barely managed to put a landline together. Telephonicus Farspeak? What a joke. Spell it out, Major."

Farley took a breath. "Yessir, Colonel. Force of habit, sir. Never jeopardize the operation. Loose lips sink ships, and all that."

"Just give me the facts, man. Where's Garrick?"

"He's gone, sir. Toast. I got the gist on the bug I planted in the boy's bandage."

"Gone?" The colonel sounded disappointed. "I liked him. He was a funny guy."

*Funny* was not the word Farley would have chosen, especially when he remembered the assassin looming over him with a bottle of ether.

"The others?"

"The boy is here, in Holborn," continued Farley. "And Agent Savano has entered the portal at Half Moon Street."

"So, no damage done?"

"No, sir. We are still running dark. As far as the future is concerned, Charles Smart's technology died with him, and we are on schedule."

"What about Charismo? Is he still nicely placed where we can use him?"

Farley ground his teeth, never happy about delivering bad news to the colonel. "Not exactly, sir. The boy set him up for a fall with the duke. They saw the mutations. I imagine he's getting his skull drilled about now. I doubt he will have enough brain cells left to play fetch, Colonel."

There was silence for a moment, except for the *thump-slap* of the colonel's masseuse at work.

"I never liked that guy and his creepy masks anyway," said the colonel at last. "We can work around him, but let's move the operation up a few weeks, just in case Charismo shoots his mouth off to someone who'll listen."

Farley dropped his hand for a moment and sighed. A soldier never knew when the colonel would go off like an automatic weapon, spewing bile instead of bullets.

"What about the boy? Should I remove him from the equation?"

The colonel mulled this over. "No. That's a plucky kid there. He could be useful, and I don't want you to get caught with your hands wet."

"Riley is a loose end, sir. And he could cause trouble."

"We know where he is, correct?"

"Yessir."

"And we can neutralize this Riley anytime we want, right?"

"Yes, we can. Easy as pie."

"Well, then, Major. Let's keep an eye on the boy for now. If he pokes his nose into anything remotely non-Victorian, then you pay him a midnight visit. How's that sound?"

Farley stepped into the street and watched Riley's form flit past a row of upstairs windows, his outline shining through the net curtains.

"That sounds fine, sir. He's not going anywhere."

"Good," said the colonel. "Now put one of your men on the kid. I need you back at the Hidey-Hole so that Malarkey doesn't get suspicious."

"On my way, sir."

Farley severed the connection and took one last look at the Orient Theatre.

"I'll be seeing you, Riley," he said to the glowing silhouette. "Real soon."

# THE HANGMAN'S
## *REVOLUTION*

Chevron Savano has just arrived home after a time-trip to Victorian London, where she helped Riley escape his murderous master. When she exits the wormhole, Chevie finds the present day very different from the one she had left. England is now being run by an organization known as the Boxites, whose members control their territory through intimidation and terror. Chevie is absorbed by this reality and cannot remember fully the history she once belonged to. Though she senses that something is wrong, she moves on with her life as a junior cadet in the Boxite police.

Gradually, scraps of information come back to her, and she begins to put the fragments together. She seeks out Professor Charles Smart, the inventor of the time machine, and in doing so sets the secret-service police on both of them. Chevie slips into the past, where, with Riley's help, she must venture into London's catacombs and derail the plans of the charismatic leader who is intent on using his knowledge of the future to seize power.

*The Hangman's Revolution* is another mind-bending thriller from the brilliant author of the internationally best-selling Artemis Fowl series.